The Last Door

BEYOND THE VEIL #3

SHEILA LOWE

Write
Choice
Ink
ESTABLISHED 2021

WRITE CHOICE INK

Praise for Sheila Lowe

BEYOND THE VEIL SERIES

THE LAST DOOR

"Voicy characters, an intriguing setting, a perplexing situation...the writing is, as always, superb." — Saralyn Richard, author of the Detective Parrott series

"I loved it from the first sentence. Your ability to create wonderful dialogue, and to thread in the story from the previous two books is wonderful." — K. Dickinson

"Great tension, great intrigue, and interesting characters" — Amazon reviewer

PROOF OF LIFE

"A delicious glimpse at what happens when the veil between the two worlds unexpectedly parts. I dare you to put this book down!" — Suzanne Giesemann, author of Messages of Hope

"A compassionate heroine bridges the divide between the spirit world and earthly evil in this well-paced thriller. Proof of Life will keep readers flipping pages all night!" — S.W. Hubbard, Author of Another Man's Treasure

"Fiction can sometimes be a powerful and inspirational way to teach us about life and the afterlife. Proof of Life celebrates this truth." — Gary E. Schwartz, PhD, University of Arizona, Author of "The Afterlife Experiments"

"A brain injury, followed by a coma opens a door wide into to the Spirit World. Proof of Life will have you on the edge of your seat, late into the night as you discover we don't die." — Sandra Champlain, author of the international bestseller, We Don't Die - A Skeptic's Discovery of Life After Death, and host of We Don't Die Radio

"A wonderfully human voice, intense emotions, and a deep dive into the Afterlife. Lowe has created a brilliant backdrop in PROOF OF LIFE, allowing readers to explore life-altering questions via the imminently like-able Jessica Mack. " —K.J. Howe, international bestselling author of SKY-JACK

"Proof of Life is a heartwrenching and heartwarming story that explores the universe beyond the veil, delving into the universal questions we all contemplate." — Connie di Marco, author of the Zodiac Mysteries

"The voices recovering amnesiac Jessica Mack hears compel her to search for a missing four-year-old boy, a quest that leads her to the doorway between life and the afterlife and challenges her beliefs on every level. This story rocks." — DP Lyle, award-winning author of the Jake Longly and Cain/Harper thriller series

WHAT SHE SAW

"Sheila Lowe's *What She Saw* is a gripping, psychologically astute thriller, with a sympathetic heroine and enough suspense to keep any reader turning the pages." — Dennis Palumbo, licensed psychotherapist and author of the *Daniel Rinaldi Mystery* Series

"Lowe spreads the mystery out one delicious morsel at a time. Both her characters and her plot are flawless." — Peg Brantley, author of *Red Tide* and *The Missings*

"From the foreboding opening chapter to the explosive climax, the reader will experience non-stop anxiety about who this woman is and what jeopardy is about to engulf

her." — Jackie Houchin, reviewer

"Twists and turns, a riveting tale of suspense that will keep you on the edge of your seat." — Connie Archer, national best-selling author of *The Soup Lover's Mysteries*

FORENSIC HANDWRITING MYSTERIES

"Dynamite" - Starred review – *Publisher's Weekly*

"Lowe wins readers over with her well-developed heroine and the wealth of fascinating detail on handwriting analysis." - Booklist

"Utterly compelling! "Outside the Lines" joins the ranks of those rare thrillers that expertly blend nonstop plotting with keen perceptions of the characters—good and bad—who populate this wonderful tale." - Jeffery Deaver, *New York Times* Bestselling Author of "The Bone Collector"

"Sheila Lowe's writing is fast-paced and suspenseful and made believable by her own background as a forensic handwriting expert. Yet another page-turner for Claudia Rose fans." — Rick Reed, Author of the *Jack Murphy Crime* Series

Dead Letters starts at high speed, and it stays there...Lowe presents a clear and compelling story—and thusly a respect for the reader's experience. - Pen World magazine

Dead Letters is an entertaining thriller set in Egypt, Gibraltar, Arizona and London, starring two heroines, an expert handwriting analyst and her intrepid niece. This novel will get your heart racing and also give you a fun education on ancient Egypt history at the same time.- Matt Witten, bestselling author of The Necklace

"Lowe expertly delivers a solid criminal investigation while guiding her readers into a unique culture where tattooing and the murder of a young girl come together on the autopsy table. Hit the lights and siren because this is one fast ride from beginning to end." — Lee Lofland, Author of "Police Procedure and Investigation" and founder and director of the Writers' Police Academy

This is a good read that's hard to put down. If you have any interest in reading handwriting, there's a lot of good information about that included in the story. You may even have to watch how you write in the future. You'd don't want anyone to think you're a psychopath... - Long and Short Reviews

A smart and likable protagonist (Claudia Rose) with an interesting and unusual occupation (forensic handwriting analysis) and a multiple mystery with plenty of suspects, each harboring a plethora of secrets.

To all the mothers and daughters, lost and found

one

Death is a human concept
Eternal life is reality
Above all, Love is never quiet
It rages or whispers
Philip Pearlman

The news landed like a drone strike, exploding everything Jessica knew about her life. And, just as in the aftermath of an explosion, silence charged the air. Only they were not on a battlefield, but seated across the desk from an attorney in a swank Beverly Hills office.

The attorney, Tanya Stewart, waited expectantly for a reaction to the letter she had just read aloud. The peculiar, implausible, unbelievable letter that made Jessica Mack and Jenna Sparks the heirs of a man whose name was unknown to them; a man who, as far as they knew, was a complete stranger. Jessica, glancing at her twin's face, saw the same stunned expression that she knew must be on her own; felt the same shockwaves thrumming through her body.

A dozen questions surged in her brain, demanding an answer—questions that stuck in her throat as undulating waves of light began to pulse at the edges of her vision, softening the periphery. The room shimmered and dissolved around her, fading into smoky shadow. Her body felt light; so light that she might float off the chair and keep going up, up, right through the ceiling and into the ether. Jessica knew what was happening and that she was powerless to stop it.

Jenna, gone. The attorney, gone...

Seated at a grand piano center stage, she is flanked by a tuxedo-clad orchestra in a darkened auditorium. Off to her right and high above, a spotlight blinks on, pinning her like a butterfly in its brilliant glare.

An expectant hush falls over the audience. Her hands rise from her lap and pause—a moment of readying before she lowers them to the keyboard. Fingers fly artfully over the keys, rendering the immediately recognizable Für Elise with such tender expression, Jessica wants to weep.

The hands behind the music are hers, but Chopsticks is more her speed than Beethoven. Someone—or something—has assumed control, causing her to play on until the last strains of Chopin's Ballade in G die away to thunderous applause.

Her hands return to her lap, her eyes falling on the silver lyre stamped above the legend, 'Steinway & Sons' on the polished black surface of the piano. She reaches out...

"Jess—*Jessica.*" Jenna's urgent stage whisper jolted her back to. reality. Her hand was reaching, not for the logo on a piano, but the edge of the attorney's desk. Jessica blinked and blinked again as she re-established her physical presence in the room, her mind racing to process what she had experienced. The occasional trances brought on by Spirit had been happening for a few months. She still came out of the mental bounces from one location to another feeling disoriented and confused. What did a piano concert have to do with—

Tanya Stewart was rising from her seat. "Are you okay, Jessica? Can I get you some water?"

Jessica managed the ghost of a smile. "Please don't bother, thanks, I'm fine."

The attorney resumed her seat. "I can see the news has come as a surprise."

"Surprise?" The ironic laugh came from Jenna. "It sounds like a joke. A stranger walks into a bar and leaves two sisters a house—"

Before she could come up with a punchline, Stewart interrupted. "Herron Pond is not exactly what you'd call a house."

"What is it, then?" Jessica asked.

Tanya held up a finger, signaling for them to wait. She tapped keys on her laptop and when she'd found what she was looking for, swiveled it to face them. A photograph taken from the sky filled the screen and left the sisters gaping. The viewer looked down on a Victorian-era mansion on a hilltop. Fronted by a semi-circular drive, the facade was cloaked in a beard of ivy. Arched turret windows gave the impression of a magical kingdom hiding behind grey stone walls.

Tanya Stewart reached over to press an arrow to page through a series of photographs: a small lake behind the mansion, an outdoor barbecue kitchen on a flagstone patio. A half-acre away at the foot of a cliff, the Pacific Ocean stretched to the horizon.

"Is this a joke?" Jenna asked incredulously.

The attorney shook her head. "Not at all. This is what Mr. Evanov left you in his will."

"It's like something out of Harry Potter," Jessica breathed.

Her sister made an inelegant sound. "Remember what happened at Hogwarts?"

"Don't be a killjoy. It's spectacular."

Jenna wasn't having it. "This is crazy. Why would someone give us a mansion? We don't know this guy from a bar of soap."

"You're *sure* he's not some long-lost relative?" Jessica asked Tanya. "You do know we were adopted at birth?"

"I didn't find any evidence that you have ties to your benefactor. But your adoption was sealed, so admittedly, that limited my investigation." Tanya's expensively threaded eyebrows rose to touch blunt cut bangs. "You really don't know Vadim Evanov? I mean, I get that you weren't aware he had made you heirs to his estate, but—"

"Not the sneakiest sneaking suspicion," Jenna said. "What can you tell us about him?" She was still speaking when Tanya shook her head.

"Unfortunately, there were no details in the letter; Just that he had made the gift and I was asked to deliver the message to you."

"Why didn't the estate people contact us directly?" Jessica asked.

"It's the kind of news that's better delivered in person, I'm sure you'll agree. Dianne Maggio, the estate attorney, contacted me and asked if I would speak to you first. I've done work for her law firm in Big Sur—that's where the estate is located—and I'm in closer proximity to you geographically. She must have thought you were acquainted with Mr. Evanov, or she surely would have said something more."

Estate. Jessica's brain grabbed hold of the word. Her eyes flicked back to the laptop screen. A place that size would definitely qualify as an estate. Could it actually be real, this gift? She looked back at Tanya. "You must know *something* about him?"

"When I got Dianne Maggio's letter, I did a search," the attorney admitted. Her mouth widened into a sugary-sweet smile. "Mr. Evanov had no Internet presence that I could find. Some people don't, especially older folks. Have you ever been to Big Sur? It's a couple hundred miles up the coast from Ventura. Why not take a drive up there? Or a train?"

Jessica, seeing the protest beginning to form on her sister's face, counted down in her head: three, two, one, wait for it...

"A place that size must take a huge amount of upkeep. How are we—"

Tanya held up her hands, stopping her. "I'm told that upkeep is included in a very substantial trust that's earmarked for the purpose. Ms. Maggio will give you specific numbers, but for now, it appears you have inherited quite a large sum of money along with the house."

The twins exchanged a wordless glance, mentally asking each other *What the hell?*

Tanya closed the laptop. "I'll put you in touch with Ms. Maggio so you can arrange to get access to the property. Look, you aren't required to keep it. It's yours to do with as you wish. If you decide you want to sell it, she can help with that. Who knows? Maybe you'll want to live there."

Three, two, one...

Jenna's objection came right on schedule. "There's no way. I have kids, my husband has a job—"

Jessica, who had begun musing on the idea, said nothing.

two

EARLY ON TUESDAY MORNING, with Jenna behind the wheel and rain in the forecast, they entered Coast Highway still bickering over whether or not their 'supposed inheritance,' as Jenna insisted on referring to it, was real or a scam. The five-hour trip north would take them to Big Sur, the area named for an undeveloped coastal expanse south of Monterey. *El Sur Grande,* the Big South, a place of giant redwoods, mountains, oceans. And Herron Pond.

The plan was to meet Dianne Maggio at the estate, where she would take give them a tour of the mansion. At her suggestion, they would stay overnight there, rather than book a room at one of the local inns. Predictably, Jenna was reluctant and Jessica jumped to accept on their behalf.

Jessica tuned out her twin's grumbling about the possibility of rain and lost herself in setting up an imaginary easel in a sunlit room at Herron Pond. Her skin prickled with excitement as she mentally mixed paints and selected the brushes she would use to paint that stunning scenery.

"If they named it Herron Pond for the bird, it's got one 'r' too many," Jenna's non sequitur interrupted the mental art project.

"I'm pretty sure they knew how to spell it."

They made it through Santa Barbara morning rush-hour traffic with a dry windshield. Forty minutes later, the Buellton exit came up, which put them a mere three miles east of the Danish Village of Solvang. Most days, it would be an excuse to pick up a box of pastries at one of the bakeries. Jenna suggested stopping.

"Not today," Jessica said. "We can stop on the way home."

"It wouldn't take long. You could run in to the bakery and—"

"If we keep going, we can outrun the rain you're so worried about."

Jenna made a silly face. "I guess you're the boss of this trip."

Jessica grinned back at her. "That's right, I am. Keep driving."

Ninety minutes later, a light sprinkle had begun. They stopped for lunch at Gino's Pizza in Pismo Beach.

"The weather guy got it wrong again," Jenna said. "Hey, we're an hour out from San Simeon. Let's go to Hearst Castle."

"Why are you so hot to dilly-dally? That place has twelve tours and you only see one teeny section, depending on the one you take." Jessica swiped her napkin across her lips and gathered her trash, ready to get back on the road.

"Hearst Castle is historic. I could tell the girls—"

"Your twins are four years old—too young to love a mommy lecture on the wonders of William Randolph Hearst. And *I* have zero interest in throwing away twenty-five bucks and a couple of hours on an uber-opulent tourist attraction. Let's go."

Jenna brought out the eyeroll she had used on Jessica since they were teens. "Tell the truth, Jessica Mack. You can't wait to see your own personal Hogwarts."

"*You* tell the truth, Jenna Sparks. Aren't you the tiniest bit curious about it?"

"Of course I am. But I still think it has to be some kind of scam."

"Jesus crumbles, Jen, give it up for a bad joke."

"You saw that house in the photo. Who gives a place like that to total strangers? I bet the real thing is nothing like the pictures we saw. Remember that Airbnb we went to in Carmel? On their website it looked gorgeous. When we got there, it was a converted garage with shag carpet from the 70s and threadbare sheets—"

It was Jessica's turn to roll her eyes. "What would an expensive Beverly Hills attorney get out of scamming *us?* You think they randomly picked us off the Internet for—what? What do they get out of it?"

"Haven't you heard about those landlord scams where they get a bunch of people to sign the same lease and—"

"Oh. My. God. Just because you married an FBI guy, do you have to be so paranoid? It's fine to be cautious, but we have to check it out. If we smell any kind of ripoff, we can turn around and leave. That's why we're taking this trip, right? To find out what's up?"

"We're taking this trip because you twisted my arm until you practically broke it." Jenna shot her a mischievous grin. "What are your woo-woo vibes saying? You can't tell me you aren't getting any clues about this whole thing."

Jessica had no comeback for that. The problem with being a twin was, even if you weren't alike in personality, all too often, the other knew what you were thinking or experiencing—especially when you didn't want them to. She was not about to admit to her skeptical sister that ever since the trance incident at Tanya Stewart's office she had indeed been receiving troubling messages through her non-physical senses. On the other hand, she argued with herself, she didn't know for certain that those messages had anything to do with the house—*the estate*—they had inherited from a stranger named Vadim Evanov.

Right.

Her 'woo woo vibes.' For five years she had fought against acknowledging the mediumship and psychic abilities that had plagued her since a devastating auto accident and head injury. She had pretended to herself that the whispers from spirits nagging her to do things for them were the product of an imagination gone wild. Or the easy explanation—she was crazy—which seemed preferable to the alternative.

That had all changed a few months ago when her friend, a FBI special agent, had dragged her into the case of a missing child. She had acquired a dizzyingly fast education in connecting with the Other Side. It had been like being thrown into the deep end of a pool without knowing how to swim—which she knew something about.

Finally, when Jessica had stopped resisting the voices and was rewarded by Spirit. They had brought her together with Sage Boles, whom she had recognized on a soul level the moment they met. The love that followed was something they both instinctively knew had bound them together through millennia. Like Jessica, Sage was an artist, and he was also attuned to the spiritual life. He had introduced her to Bella Bingham, an experienced medium and teacher, who settled comfortably into being her mentor.

And yet, with Jessica's uninvited abilities in their infancy, not even Bella had been able to help her control the unexpected trances, like the one in Tanya Stewart's office.

The concert stage, the music, the invisible pianist controlling her hands—since the meeting with Tanya, the scene had rerun every night in her dreams. Jessica was too new at trying to interpret what the dreams meant to figure it out, and she couldn't share them with Jenna. As much as Jenna tried to accept it, Jessica knew that her twin still feared her ability to communicate with spirit and her habit of 'disappearing' into trances.

Most of the time, the recurring dreams she had were from a spirit desperate to get a message through to someone living on earth. She was rarely frightened by them, but the spirits tended to be persistent, not giving up until she had figured out what they needed to get across and how she was supposed to deliver the message they were insisting she bring through.

The landscape hurtled past outside the window. Jenna chatted on about her preschoolers, Emma and Sophie, talking about going with the girls to Legoland. Keeping half an ear on what her twin was saying, Jessica's mind drifted to her dreams. Her playing the piano on a concert stage didn't make sense. She had known since she was eight years old that she loved art more than piano lessons. Why would spirt want her to be in that scene?

She knew there was a difference between these dreams and others she'd had. She'd tried to look into the front rows of the audience, but the faces were a blur; there was no one she could identify as a spirit stuck between worlds, or one who needed her help to resolve a grudge. Or to tell someone they were sorry for the way they had behaved in life, or that they loved them.

The music in the dream—always *Für Elise*—and inevitably, the piano keys moving under her fingers, sometimes whimsically, but often with a melancholy inflection, left Jessica unbearably sad when she awoke the next morning.

"You're not listening to me." Jenna's voice penetrated the reverie.

"Yes, I am," Jessica said with a guilty start. "Legoland."

"Uh huh. You thought you cleverly ducked my earlier question about getting any psychic clues. Are you?"

Lying to her twin didn't work, but not finding a way to explain what she had seen, she deflected the question. "Since when do you want to know about my 'psychic stuff?'"

"Since we're going into this weird situation."

"No, and I couldn't find anything on the Internet about Vadim Evanov, either. I tried every which way I could think of. It has to be a Russian name, or one of those other Eastern European countries, maybe Slovenia or Ukraine."

"There could be information about him in Russian," Jenna said.

"Do you read Russian, doofus? I didn't think so. Maybe you could ask Roland to have him checked out."

"You know he can't use those resources for personal things."

"How did you get to be so prissy?" Jessica said. Taking out her phone, she started to ask Siri about the origins of the name 'Evanov.'

"Siri is not available at the moment," the phone announced. She checked the bars. "There's no cell service up here."

"Wait—what? You know I have to be able to call Roland and the girls."

Jessica laughed at her stricken look. "Did you know your voice gets all squeaky when you're anxious?"

"It's not nice to make fun of your little sister."

"You're ten whole minutes younger. Don't get your panties in a wad. There's gotta be Wi-Fi at the house, or a Sat phone or something."

"But what if there's not?"

"If there's not, we'll find a place to stay in Big Sur Village. It's not totally cut off from civilization. There are tons of inns and B&Bs around there."

Reverting to a childhood gesture, Jenna held out a pinky for her sister to link with her own. "Pinky swear as a twin?"

Jessica solemnly gave the little finger an extra-firm squeeze, to be held in the highest regard of any promise. "Pinky swear as a twin."

***

At barely past two pm, the hour the estate attorney had arranged to meet them, the journey came to an end. They were facing a pair of tall iron gates set in the river-rock wall that secured the property. The branches of a flat metal tree spread across each gate and rose above it. The word 'Herron' was etched on one gate, 'Pond' on the other.

To keep intruders out? Jessica wondered idly, considering the gates. *Or to keep someone in?* She laughed at herself, recognizing Jenna's angsty influence. The artist in her craved the quiet solitude of both the untamed and the beautiful landscaping. If she lived here, she would never want to leave it. She could pour herself into her painting and sculpting and creating miniatures.

"Maybe Dianne Maggio is already here," Jenna said. She stopped the car at the intercom outside the gates. Lowering her window, she was reaching for the call button when a Mercedes came up behind them. An attractive blonde in a tailored pantsuit climbed out. She leaned down with a pleasant waft of floral scent. "Hi, I'm Dianne Maggio, we spoke—" The rest of the sentence died out.

The twins, used to surprising people with their virtually identical faces, had designated Jenna as the one to introduce them. "Hi, Dianne. I'm Jenna Sparks. You spoke with my sister, Jessica Mack. She's the one in the passenger seat."

The attorney's welcoming smile revealed even, white teeth. "Great to meet you both. I was expecting sisters, of course, but nobody mentioned twins. Wow. I bet you're sick of hearing how amazing it is that you look so much alike."

She was right; after thirty-three years they *were* sick of it.

"We don't dress alike," Jessica said. "So, you'll be fine if you keep in mind that Jenna is wearing green and has her hair straight, and I—Jessica, have curly hair and am wearing blue. See how that works? Easy."

Dianne laughed. "Thank goodness for that." She pointed a remote at the gates, and as they opened said, "Follow the road about a half-mile to the house; I'll be right behind you."

She returned to her vehicle and the sisters exchanged an astonished glance. "It looked humongous in the picture," Jessica said, "but a *half-mile* long driveway?"

"I mean, seriously."

They drove slowly forward under the grove of old-growth trees that lined the road. Their bare branches reached for each other like the arms of bereft lovers, forming a bower for them to drive under. Jessica found it haunting and hoped that once winter had gone and spring leaves dressed their limbs, the trees would appear more welcoming than they did today.

She wanted to pinch herself. How was it possible that all of this suddenly belonged to her and Jen? And again, who was this man, Vadim Evanov, that he had wanted them to have it? Had there been some kind of mistake? She had asked herself the same questions over and over and come up with no reasonable answer.

"I called Lorraine," Jenna said, reading her thoughts. "I figured if this Evanov guy was connected to us in some way, she would be the one to ask."

At first, Jessica said nothing, as she tended to do when their mother's presence was invoked. She had gradually come to accept a painful truth about the woman who had raised them. Lorraine Marcott was a narcissist who was as incapable of compassion or empathy as a rock. Nothing existed outside her own ego. She was a mother who had never seen Jessica for who she really was, nor cared to. On the single occasion Jessica could recall her showing the slightest interest in a piece of art she had produced—a rainbow-hued unicorn—rather than praising it, their mother had chided her for being 'too fanciful.'

What would Lorraine have said had she known that most of Jessica's actual fancies featured herself as a magical being, forced to live in a love-impoverished human household until she could be rescued by someone from her own world who understood her? A little bit Harry Potter, a little bit fairy princess.

"The adoption stork dropped me at the wrong house." Jessica said. "How can you stand to talk to her?"

"Maybe if you tried a little harder at not being so resentful—" Jenna said, cutting her eyes at her.

And Jessica immediately regretted raising the old argument, which would probably never be peacefully resolved. "Let's not go there," she said. "Did she Lorraine know who Mr. Evanov was or why he would do this?"

"If she was being honest—which as you know is always a big *if* with Lorraine—she had no idea. She reminded me—as if I didn't know—that with the adoption sealed they never knew where we came from. Plus, it was sealed from our birth mother, too, so she didn't know who got us."

"That's a dead end, then."

"She was stoked about the whole 'inheriting an estate in Big Sur' thing. After I sent her those photos of the mansion, she was ready to pack her bags and meet us there."

"I'm sure she was," Jessica muttered.

"It was worth asking her," Jenna said, as if she needed to excuse herself for making the contact.

Asking Lorraine was the logical thing to do, Jessica told herself. She would never have done it, so it was an avenue she should thank Jenna for exploring.

Jessica had always resented the fact that Jenna had worked hard to be good and do right, to get good grades and please their parents, gratefully accepting any scraps of affection they doled out. What for Jenna had been the 'good old days,' for Jessica had been an endless series of days-long dark moods of despair; of hiding, even from her twin, taking refuge in the garden shed.

Jessica had never lost the yearning for what she couldn't have that everyone else seemed to—a family where the parents adored their kids. She was well into adulthood when she finally admitted to herself that few families actually lived in that kind of a sitcom household.

The silence stretched between them as they continued along the driveway. *Für Elise* began to play softly in Jessica's head, pulling her attention away from the sting of past memories. She knew with utter certainty that the music vision and the dreams were intimately entwined with the house they were about to see. Why else would she hear that particular melody whenever thoughts of Herron Pond came to her? One thing she had learned about the spirit world was that nothing was random. Every symbol had a meaning.

The tree-lined avenue narrowed to a lane that opened onto manicured parkland. Too stunned to speak, the sisters followed it around the shore of the lake, past a boathouse and a gazebo. The twins gasped a simultaneous breath. At the end of a wide circular driveway, the house seemed like a small palace.

The photographs on Tanya Stewart's computer screen had been impressive. In no way did they do justice to the grand old Victorian mansion that glowered down at them like a haughty dowager duchess.

three

OVERWHELMED, THE TWO OF them stood in the foyer, gawking up at a magnificent stained-glass wall that rose to the second-floor ceiling. A shaft of refracted light poured through the glass, illuminating the grand staircase with a rainbow of color. Contemplating the designs in the various panels, Jessica wanted to stand there all day and drink in the artistry. She recognized the meaning of the scenes. The renaissance figures told the story of good and evil in the Garden of Eden. If she could politely have asked her sister and Dianne to leave her there alone, she would.

Her imagination took her to the long-ago days when the house was new. The late 1800s, Dianne had told them. With authentic Victorian details all around them, it was easy to picture being tightly laced into a corset and layers of petticoats, a beribboned and laced gown worn over them. How many babies had come into the world here? How many weddings celebrated, funerals held, tears shed? These old walls had soaked up more than a hundred years of history. Jessica hoped the Herron family and its successors had seen more smiles and laughter than sadness. On a sigh of pure pleasure, she found her voice. "It's remarkable."

"Isn't it, though?" Dianne said. "It's a lot to take in."

Jenna's attention had wandered almost immediately from the stained-glass artwork. She wandered away from them, rambling through the foyer, stopping to look at each of the faithfully preserved Victorian-era details.

"Mr. Evanov bought the property in the early seventies," Dianne said like a tour guide, while following Jenna's movements with her eyes. "This wing is more or less the same as when it was originally built in the late eighteen-hundreds. You'll see the extension, which was added much later. It has a beautiful new kitchen and living space. With the other wing being contemporary, it's like two houses in one. The old kitchen is on this side, but these days—well, when Vadim was alive—it was used for staff to take their meals, and as an adjunct when there was something going on in the public rooms." She paused, giving them a chance to ask questions, but Jessica was rendered speechless, and Jenna had not had her fill of browsing.

Dianne started moving toward the staircase. "We'll take the stairs to the second floor. I'll show you the bedrooms on this side first. After that, we'll see the public rooms down here, and then end up at the new wing. This side has a lot more that's interesting from an architectural and décor point of view."

Jessica moved to follow her, but Jenna, rejoining them, raised both hands in a 'stop' motion. "This is all very interesting and important, Dianne, but you're right, it's a *lot*. And frankly, we're reeling from it all. And now that we're here—"

"Of course," their host interrupted. "I apologize. I should have asked what you would like to do first. Do you prefer to rest up for a while after that long drive? I can show you around a little later."

"What we would like most," said Jessica, "is to understand why Mr. Evanov made us his heirs when we have no idea who he was. As far as we can tell, he didn't know us either, so—"

"Naturally you're curious, to say the least." Dianne gave them an appraising look and seemed to come to a decision. "How about I take you to that kitchen I mentioned in the new wing? We can chat over a cup of coffee."

"I could use some coffee," Jenna admitted.

"Sounds good to me, too," said Jessica, peering down the long hallway, where she could see wide arched doorways. "Are we going to need a map to find the kitchen?"

"Not while you've got me here," Dianne said with a grin. "You might later, though."

How can all this be ours? Jessica asked herself yet again.

Jenna, perhaps sharing the thought, linked arms with her as they followed Dianne, who pointed out various pieces of furniture they passed. Some had been imported from Europe and England, she told them. The stained glass in the foyer wall had come from an Italian church. When Jessica asked how Mr. Evanov had gotten it out of Italy, Dianne said it was a question best not asked.

They entered a formal dining room, which the attorney told them was the way into the new wing. As she took them past a long black marble table surrounded by ten upholstered chairs, an odd quiver passed over Jessica that made her wonder.

At the rear of the dining room, wide French doors opened onto a stone-paved patio that looked out onto the grounds, with the eponymous pond in the distance. Dianne showed them a keypad hidden in an unobtrusive alcove. "This door separates the two wings of the house," she said, tapping in the code. A door concealed in the paneling slid aside on a well-oiled track and she signaled for the twins to precede her.

"Like something out of Clue," Jessica said, suppressing a giggle. Jenna snorted in apparent agreement and they stepped through the opening.

Moving from the Victorian dining room into a short passageway, she had expected that although they were going into the new wing, it would be furnished consistent with the Victoriana they had seen so far. She could not have been more mistaken. Following Dianne into an ultra-modern kitchen, she got the eerie feeling of having time-traveled more than a hundred years from the Victorian past to the twenty-first century. It was like coming out of a split-second trance.

Glancing at her twin to see whether she had experienced the same sensation, Jessica noted that Jenna's slim jaw was clenched, her lips closed in a tight line. What was going on in that perfectionistic head of hers? There were times when she thought maybe Jenna had psychic flashes, too, and was afraid to admit it.

Dianne studied them both impassively, waiting for a reaction. Jessica made admiring murmurs like, "Wow," and "Amazing." It probably wouldn't be appropriate to share her private opinion that the stylish modern rear of the house clashed with the antique front like a beautiful gown that pinched at the waist. She had to admit, though, it was a fabulous kitchen for any home, and for someone who loved to cook—which was not her—a piece of heaven.

Jenna was a natural homemaker. The oversized luxurious appliances seemed to have drained the earlier disapproval out of her. She dashed from one gadget to another, all but drooling.

"Omigod, look at the size of this oven. You could cook a banquet in here." And, "Is this a Dacor refrigerator? I would so love to have one, but it would never fit in my little kitchen."

Jessica grinned, enjoying her twin's excitement and hoping it lasted. Was it possible that it would be the kitchen that won her over to Herron Pond? "Hey, *this* kitchen is big enough for your girls to ride their trikes in," she said. "Think of all the fun they'd have."

Jenna frowned. "Are you insane? I would never let them—"

"Sense of humor, Jen, I'm joking."

"How many kids do you have?" Dianne asked, correctly guessing that the quickest way to earn brownie points with her was to show an interest in her children. When Jenna fished out her phone and thumbed to the latest photos, showing the attorney her two little redheads, mirror images of each other, Dianne made the appropriate cooing noises.

"This is Sophie and this is Emily. As you can see, they're twins, same as Jess and me. They were four last month."

Dianne reciprocated with pictures of her grandchildren. While the two of them chatted about pre-schools and playdates, Jessica wandered over to the wide windows that looked out on an avenue of potted dwarf palms that led down to the pond. Even someone as undomesticated as she couldn't object to washing dishes with that view.

At the other end of the outsize kitchen was a double-sided fireplace flanked by a river rock fireplace. Jessica followed the wall around to an elegant breakfast room. Curved window walls revealed the same stunning view of the lake as the kitchen.

Jenna and Dianne joined her.

"Have a seat in here and I'll make the coffee," Dianne said. "How do you take it?"

"Black, please," said Jessica.

"Cream and sugar if you have it," said Jenna simultaneously.

Dianne laughed. "Is this a case of everything being opposite?"

"Pretty much," the twins agreed.

As the attorney took herself off to the kitchen, Jessica could practically hear her sister thinking, *"Chandelier in the breakfast room—la di dah!"*

"That's the actual pond in Herron Pond that you can see behind the house," Dianne called out. "The house was named for it. The original owners were Herrons."

"That explains the spelling," said Jenna.

"Looks more the size of a lake to me," Jenna said, moving to take the tray from the attorney as she entered the breakfast room.

"I'm told it started out as a pond and was enlarged later. 'Pond' was in the name of the property, so it stuck. We use 'pond' and 'lake' interchangeably. Take your pick."

The three of them sat at the table, Jenna distributing the mugs of steaming black coffee from the tray. "What happened to the Herrons?" she asked.

Dianne stirred a packet of sweetener into her mug. "I only know of the last generation that lived here. I believe there were four or five daughters and one son. They all grew up and got married, built homes of their own; not the size of this one. Unfortunately, over the years, the house fell into disrepair. The parents eventually died. It was quite old by then and it needed considerable work. It's sad, really. It was sold once or twice prior to Vadim—Mr. Evanov—acquiring it."

"So, the kids all moved away?"

"There is one Herron that I'm aware of in the area—Amy. She's the realtor I intend to introduce to you. She can help with an appraisal and all of the details if you want to sell the property."

Jenna blew gently on her coffee, eyeing Dianne over the rim. "Isn't it kind of cruel to ask her to sell her old family home?"

"It's been out of her family for an entire generation. Not to mention it's worth quite a bit of money and she'll make an excellent commission when it's sold—if you decide to use her as your agent."

"It's a little soon to talk about selling," Jessica said. "We haven't really seen it yet." She was already infatuated with Herron Pond, especially the

Victorian side, and there was a lot more to see. It wouldn't take much to tip her into falling in love.

Jenna's hand paused over the cream jug. "What are you talking about, Jess? There's no way we can keep it. Even with the money Mr. Evanov left, can you imagine what it must take to run? It would be a full-time job."

"We just got here, Jen. Let's talk about it later, after we've had a chance to look around. We haven't seen enough to make any kind of informed decision."

"You're correct, Jenna," Dianne added. "It's far from being a low-maintenance property. It takes a full staff to keep it up." She sipped her coffee, giving them time to think about what that might amount to. Tanya Stewart had indicated that the maintenance costs were covered in the will, but there was the management to consider.

"Let's go back to our original question," Jessica said. "Why are we here?"

There was a prolonged silence, while the twins waited for an answer. Finally, Dianne huffed a sigh. "I'll tell you what I know, though I may not have what you're looking for."

"First," Jenna said, "Why didn't you call us? Why go through Tanya Stewart?"

"I would have contacted you directly, but this is the kind of news you need to hear in person. Ms. Stewart's office is so much closer to you, it seemed like the logical thing, to ask her to meet with you on my behalf. If I had called out of the blue to say you had inherited a large property, you would have thought it was some kind of scam, don't you think?"

Jenna nudged her sister as if to say, "I still do."

Catching the gesture, Dianne chuckled. "There's that old saying about looking a gift horse in the mouth, but you are absolutely right to be suspicious of something of this magnitude."

Jenna's phone buzzed and her mouth softened into an affectionate smile. "Roland. Texting to make sure we got here safely."

"He's such a great husband," Jessica told Dianne. "See, Jen, I told you there would be Internet."

Dianne moved the tray off the table and stood it against the wall. "Well, there is and there isn't."

Jenna looked alarmed. "What does that mean?"

"Back here in some of the newer areas of the house, you can usually get Wi-Fi, but it can be a little, um, temperamental. You see, Mr. Evanov never used the Internet himself. He was, you could say, reclusive. He didn't want anything to do with it. I think it might have been something to do with his old life in Russia. He finally broke down and had it installed because the current estate manager, Darryl Andrews, wouldn't come to work here otherwise. Darryl, and more or less everyone ever interviewed. So, he caved in and had it installed. The Wi-Fi is fairly basic, though."

"What exactly is 'basic'?"

"The bandwidth can be quite low. So, if you were on a Zoom meeting, for example, you'd want to be on this side of the house and not have anything else running in the background. Otherwise, people tend to freeze on screen. You could get your email, no problem. Usually."

While Dianne and Jenna were discussing the WI-FI, Jessica's brain had skidded to a halt at *estate manager*.

"Will we meet Mr. Andrews today?" she asked.

"With no one currently living here, he doesn't need to be on the property full-time anymore," Dianne said. "Since Mr. Evanov passed away last October, Darryl has been coming up once a week or so to supervise the cleaners and check on things. He's got a condo in Carmel where he stays. I'll arrange for you to meet him while you're here."

"I thought an estate attorney handled the paperwork," Jenna said. "It sounds like you're a lot more than that."

"That's because I am the executor of the estate. I became Mr. Evanov's estate lawyer several years ago and we got to be friends. He started entrusting me with certain tasks that he needed help with and didn't want handled by anyone else."

Jenna eyed her over the rim of her mug. "Am I right in guessing that an estate manager isn't the same as a housekeeper?"

"For a house this size, it's a lot more complicated than a housekeeper job." There was something faintly patronizing in Dianne's smile. Maybe she thought they were philistines who didn't know a mansion from a McDonald's. Jessica couldn't blame her if she did. It wasn't that far from the truth.

"The manager's job is to keep everything on the estate running smoothly. Darryl handles the staff. He coordinates the schedules of the cleaners and landscapers and arranges for any necessary repairs. He worked with the chef, too, planning menus. Basically, he has his hands on everything. Occasionally, he would take Vadim to the doctor or other appointments, when Vadim's secretary, Wanda, wasn't available." She glanced away, her eyes drifting to the window and the pond outside. "There were dinner parties to supervise, too. Not to mention the occasional piano recital and—"

Jessica missed the rest of what she said. Her vision lost focus as a tunnel opened in front of her. *Für Elise* played gaily in her head, a vastly different tone than the melancholy accent she usually heard. Sparklers and shimmering sprinkles of light were showering her like a Fourth of July fireworks spectacular. With a jolt, she became aware that Dianne was looking at her with concern. How long had she been spaced out?

"Recital?" Jessica said, fighting for composure. The strange look Jenna gave her let her know that the question had been hanging unanswered long enough to be weird. But if Dianne thought so, she was too polite to let it show.

"My apologies," she said. "I keep forgetting you didn't know him. Vadim Evanov was highly respected in musical circles. After he ended his teaching career years ago, he kept up an interest in what was going on in the classical music scene."

"If that's true, why couldn't we find anything about him on the Internet?" Jenna asked.

"It was a long time ago that he was on the concert stage. Not everyone is on Google—it's only been around since the late 1990s. Plus, he went out of his way to resist anything that smacked of social media when that came along. I can assure you, whether it comes up in a search or not, he was famous in his day, and piano teachers brought their young prodigies from all over the world for him to hear and critique, right up until he died."

The windows were closed but an icy breeze rippled across Jessica's shoulders. Was their benefactor letting her know he was with them in spirit while they sat at his breakfast table having a conversation about him?

"Für Elise."

Dianne cocked her brow in a question. "Excuse me?"

She had spoken aloud without realizing it. "The piece by Beethoven— *Für Elise?* It's a recital piece, isn't it?"

Jenna's expression was one of dubious curiosity, letting Jessica read her thoughts: *What the hell do you know about what's played at recitals?*

Dianne nodded. "I'm a rock fan myself, but yes, I think that's a piece most people would recognize, even if they couldn't name it. Do either of you play the piano?"

"I used to," said Jenna. "Since the twins came along, I don't have time to practice. I'd love for them to start learning when they're old enough."

"Emily would never sit long enough; Sophie would, though. They're like the two of us," Jessica chuckled, explaining to Dianne. "Sophie is prim and proper like her mother. Emily is a savage rebel like her aunt."

"They must be a lot of fun. And a handful, I bet."

"That's the truth," said Jenna, like the proud mom she was. "I should get serious and start looking for a good piano teacher. The piano will need tuning, too. If Sophie starts, Emily will want lessons, too. They're like us—ten minutes apart in age, but Em is so competitive with—"

And she's off, Jessica thought with an inward grin. Tuning out Jenna's happy chatter, she got busy processing the new information about their benefactor. Was it the spirit of Vadim Evanov that had shown her the vision of a piano concert? Kept repeating it in her dreams? In light of what they had learned, it would be reasonable, especially if his students had performed at Carnegie Hall.

"How about you, Jessica?" Dianne interrupted her mental meandering. "Do you play, too? I can picture you two girls playing duets together."

"Definitely not me. I gave it up after a few lessons. I was more interested in art than music."

After that, the conversation turned to the intricate miniatures Jessica fashioned, often from repurposed materials, and the sculptures and paintings she had exhibited in galleries. As soon as she could, she brought the talk around to the topic that most interested her.

"You mentioned that Mr. Evanov was a piano teacher?"

"Yes, though not in the standard definition of the word. He started his career as a concert pianist and played all over the world—the Royal Albert Hall in London, Carnegie Hall, that kind of thing. And as I said, when he wasn't performing on stage any longer, he trained others—world-class pianists. He was invited to officiate in international juried piano competitions."

Piano competitions

Carnegie Hall

Für Elise

Jessica's heart pitter-pattered. As well-acquainted with him as Dianne had been, she must have the information they were seeking. New questions were forming too fast for her to articulate. "Why do you think he quit performing?"

"Nobody I've spoken to seems to have a clue," Dianne said, dashing her hopes. "He retired from the public eye when he was relatively young and stopped taking on new proteges. That was a long time before we met. The rumor goes that he stayed holed up in the old house, alone for a long, long time. It does make you wonder what happened. He was a very private person, so—"

"So, he didn't confide in you as a friend?"

"No. When I say we were friends, we shared similar interests, went to the theater together; things like that. But he was very closemouthed about anything personal. I think maybe his Russian upbringing—"

"It would have to be something serious to quit a good career and go into hiding like that," Jenna interrupted.

"She didn't say he was in hiding," Jessica snapped, irritated and not clear on why she felt the need to defend a man she had never met, and yet something prompted her to do just that.

Dianne raised an eyebrow. "Whatever the reason he quit, he came out of retirement not long after he built this extension. Maybe it gave him a 'new lease on life,' as the saying goes. He invited some of the top names in the field to come and visit. If you've ever heard of Claudio Arrau, Murray Perahia, Lang Lang—they all admired him. He was thought of as a great virtuoso."

Jessica, who was only vaguely familiar with the pianists Dianne listed off, sat in perplexed silence, her mind jumping. What had made Evanov leave the concert stage? And what had later brought him out of his shell? Even Jenna had nothing to say on that score.

Dianne gave the sisters time to digest what she had told them. When she spoke again, she sat up straight, every inch the lawyer and executor of the estate, ready to get down to business. "Now, getting to the question of why Vadim decided to make the two of you his heirs, I'm sorry to disappoint you, but the bottom line is, I have no idea. That was something else he never confided in me and when he didn't want to talk about something, his lips had an iron padlock; nothing would move them."

Disappointment rolled over Jessica like a wave. "You can't be serious. If *you* don't know why he did this, who else would?"

Suddenly, Dianne's lips began to quiver and the gleam of tears filled her eyes. Jessica saw it then—the grief she had been hiding. Vadim Evanov was someone she had cared deeply about.

"One thing I can tell you—" the attorney said, pulling herself together. "—although I shouldn't. Until five or six years ago, Vadim's intention was to leave everything to Amy Herron, the realtor I mentioned whose family once lived here."

The sisters' bewildered gazes were living reflections of each other. Jenna spoke first. "What do you think changed his mind?"

"I couldn't say. And to my knowledge, Amy never knew she was named in his will, so there's no need to worry about her resenting you for inheriting. She's not that kind of person anyway."

Jessica's curiosity about the man who had owned Herron Pond was increasing with everything she heard about him. "Didn't he marry, have a family?"

"He did have a wife. You'll see photos of her in the old part of the house. I believe she died fairly young and he never re-married." Sadness shadowed Dianne's eyes. "I hate to think of him living here as a young widower, all alone."

"Do you think that's why he quit performing?"

"Save that for later," Jenna said, and her tone was sharp with annoyance. "You're telling us that you're in the dark just like we are. How can that be?"

Dianne wrapped her hands around her coffee mug as if drawing warmth, or whatever she needed, from it. "I'm sorry, girls. When he called me to come over and re-draft his will, I did ask his reasoning. As his attorney, that was my job. It seemed a little strange, to say the least. But he got testy about it and told me in very plain terms to butt out. Vadim could get a little cantankerous." Her lips puckered into a cynical moue. "Okay, a *lot* cantankerous. Enough that I wasn't about to press him and get my head chewed off again."

"We thought you were going to solve the mystery for us," Jessica said with a defeated sigh.

"I wish I could. All I can do is show you what you've inherited. And of course, I'll get you a copy of the will so you can read it for yourselves. You can be assured that there is plenty of money to take care of the upkeep until you sell it."

Jessica bit off the question that wanted to spring out of her mouth: *why are you so hot for us to sell?*

Jenna drained her mug and set it on the coaster. "How old was Mr. Evanov?"

"He was elderly—in his 70s—but he didn't have dementia, if that's what you're thinking. His intellect was as sharp as a tack, if you'll excuse the cliché."

"That's relatively young," Jessica said. "What did he die of?" She leaned forward, suddenly impatient for the answer.

Dianne's lips flattened as if she wanted to keep the words from spilling out. "An accident," she said at last. "An unfortunate accident."

four

AN ACCIDENT. JESSICA FLASHED on an image of an old man tumbling down that long flight of stairs in the old part of the house and dying, alone. *Hopefully, nothing more than my ridiculous imagination.* "What kind of accident?" she asked, afraid to hear the answer.

Dianne rose from the table and walked to one of the curved windows, where she stood in silence for what felt like a long time, gazing out at the pond. Finally, she cleared her throat. "He was on his way down to Paso Robles for the Paderewski Youth Piano Competition. Darryl Andrews was supposed to take him because his secretary wasn't available that night. But for some reason, Vadim decided to drive himself." She returned to the table and sat down, her hands clasped tight in front of her.

"He had no business driving," she said, sounding angry. "He didn't have good night vision, and he'd had heart surgery a few years ago. The coroner's office said he'd had a heart attack, but they couldn't tell whether that was what caused him to veer off the road or it happened because of the accident. The Highway Patrol thinks he may have been distracted by something. Could be an animal ran out in front of the car. We'll never know." She paused as if gathering strength. When she spoke, her gaze had gone distant, and Jessica suspected that she was seeing neither of them.

"His car went over the cliff and onto the rocks, into the ocean. Coast Highway in that area isn't called one of the most dangerous roads in California for nothing." Her eyes welled up and she spoke haltingly. "It's so narrow, only one lane in each direction for quite a long way. Even in good weather—they didn't find him until two days later." A tear spilled onto her cheek, followed by another. With a murmured, "Excuse me," she stood up and hurried from the breakfast room, leaving the twins with the sound of muffled sobs.

They looked at each other.

"Don't say it," Jessica warned, well aware of what was in her sister's thoughts: Her acquaintance with the spirit world had followed an accident not dissimilar from what Dianne had described. An accident caused by Greg Mack, the man she had married; the father of her toddler son, Justin, who had been killed instantly. For a long time, the shadow of Justin's death had threatened to pull Jessica all the way into the black hole where her heart used to beat; a hole so black, no light could get in or out.

Understanding that talk of a car crash, particularly one that involved plunging off a cliff, might trigger those devastating emotions, Jenna reached over and squeezed her sister's hand. Jessica squeezed back; no words needed. The sisters were often at odds, but there were times when having a twin who knew what you were thinking was the best of all comforts.

Something more than her own memories was nagging at her, though. Some instinct, maybe a psychic message, that told her Vadim Evanov's accident was about to impact her and Jenna in ways she could not predict.

Dianne returned, dabbing a tissue to her flushed face. "I apologize for letting my emotions get the better of me," she said, sitting back at the table. "It's just, it was such a ghastly tragedy; so completely unexpected and traumatic."

"Please don't apologize," Jessica said. "We're very sorry for the loss of your friend."

The attorney wrung the tissue in her hands, clearly trying to get the better of her emotions. "He was in his late 70s, but he wasn't nearly ready to die."

"That's just awful." Jenna reached out and patted her hand. "We don't have to talk about it anymore. Let's change the subject."

"Yes, thank you, let's."

"You mentioned that it was several years ago when Mr. Evanov decided to leave his estate to us and changed his will—"

"There's nothing unusual in the terms of a will not being disclosed until after the testator has passed on," Dianne said, anticipating Jessica's question. "In this case, Vadim *insisted* it be kept completely confidential. It was completely up to him to tell you when he was ready." She spread her hands, her expression one of regret. "You have to understand that as his attorney, I was bound by law, under obligation not to divulge the information until after his death. I suspect he intended to contact you at some point. We'll never know."

"He died last October?" Jenna asked.

"Yes, and it took a while for you to be notified because when the will was redrawn all those years ago, you were both living in different areas and had different last names and addresses. I had to hire a private investigator to track you down."

She fixed a speculative gaze on Jessica. "The investigator came up with some interesting media stories about you finding that little boy last year. That was amazing what you did."

Jessica, who had no desire to revisit an experience she would be happy to forget, brushed off the comment and changed the subject. "I don't get it, Dianne. If Mr. Evanov wanted us to have—" she waved a hand, "all of this, why wouldn't he have arranged to meet us? Why not introduce himself?"

"There has to be a reason for it," Jenna agreed.

"Sure, he would have had his reasons for waiting. I never knew him to do anything without one. As I said, he may have had every intention of introducing himself."

"Isn't there anyone we could talk to who knew him?" Jessica asked.

"He didn't socialize locally. Like I said, he invited celebrities here from the music world, but I can't imagine he would have discussed his will with any of them. If he had any close friends, he didn't tell me. As far as I know, I was as close as it got."

"There must be *something* that would give us a hint." Jenna's tone said she was not buying it.

"I do believe you two are going to have to find any answers yourselves," Dianne said.

"How are we supposed to do that?" Jessica asked.

"I would think that if there *are* any answers, they might be in his personal papers, which would be in his study in the old wing. As his beneficiaries, you have a right to—"

Jenna broke in and started objecting. "It could take forever to dig through a bunch of old papers when we have no idea what we're looking for. My husband took two days off to take care of the girls. He has to work on Thursday. Jess and I have to be out of here by noon tomorrow, latest."

Dianne put out a pacifying hand. "Please don't worry, Jenna, there's no rush at all. I'll give you the security codes and everything you need. You can come up here at your leisure."

"Maybe we'll find something if we start looking this afternoon," Jessica said. "I don't want to leave until I understand why Mr. Evanov did this."

"I can show you his study and—" Dianne broke off, interrupted by Jenna's phone, which she had left on the table.

Excusing herself, Jenna took off around the corner to the kitchen, taking the call as she went.

"That's her husband's ringtone," Jessica explained with a small stirring of alarm. "Something must have happened."

"I hope it's nothing serious," Dianne said. "We'll wait for her before continuing."

As the seconds added up, Jessica's psychic antenna was vibrating loudly. She felt the urgency building in her gut.

"Who's hurt?" she asked when Jenna reappeared, but the question was a mere formality. She already knew the answer.

"Em had a fall at the playground and cut her forehead. They're on the way to the emergency room and Roland has completely lost his cool and is on to freaking out." Jenna managed a feeble smile. "Here's a guy who has no problem dealing with serial killers and kidnappers, but when it comes to his baby girls—"

Jessica responded to Dianne's unspoken question. "Her husband is an FBI supervisor."

"Ah—"

"I'm so sorry, I'm going to have to go." Jenna stooped to pick up her purse. "He thinks she's going to need stitches. I have to be there."

With a twinge of regret, Jessica got up, too, and made to retrieve her jacket from the chair where she had draped it. Jenna stopped her. "Why don't you stay here. There's nothing you can do if you come with me."

"I can take care of Sophie for you."

"No need, Roland is dropping her off with his sister on the way to the hospital."

"Are you sure? I could drive. You shouldn't be driving when you're upset."

Jenna gave her head a firm shake. "I'm fine, but I need to hit the road. It's going to be the same five-hour drive going home as it was coming up. Longer at this time of day."

Jessica knew she ought to object further. She also knew that in spite of her misgivings, her twin was aware that her protest was as weak as Jenna's own desire to leave was strong. She held her sister's eyes. "Are you *sure* sure? I think I should go with you."

"I'm *sure* sure. We don't need to do this, okay? You stay here. I know you want to. Have Sage come and get you. You can show him what we've inherited—for some inexplicable reason."

It was easy to see that despite seeing Herron Pond in person, Jenna was no less skeptical about the inheritance. "He's at a seminar until the weekend," Jessica said. "I guess if I stayed that long—"

"Sage is your husband?" Dianne asked.

A blush warmed her cheeks. "We haven't got to that stage. We met a few months ago. But I'd love him to see the place."

She followed Jenna outside to get her overnight bag from the trunk. When she made to say goodbye, her sister embraced her in a tight hug. "I love you, twin. Last chance. You really want to stay here all alone, as isolated as it is?"

"Yes, I'm fine with it."

"Okay then, if you're—"

"Stop it. I'm sure." Jessica hugged back. She had looked forward to exploring the old house with Jenna, had hoped to see her persuaded to see it as she saw it, but the prospect of doing it without fending off critical comments was even more exciting. With no more than a tiny pang, she said, "I love you, too. Please be careful, and watch out for jerks on the road."

"Don't worry. I don't want to end up on the rocks like our 'fairy god father.'" Jenna clung to her for longer than a quick goodbye called for. "I wish you would go with me."

"Jeez, Jen, pick a side. First, it's okay for me to stay, now you want me to go with you."

Jenna's cheeks puffed out on a long sigh. "It's just—I don't know, something doesn't feel right here."

Her attitude threw a pall of gloom over Jessica's enthusiasm. The thrill of seeing the estate had allowed her to neglect the itch that had been niggling at her ever since their arrival. She had been feeling the 'something,' too. She gave a weak chuckle. "Don't tell me you're getting psychic?"

Jenna looked aghast at the idea. "Don't be ridiculous. I'm just nervous about leaving you alone here. But I have to go—"

"Em's going to be fine. And you'd better text me the minute you get to the hospital. Give the girls a big kiss from Aunty Jess."

"You're too damn stubborn, Jessica Mack," Jenna said, plainly unhappy with the impasse they had reached.

"One of the less admirable traits we share, dear twin." Jessica gave her a little push toward the car.

Watching her go with promises of an update when she got to St. John's hospital and knew more about Emily's condition, the cynic in Jessica couldn't resist a smirk. The way her sister had pounced on the opportunity to leave Herron Pond carried an enthusiasm that smelled a lot like a reprieve.

five

THE BEDROOMS IN THE Victorian wing were on the second floor, generously spaced along a landing nearly as wide as the living room of the cottage where Jessica lived. Silenced by the grandeur, she drank it all in. The dignified grandfather clock ticking loudly in one corner. The elaborate arrangement of fresh flowers on a table that rested on a Persian rug. An immense floor-to-ceiling pier mirror on the side wall, encased in carved wooden surrounds—a regal centerpiece for the landing.

"—more than eight thousand square feet of living space," Dianne was saying, pulling Jessica's attention to her. "Five bedrooms on this side and three very nice guest rooms in the new wing. Seven baths in all."

"That's a lot to maintain."

"Yes, it is. It's my understanding that it was after building the new wing that Vadim started holding recitals again and invited special guests to stay over."

In keeping with the Victorian era, the first three bedrooms they entered were furnished with heavy oversized armoires and dressing tables. Jessica, whose education in antique furnishings was rudimentary at best, had expected to see four-poster beds hung with fusty draperies. These beds had carved wooden headboards and footboards and sumptuous velvet coverlets.

The house had bewitched her. She had to find a way to get Jen to feel the same way so they could somehow hold on to Herron Pond. If Jenna insisted on selling, there was no way she would be able to buy her out.

They had reached the end of the landing. Dianne led her around the corner to a suite of rooms set off on its own. "These were Vadim's rooms. You're welcome to use them while you're here. His clothes were given to a charity, so it shouldn't feel like you'd be staying in a, you know, deceased person's room."

Like that's not a creepy way to put it, Jessica thought, following her into the bedroom. Unlike the other bedrooms, the design was open and airy with plenty of space, though the furnishings followed the same Victorian conventions as the rest of the wing. As Dianne had said, most of the evidence of an elderly gentleman occupying the room had been cleared away, leaving it as impersonal as a home on the market.

The attorney walked deep inside the bedroom with such easy familiarity that Jessica wondered, not for the first time, whether she had shared something other than friendship with their benefactor. Evanov must have been a good twenty years older than her—not that age had to be a barrier in a relationship, if there had been one. The question was too personal to ask of someone she didn't know.

Dianne flung open the wide French doors and brought in a blast of March air. "Come and take a look. You can't see the private beach down the cliffs from here, but you can see the ocean."

Jessica stepped onto the veranda and took in a lungful of brisk air. The storm clouds had blown away for now. The acres of land on which the house stood stretched all the way to the Pacific, which winked in the distance like facets of a blue diamond.

"This is incredible. Living here would be like a permanent vacation."

"He liked to sit out here and watch the sunset."

If there had been no personal relationship between Vadim Evanoff and his attorney, Jessica was a lousy judge of character. "You really cared about him," she said, deciding to take a risk.

Dianne sauntered past her with a Mona Lisa smile. "He was a dear friend." Beckoning Jessica to follow, she started to retrace her steps toward the main staircase. "There's a lot to see downstairs. His study, as well as several public rooms and the—"

"Wait a sec. Didn't you say there are five bedrooms in this wing? We saw four."

For a moment, she looked flustered. "Oh. Yes, yes, there are five. You don't have to stay in Vadim's rooms. Feel free to stay in any of the ones I've showed you, or the guest rooms in the new wing." There was a slight hesitation. "Any of them are fine, except for the last door on the landing. You won't want to go in there."

A chill as cold as a kiss from frozen lips touched the nape of Jessica's neck. "Um, why?" she asked, stifling a shiver. "Do you have Bluebeard's wife hidden in there?"

"Nothing so gruesome, thank goodness." Dianne chuckled but her eyes slid away from Jessica's frank gaze. "It isn't actually used as a bedroom. It's become a kind of er, storage room. It's not ready for visitors."

It could not have been clearer that she was lying, and Jessica wanted to know why. So far, the other woman had been warm and welcoming. For some reason, this subject was making her uneasy.

"Well, I'm not exactly a visitor," Jessica said, refusing to be sidetracked.

"That's true in the strictest sense. But the first time you see the house, it should be at its best. You don't need to start with a lot of old junk that needs getting rid of."

"Isn't there an attic to store old junk?"

"As it happens, there is, a very large one. But you know how it is. People get lazy and start throwing things into a spare room. You don't realize how much has accumulated over the years until you look at it through someone else's eyes. Like when you were coming here today. We suddenly realized that this was something that needed handling. It was best that everything you were going to see was presentable for you and Jenna. It's just, there's been so much to do since Vadim passed on that it hasn't been possible for Darryl to do everything." Dianne herself cut off. She straightened her spine and firmed up her tone, too. "You'll want to wait until Darryl and I can sift through everything. We wouldn't want you to get hurt by some stray piece of furniture falling on you, right?"

Without waiting for a response, she started down the magnificent staircase, trailed by an unsatisfied Jessica. If she and Jenna had inherited the furnishings as well as the house, shouldn't she be the one to sift through the items, even if they had been tossed into a storage room? She started to say so, but thought better of it. No need to create conflict at the outset. There would be plenty of time to speak her mind about it.

Ignoring the slight awkwardness that had fallen between them, Dianne continued her monologue. "Did I mention there's a large apartment above the garage? Darryl stays in it while he's here. And, let me see, what else is there to tell you? Oh, the pond—or lake, if you prefer. It isn't all that deep—about ten feet, I think. There are canoes in the boathouse. So, if you want to take them out any time while you're up here, you can call Captain Steve. He'll drive up and get them out for you."

"There's a captain?"

"Yes, Steve Flynn. He takes care of any boating needs in the neighborhood. Which reminds me, I need to show you the passcodes for the gate and the contact information for any vendors you might need to call."

Moving back to the kitchen in the new wing, Dianne showed her where to find a laminated sheet with a printed list of phone numbers and email addresses for service companies and vendors. "The WI-FI password is at the bottom."

A concerned frown had formed between her brows. "Are you really okay staying here by yourself? If you decide otherwise, there are some inns not too far away. I can make arrangements—"

"Please don't worry about me, I'll be fine."

"It's too bad you won't have your sister for company."

"I'm okay being on my own. Seriously, I'm kind of a loner."

Looking cheered by her statement, Dianne gave up the debate. "If you say so. By the way, in case you do need to go anywhere, you'll find some vehicles in the garage." She jerked a thumb toward the rear of the mansion. "You inherited them along with everything else. Vadim was driving the Bentley when the accident happened, so of course, it's not there. You'll find a BMW and a Prius. They're both in excellent shape. Darryl has been taking them out regularly to keep the batteries charged and so the oil doesn't gunk up." She indicated a drawer in the kitchen island. "The remote for the garage and the front gate are in here."

The degree of relief that rippled over Jessica took her aback. She had meant it in principle when she said she didn't mind being alone. Learning that she was not without resources made her realize that she had not relished the idea of being alone in a huge isolated house *and* without transportation. "Please don't worry about me," she repeated. "As long as I brought my phone charger—"

"There's a land line for emergencies. You'll find an extension in the kitchen and one in Vadim's study. Oh dear, I haven't taken you there, or the public rooms—" Dianne darted a surreptitious glance at her wristwatch.

"I can finish showing you around quickly, but I do have another appointment I need to get to."

"Please don't bother. I'll explore on my own."

"If you're sure? That could be...er, fun." The attorney looked as convinced as little Sophie when Jenna was trying to persuade her daughter that veggies were as yummy as ice cream. "It's been such a pleasure meeting you and your sister. I hope your little niece isn't badly hurt."

"Thank you," Jessica said. "I suspect Roland is overreacting." *And gave Jen an excuse to hightail it home, long drive notwithstanding.*

With Jessica making a mental map of the route to the front of the house, they backtracked through the passage and into the old dining room together. She memorized paintings on the walls, ornaments on tables, the number of doorways they passed.

They went out to the driveway, where Dianne's vehicle was parked in front of the mansion. She extended her hand and took Jessica's in a warm grip. "Please, Jessica, don't hesitate to call me anytime if you need anything at all."

"I will. And thanks for welcoming us. It's going to take a while to process. It feels like I'm living in a dream."

"That's not surprising, all things considered." She climbed into the driver seat and the window slid down. "Oh, and Jessica—"

"Yes?"

"Since you will be staying alone, I feel like I ought to warn you that in a great big old house like this, you're probably going to hear all kinds of strange noises, especially at night. So, if you do decide to use Vadim's or one of the other rooms in the old wing and you hear weird creaks and pops and wonder where they're coming from, don't let it spook you."

Jessica thrust down the impulse to snicker that bubbled up. Dianne would be shocked if she knew some of the *truly* spooky things she had experienced. Nighttime noises in an old house were at the bottom end of that scale. She gave the attorney a nod and a smile. "I'll keep that in mind."

As the Mercedes made the semi-circle and disappeared along the avenue, Jessica stood on the driveway with a final wave at the attorney. Once the vehicle had left her view, she ran up the front steps, eager to start exploring the house. Her sneaker had scarcely touched down on the top step when the front door, which she had left standing open, slammed shut in her face.

six

JESSICA FROZE, THE FINE hairs bristling on her arms and the half-oval windows rattling in their frames. She looked at the trees that lined the driveway. They were rustling with the slightest of breezes; not strong enough to shut that sturdy door. It smirked at her as if daring her to enter. Trying to make herself laugh at the fanciful notion was an epic fail.

If the front door was self-locking, she would be in a fine mess. Her phone was in the kitchen in the new wing. What would she do, already shivering, stuck outside on a winter afternoon with no coat or phone, or a way to get to a neighbor in this remote area? On the drive up the winding mountain road, she had not seen another house for miles. If there were any, they were well hidden behind the huge old trees.

Jessica lifted a hand, mentally crossing her fingers for good luck, and reached for the knob. The door swung ajar without her touching it.

Her experience as a medium did nothing to prevent the frisson that traveled up her spine. Did Herron Pond have a poltergeist—the kind of supernatural being that thought it funny to play tricks on the unwary? She flashed back to the cold feeling on her neck earlier and knew it was entirely possible.

Alarm bells clanged in her head like a train signal. Toeing the door open, she stepped inside and shut it, pushing hard against it to make sure it was secure. It's just a quirky door, she told herself, staring it down, waiting for it to defy her and re-open itself. The house appeared to be in excellent repair, but at more than a hundred years old it was not unreasonable to think the door might be loose in its frame.

Pivoting in a slow circle, she once again took in the polished oak staircase, the side table graced by a gorgeous Tiffany lamp, the stately oak hall chairs. And of course, the stained-glass wall. She wanted to get acquainted with it all as intimately as its previous occupants had done.

She spoke aloud to the house as though it could hear her. "Where should I start?"

Near the staircase a creak sounded as though someone had stepped on a wooden floorboard. A feeling of deep antipathy suddenly flooded the cheerful entry hall and thickened the atmosphere with gloom. A hoarse whisper skimmed her left ear.

"Go away."

Even before she jerked around to see who had spoken, Jessica knew that the foyer would appear as empty as when she had entered it. "Who's there?" she asked into the silent hallway. "Who are you? What do you want?" The surprise jump-scare of the whisper had set her heart knocking against her ribs and dampened her palms.

The brilliant afternoon light that had streamed through the stained glass was transmuted into grey, casting the foyer into deep shadow. No invisible breezes slamming doors shut and reopening them. No more whispers in her ear. The house was oppressively silent.

Bella Bingham had taught Jessica a simple protection ritual early in her mediumship studies. Calling it up now, she took three deep, cleansing breaths and visualized a shower of pure white light flowing all over her body, constructing a spiritual shield to insulate her from any harmful entities.

Once her pulse was back to normal, she remembered that the whisper had come in her left ear. She had learned to associate that side with female spirits. There was certainly nothing welcoming in those two words, *'Go away.'* she had not imagined the menace in them. She couldn't stop the shudder that came. It crawled over her like the hairy legs of a spider. Who or what might not want her at Herron Pond?

Jessica scoffed at herself. If most people knew the details of her life, they would question her sanity. For a medium to be scared by a ghostly whisper was nothing short of silly. The most likely explanation was, the whisper was an echo, an endless psychic imprint left behind by a resident who had died at the house. Nevertheless, she had been a little bit scared.

The house felt as enormous and empty as it was. Maybe staying on without Jenna wasn't the best choice after all. She found the dimmer that controlled the chandelier above the staircase and lit the hallway as bright as day. Maybe the heavier energy of the Victorian side was better explored in the morning.

What she wanted most was to call Sage and let the warm honey tone of his voice make her forget the psychic echo, or whatever it was that had whispered to her. But today and tomorrow, he was attending a seminar in Santa Barbara, one of the legal hoops he had to jump through to keep his license current for the Center he owned and operated. If he could sit through the dull as dirt lectures he was enduring with good grace, she could wait until later to talk to him. She settled for a short text about Jenna's unplanned departure.

"The Universe has an interesting sense of humor," Sage had said when she told him about her and Jenna being Vadim Evanov's unlikely heirs. His unique sapphire-blue eyes had gleamed with amusement. They both had to laugh at the irony. He had funded the Regina Boles Center for Traumatized Children using the fortune his aunt left him to serve twenty kids at a time at no cost to their families. Jessica volunteered there, reasoning that if she couldn't be with her own child, the satisfaction she got from teaching art to little ones who were recovering from shocking abuses was the best substitute.

"You really believe it's the cosmic jester at work?" she said. "First, you inherit a big pile of money and a house from your aunt. Now Jen and I inherit an estate in Big Sur. There's something weird about that picture." She stretched on tiptoes to reach his lips with hers. "You think it was the Universe that told this guy to suddenly decide to leave Herron Pond to us?"

"I don't know, but there is no way it's random, my beautiful girl." Snagging a lock of her unruly blonde mop, Sage twirled it around his finger and pulled her in for a deep kiss that left her shaky. "It is *exactly* like me getting the money from my aunt out of the blue. You'll see, angel. I don't know when or how, but I'm one hundred percent positive there's a bigger reason behind a gift like this. It's not about inheriting a house and some land. Whatever it is, trust me, you'll understand when you see it."

And then they'd made love and Jessica didn't care why or when or how she and Jenna had become Vadim Evanov's heirs. When she was wrapped in Sage's arms, nothing else mattered.

Punching in the code and making the door slide open between the wings, Jessica congratulated herself with a Sam Adams that she found the well-stocked refrigerator. She was twisting off the cap when Sage's ringtone sent her hand diving into her pocket. After the incident with the front door, she had pledged to herself that for as long as she was at Herron Pond, her phone was not going to leave her possession at any time.

"Hey, cupcake." His rich voice wrapped her in exactly the kind of glow she needed. "We're on break. I got your text. Too bad Jen had to leave so soon."

"Don't worry about Jen, she was thrilled for an excuse to go."

"Seriously?"

"Herron Pond hasn't affected her the way it has me. I love it."

Mostly.

"You know how she is," Sage said, and Jessica could hear his smile over the phone. "Anything *you* love—"

"She refuses to. She does that on principle."

"What about little Emily? Will she be okay?"

"Going to the emergency room is a big deal for anyone, let alone a four-year-old, but I have a feeling she'll be fine."

"A psychic feeling?"

Jessica laughed. "A feeling. I'm not questioning where it came from."

Chatting with him in the modern, well-lit kitchen, so efficient and utilitarian and unlike the Victorian side of the house, no differently than the way they connected every day made the ghostly whisper in the foyer seem far away and not so fraught. She might have imagined it. *Almost.*

"What else is going on?" Sage asked.

She hesitated, not wanting to worry him. He understood her in ways no one else did, not even her twin. He was the most accepting partner she could have asked for. Even so, it didn't seem fair to burden him with her misgivings when he was two hundred miles away.

"Not much," she said. "I'll tell you all about it later when we have more time."

He could read her better than a clairvoyant gazing into a crystal ball. Perhaps it was that psychic link that had made him call at this very minute.

"You have all the time you need," he said. "We're not ending this call until you tell me what's bugging you."

A few seconds ticked past. "Angel?" he prompted when she didn't answer right away. When it came to her, Sage had all the patience in the world and Jessica was fully aware that he would not let it go until she had given him an answer. She went to room she thought of as the den because it had a big screen TV and plunked onto the sofa.

"It's just that something happened after Dianne Maggio left. It was, um, a little weird."

"What kind of weird?"

"Well, like a whisper."

"A whisper?"

"A spirit asking me to leave."

He didn't ask for more specifics. "If I leave Santa Barbara right away, I can be there—"

"No, Sage, I'm fine, seriously. I think it might have been one of those echo loops, like an old tape recording that plays over and over. It'll probably happen every time I go to the foyer. You stay there and get those credits you need. There's nothing to worry about. It's nothing I'm not used to. It was just surprising."

And a little menacing.

"You mean more to me than any credits, Jess, don't you know that by now? I can make them up—"

Gently, she cut him off. "I don't want you to come tonight and this is for purely selfish reasons. I found out today that Mr. Evanov was killed in a car wreck on Highway 1. I don't want you driving the Tesla on that stretch, especially when you're rushing."

"It would take too long to go home and get the truck."

"Please, Sage, stay there and do what you need to do. Nobody knows better than you that I've dealt with far worse than a ghost whisper."

She heard him curse under his breath. It would drive him crazy to be stuck on the sidelines when he did know what she had been through a few short months ago. Hell, he had been at her side during some of the most sinister events she had experienced. Through the phone, she could hear the seminar being called to order. "I'll be fine, honest," she pressed. "I'm not sensing any activity here in the new wing. I'm going to sleep on this side."

His prolonged sigh was one of defeat. "Promise you'll keep your phone with you. Don't go setting it down and forgetting where you left it the way you do. And be sure it's fully charged."

"I know, I know. I promise. As soon as we hang up, I'll plug it into the charger. And I've done that protection routine Bella showed me. Don't worry, if there *is* a spirit on the Victorian side, it just needs to get used to me being here."

"That doesn't make me feel better. I wish Jenna could have stayed with you."

"Are you kidding? If she'd heard a spirit say 'Go away,' she would have taken off like the proverbial bat out of hell. That's what she did even when nothing happened and she just had a 'funny feeling.' Go, Sage, get your credits, and call me when you get home tonight."

"Angel, just so you understand, I don't give a shit about the seminar. If you need me *any* time, call me."

She pictured him closing his eyes and shaking his head, wanting to be with her and agitated that he couldn't be. "I love you," she said, meaning it with all her being.

"I love you, too."

As brave as she had sounded, when they ended the call, she weighed the option of taking one of the cars Dianne had said were in the garage and booking into a hotel. She could wait to explore the house until Sage drove up on the weekend.

Nope; not gonna cut it.

She was too curious about Vadim Evanov, the man she was beginning to think of as their phantom benefactor, and his motivation for giving his entire estate to two complete strangers. Besides, as she had said to Sage, she had survived far worse than a whisper.

It was getting dark outside as she speed-wheeled her overnight bag from the foyer to the new wing without running into an unfriendly spirit. Her first act was to plug her phone into the charger and set up the laptop in the kitchen.

The lake was no longer visible through the windows in the falling dusk. Jessica went around switching on as many lights in the new wing as she could find. They could burn all night as far as she cared. She had no intention of waiting in the dark for the mansion to become a scary place.

Even if you didn't count the Victorian side, the new wing was in itself a huge house. She took a walk through it. On both sides of the mansion, the downstairs rooms were accessed through wide arches. In addition to the new kitchen, and the breakfast room where she had spent most of her time while indoors, there was a large, open plan living room and the library-cum-den with its big screen TV mounted on the wall. The three upstairs guest rooms were as luxurious as the best suite at a boutique hotel. One of the bathrooms featured marble floors and a Roman-style bath set in a windowed alcove, steps leading up to the sunken tub.

Jessica rambled through the rooms, trying again and again to guess at Vadim Evanov's reasoning. What was it about her and Jenna that prompted him to make such a consequential decision? Then she remembered, Dianne Maggio had said it was five or six years since he changed his will in their favor.

It wasn't difficult to recall what was going on in her life during that time. It was a few months after the accident that took Justin from her. Well-meaning people frequently said there was nothing worse than losing a child, and they were right. What they failed to understand was that losing Justin had killed something in his mother, too.

Not long after that tragedy and her recovery from the head injury, both twins had become innocent victims in a freakish and sensational crime. Jenna was kidnapped and Jessica, traumatized all over again, lost her memory. After they were rescued, they had tried to put the drama behind them, but it was impossible with reporters continuing to dig into their story with the relish of a dog hunting for a buried bone.

Being twins had added an extra fillip to the story. Despite their steadfast refusal to appear on the popular shows and magazines, their virtually identical faces had been splashed across the media the world over. When at last the next salacious news item came along and pushed them off the radar, it could not have been more welcome.

Jessica assumed that Vadim Evanov must have read about their misadventures and for whatever freaky reason of his own, altered his will in their favor. Maybe he was *that* eccentric.

The more recent story Dianne had brought up, where Jessica had been made into an unwitting media darling again, had occurred around last Christmas. She and Sage had been instrumental in locating a missing child, which had resurrected the older news stories for a while. But that was not the answer to her question. According to Dianne, the changes to the will had been made well in advance of Vadim Evanov's October passing.

It had been while she was recovering from the loss of her memory that spirits started speaking to her. After denying it for years, her 'gift' was not something she had ever advertised or shared with anyone other than those closest to her. Yet, somehow, random people heard about it. They came to her grieving for a lost loved one, begging her to contact them, expecting it to be like using a phone to 'dial up the dead.' It wasn't like that at all. The best she could do was attempt to tune in and make a connection with the energy of the person who was asking—the sitter—and see who showed up. There were times when the spirit who came through at the session was not welcomed by the sitter.

Jessica had learned through experience that whatever Spirit did, there was always a reason for it. She never knew who would show up at a reading. The people who stayed and listened to whichever spirit appeared tended to leave happy. When a sitter left disappointed, it was usually due to their unreasonable expectations. If she could get in touch with Evanov on the Other Side, it was possible that he would tell her what had motivated him to make this gift.

It was an iffy proposition at best. All she could do was open herself to the spirit world and ask. But not tonight. Not in the new wing.

Her stomach reminded her that it was time to eat. The refrigerator was stocked with fresh fruit and produce, the pantry with everything a visitor might need or desire. She made a simple cheese and mushroom omelet, tossed some salad greens, and opened a bottle of white wine. The winery label was unfamiliar—a lot classier than she normally drank, she gathered, and poured a healthy glass.

Consuming her solitary meal in the breakfast room, her mind continued to churn over the ghostly command to '*Go away!*' Who had delivered that message? Some longtime ghost from Herron Pond's Victorian past? She could rule out the most recent decedent. For whatever reason of his own, Vadim Evanov had intended for her and Jen to be here. There were plenty of questions with no good answers.

Once the dishes were cleared away, Jessica relegated Evanov to the recesses of her mind and opened a browser on the laptop. She would make notes of anyone else she could find who had owned the house, then search on what had happened to every one of them—if someone had died here—someone whose spirit might be hanging around and objecting to her presence, knowing who they were might make it easier to negotiate a peace settlement.

Negotiate with a ghost? Jessica Mack, you have gone right over the edge.

She called up the real estate app Zillow and entered the address of Herron Pond, but the notepad remained blank. The site listed homes currently for sale, which Herron Pond was not, and would not be for as long as she had a say in it. Querying Google, Jessica learned that the best way to track the historical ownership of a property in California was through the County Clerk or County Recorder's office. It was past five o'clock. Both offices would be closed until tomorrow.

She was thinking about what step to take next when a text came from her twin. Jenna had arrived at St. John's Hospital emergency room in Oxnard. As she had suspected, Emily's injury was not as serious as Roland made it sound. The blood had been easily stanched; no stitches were required. The worst of it was the possibility of a tiny triangular scar under her hairline.

Jessica texted how happy she was to hear the news and made a promise to bring her niece a special treat when she left Herron Pond.

Sage called again and they chatted until he had assured himself that she was safe and comfortable in the new wing of the house. After they said goodnight, she returned to the laptop and opened the Google Search window.

Following their visit with Tanya Stewart, the lawyer, she had searched extensively and in vain on Vadim Evanov's name. Tanya—or was it Dianne—had been correct when she'd said that not everyone had an Internet presence. No reason to go that route again. She switched her search term to 'Amy Herron.'

Images of several different women with the same name appeared on-screen. Only one of them was a realtor in the Big Sur area. The woman Dianne Maggio said she would introduce to the twins if they decided to sell the house.

Clicking on Amy Herron's LinkedIn page, Jessica was met by the smiling face of a youngish woman with a mane of long, tawny hair. There was nothing in the description of her background or education that gave any helpful hints about her, but with Amy being a local realtor, and as members of the Herron family were the original owners of the Victorian house, she must know something of its history.

Right after the meeting with Tanya Stewart, Jessica had looked up Herron Pond on Google Earth and was astonished by the amount of land it encompassed. On either side, the nearest neighbors were more than a mile away, with homes that appeared to be every bit as large as this one. The fourth boundary was a cliff, at the bottom of which was the Pacific Ocean and the private beach that belonged to the property.

She tapped a direct message inviting Amy to meet for coffee. No reason to wait for Dianne to introduce them.

Jessica got up and stretched, refilled her glass. She was just beginning to feel the full impact of what they had inherited. As Jenna had pointed out more than once, an estate of this size would require a tremendous amount of care and maintenance—enough to need an estate manager. A huge responsibility not to be taken lightly.

On emotional overload, she powered down her laptop and showered in the downstairs bathroom. It was not as grand as the Roman bath upstairs—that one required a long soak, which she would save to experience with Sage. After the long drive, what she needed was something simple.

Later, in her pajamas and a pair of Sage's socks she had appropriated on one of his sleepovers, she considered choosing a guest bedroom. She thought of lying alone in one of those king size beds. Everything she needed was down here on the first floor. Better food and drink than she would have bought for herself, more bathrooms than she could count. And best of all, she had not encountered any unfriendly entities in this wing.

Jessica curled up in a warm throw blanket she found in the den and made a place for herself on the sofa. She was half asleep when Dianne's strange admonition sneaked into her head.

Feel free to go anywhere except the last door on the landing.

It didn't take a psychic to pick up on the attorney's nervousness when she had pressed her about the odd warning. Either Dianne had been lying or was withholding something critical.

As familiar with the house as the attorney appeared to be, Jessica wondered if she had run afoul of the unfriendly entity who resided there, or been aware of it and had not wanted to tip off the twins. That kind of information could ruin the chances of a sale, which she seemed to be pushing. Though why Dianne would care whether they sold it or not was outside the limits of Jessica's understanding.

...except the last door, the attorney had said.

Go away, the entity had said.

The two warnings were not all that dissimilar and Jessica began to ask herself if there might be a link between them. After pondering the question for a while, she decided that she was less afraid of the entity than she was curious about it. She wanted to know who it was and where it belonged, and why it wanted her to leave Herron Pond.

Maybe it was one of those spirits that got stuck between worlds on its way to the Afterlife. Maybe it needed some encouragement to move on, or 'Go to the light,' as the New Agers liked to say. Bella Bingham had told Jessica that in such cases, you usually needed to let them know that they're dead and it's okay for them to leave the earth plane.

That whisper in her ear had been so sudden and unexpected and hostile that it had not occurred to Jessica that it *might* be a spirit needing help.

"Go away," didn't sound like someone who *wanted* help.

Next time—if there was a next time—she would be prepared. For tonight, though, she had no desire to go in pursuit of that entity, or ghost, or whatever it was. She would remain under her blanket in the new wing, with the fervent hope that whoever or whatever *it* was would remain on the Victorian side.

seven

MOTHER-OF-PEARL LIGHT FILTERED THROUGH the uncurtained windows and woke Jessica from a surprisingly sound sleep. Most of her nights at in her own bed were populated with full-color dreams. After her encounter with the presence in the foyer at Herron Pond, she had readied herself for nightmares. Rolling off the sofa with a yawn, she was amazed not to recall a single dream.

A pot of hot, strong coffee brought her fully alert and ready to explore the grounds and the beach.

I own half a beach! How incredible is that?

Herron Pond was the size of a boutique hotel, but the route from the new wing to the Victorian foyer was beginning to feel familiar. Psyched for a confrontation with the unwelcoming entity, Jessica entered the old wing through the door that divided the two sides of the house and made her way to the entrance hall.

When she arrived in the foyer, the silence there mocked her intentions. Was the entity playing hide-and-seek? She waited a while, not sensing any paranormal energies. Curbing the temptation to shout, "Come out, come out wherever you are," she reached the conclusion that the spirit behind yesterday afternoon's unfriendly whisper was not coming out to play.

Unlocking the front door with a sense of disappointment, she stepped onto the porch. A celestial artist had daubed violet-hued brush strokes across the clouds, making Jessica wish she could set up her easel, although it would be too chilly to paint outdoors without wearing gloves. She ran down the steps and walked briskly to the rear of the house.

A freestanding building housed the four-car garage Dianne had mentioned. Peeking through a side window, Jessica was reassured to see the two vehicles the attorney had said were there, along with two empty spaces. That she had never met Vadim Evanov did not stop emotion from rolling over her when she pictured his terrible fate. What sort of man had he been, this internationally renowned musician and teacher? She had not had time to develop enough of a sense of him to figure it out.

Jessica passed the outdoor kitchen she had seen from the window—Sage and Roland would be in seventh heaven when they saw it—and crossed the grass to the boathouse at the rim of the pond, which she decided that, as large as it was, she would think of as the lake. Four canoes hung on the boathouse walls. In the heat of summer, it would be fun to row out to the middle of the water and recline on a comfy cushion, reading, trailing her fingers in the water. In theory, anyhow. Ever since being pushed into the deep end of their pool by her mother, who chose that method to supposedly make a frightened eight-year-old learn to swim, Jessica had avoided any body of water deep enough to cover her head. That meant deeper than five foot three. She would ask Sage to come in the canoe with her. She would not be afraid with him there.

That was when it hit her. By summertime Jenna might have forced her to sell the estate. The sisters looked alike, but were remarkably different in the way they thought. Why did Jenna have to be so perfect all the time, so on edge? The little twins, Jessica's nieces, would love digging in the sand with their plastic spades and buckets, paddling around the shore. In the evening, when the girls were sleeping, the grownups would barbecue and drink beer or wine. In her mind it was an idyllic scene that Jenna *must* go along with.

Right.

Continuing in a westerly direction, Jessica made her way to the far side of the lake, where the trees dotted the shoreline and reflected at her on the water. The feeling of being in a waking dream kept making her want to verify that she really was walking through grounds as well-kept as a manicured palace garden.

Keeping to the path, she came, eventually, to a sturdy, waist-high redwood railing close to the cliff. Without the railing, a strong gust might send a person of Jessica's size sailing right over. And that thought made her picture Vadim Evanov's fate. If Jenna and Roland ever did bring Em and Sophie up here, they would have to keep a close eye on the two little girls, who were virtually impossible to corral on flat ground.

At the top of the long flight of steep wooden steps that led down to the private beach, she caught a whiff of seaweed and tasted the salty tang on her tongue. The frigid wind lashed her hair across her face and stung her cheeks. She loved the sand and the ocean, but this was not the kind of day that invited a descent.

Huddled into the warmth of her jacket, Jessica abandoned the beach path and headed for the house. Its massive roof in the distance was a lodestar calling to her. Compared to Herron Pond, her cottage was the size of one of the miniatures she created. And when Sage was there, too, it shrank even smaller.

Thinking of Sage, picturing herself in the circle of his arms, his warm breath on her hair, made her smile. His strong yet delicate artist's fingers caressing her face, her arms, her body—and her touching all the landmarks of his skin. When they were together like that, no words were needed. All at once, she longed for his physical presence.

After losing her son in the car crash and divorcing Gregory Mack while he was serving a prison sentence for the DUI, Jessica had wanted never to experience any emotion ever again, let alone allow herself to love anyone. Living the half-life of a zombie was easier than feeling flayed alive, naked and defenseless in her grief.

The doctors believed that was why she took refuge in amnesia, where she was no longer forced to remember that she was a bereaved mother, or that she had a twin sister whom she believed had been murdered while she watched.

Much later, after her memory returned and they had been reunited, Jenna, in a misguided attempt to move her sister's healing forward, had pushed her to "get out into the dating scene and live again." And Jessica had tried, unenthusiastically, over one summer, when a handful of disastrous Internet dates had confirmed what she'd known in every cell in her body: that her ability to love had died with her precious baby boy. Why couldn't her twin understand that?

Immersed in her art, five years passed. And then came Sage, and everything in her life had changed for the better.

Though the house was a distance away, its turrets rose above the trees that surrounded it. She stepped off the path, not quite ready to leave the gardens and in the mood to explore, and wandered past flowerbeds and grassy patches, arriving at the crest of a gentle slope. It didn't qualify as a hill, but the elevation made it high enough to see the lake. She looked down the other side of the rise, surprised to see that it ended at a copse of untamed trees and scrubby bushes. Why was this small area allowed to grow wild, as out of place as a barbarian at a cocktail party?

Something was nudging her to check it out. Slip-sliding to the bottom of the slope, which was muddy from the recent rain, she came closer to the thicket of trees, whose untrimmed branches stuck out from the hedge. What from a distance had appeared to be a slight gap in the bushes was in actuality a wide space between them, rather like an overgrown aisle.

Stepping into the gap, Jessica emerged into a clearing. A pocket-sized family cemetery was the last thing she had expected to see. The two oldest of the five gravestones, their names largely obscured by moss and dirt and mildew, leaned drunkenly against each other. Digging a crumpled Kleenex out of her pocket, she cleaned away as much of the muck as she could. At length, the words etched into the stone became a little easier to read. She could just about make them out:

Here lies Thomas Herron, loving husband and father. 1868-1953

Here lies Hannah Herron, devoted wife and mother. 1870-1952

Thomas and Hannah were the only two Herrons in the little plot. According to Dianne, the Herron children had been eager to leave Herron Pond. If there were any other members of the family who had died, they must be buried in some other graveyard. What had begun as a family plot had not been used for nearly thirty years.

Moving to the next headstone, Jessica read:

Nika Inessa Evanov, beloved wife. 1945-1982

Vadim's wife, as Dianne had correctly guessed, had died young. The most recently dug grave was next to Nika's final resting place.

Vadim Ilya Evanov. 1940-2021

In the months since his interment, the burial mound had settled into the earth. Jessica knelt on the grass and spoke to the spirit of the man her sister had facetiously referred to as their 'fairy godfather.'

"I wish we had met you, Mr. Evanov. I'd love to know what you were thinking when you made us your heirs." Jessica spoke in the hope that he heard her on the other side, and would send her a message. When none came, she bowed her head and said a silent blessing for his well-being in the spirit world. She rose, dusting off her damp jeans. "It's very weird that you did this, Mr. E, and I want to say, whatever your reason was, thank you."

The final grave in the clearing was about half the length and width of the others. The inscription brought a lump to Jessica's throat: *Ilya Evgeny Evanov. 1992-1999.*

Seven years old. Her firsthand knowledge of burying a child made it too easy to empathize with little Ilya's parents. Ilya Evgeny had been born two years after Jenna and her. Had he lived, he would have been close to their current age. Tears blurred her vision and she let them fall freely, for the Evanov family, and for herself. Giving herself over to emotion was something she rarely allowed, but for a few moments, that's what she did. And when it was over, she packed it neatly away in the box where she kept her grief and her guilt.

Using the dates on the headstone, she did a quick calculation. Vadim would have been 52 when Ilya was born. It was not uncommon for an older man to become a father. But his wife, Nika, had died twelve years previously and there was no indication of a second marriage. What might it mean? Apart from sharing Vadim's middle name and surname, nothing on the boy's headstone designated their relationship. Was little Ilya his grandson? If so, where were the boy's parents? If they had died, too, wouldn't they also be buried in the family cemetery? And if, more than thirty years after Ilya's death, they were alive, where were they today?

If Vadim Evanov had a son, he was the one who should rightly have inherited the estate. So, he must have died and been buried elsewhere. And what had caused the death of little Ilya at such a young age?

Jessica had not welcomed the awakening of her psychic abilities, especially when they pecked at her like a relentless chicken until she listened.

Like now, when her sixth sense was doggedly insisting that she find the answers to these questions—questions that kept piling up, waiting for the right answer to set off an avalanche.

Was little Ilya the whisperer in the foyer?

She thought not. The demand for her to leave had come in her left ear, which was her sign that the spirit had been female while residing on the earth. That raised another question. What if the whisper had come from Vadim's wife, Nika? Might she resent the intrusion of the twins—two strangers—in her house?

A sharp breeze moaned through the trees. Glancing up, Jessica caught sight of a hawk keeping an eye on her from a high branch. Bella Bingham had taught her that the appearance of a hawk was symbolic of spiritual awareness and clairvoyance. Had it come to give her a message?

Sage was certain that when she understood the reason for Vadim Evanov's extraordinary bequest she would know why she was here. This inheritance might have something to do with her spiritual development. Or not. She was beginning to feel like a random piece in the middle of a puzzle that pressed for completion.

Puzzle imagery was not new to Jessica. When she had met Sage, her imagination had shown her the pieces of a puzzle shifting until they came together to make a whole picture. So far, most of the pieces of the Herron Pond puzzle were missing. If she was patient, she would find them and fit them into their proper places.

As she stepped out of the thicket, the branches closed across the gap through which she had entered, erasing any evidence that she had visited the little burial ground and its five lonely graves.

Jessica made her way up the gently sloped hillside. Vadim Evanov must have deeply loved his wife and Ilya Evgeny to bury them together in such close proximity to the house, she decided. With this new wrinkle in

Vadim's story revealed, she visualized a sad, pensive widower who had kept to himself in his mansion and seemingly boundless acres of grounds as he aged alone. For some reason of his own he had decided to come out of his self-imposed confinement and build a new wing onto his house and hold recitals there. And finally, he had willed his estate to two strangers.

What had changed in him? Had he decided he had done enough mourning? Had he, like Jessica, met someone who made him want to live again? When had Dianne come into the picture, she wondered, stopping to pick a few of the California wildflowers that grew in a lush blanket of lavender and gold. Poppies and seaside daisies, yarrow, and Mariposa lilies. They could not match the extravagant arrangements Jessica had seen throughout the house, but in a glass jar, they would be more beautiful in their wildness.

Her phone pinged in her pocket with a text from Jen—a photo of Emily pointing forefinger to a super-sized Band-Aid nearly hidden under the fizz of rust-colored hair that covered her forehead. The little drama queen was making the most of her injury, using it to get her sister, Sophie, to serve her, hand and foot.

Jessica loved those precious twins as much as she loved anything. But with every glimpse she was reminded of her loss; her longing to hold Justin on her lap as he named every animal in the zoo for her, recited his ABCs, counted to twenty. She craved to stroke his hair, which was the same shade of honey blonde as hers. To feel his baby arms around her neck and hear him say, "I love you, Mama."

Losing Justin had been the harshest of punishments for her failure to keep him safe. Safe from his father, who had been three sheets to the wind as he so often was. Jessica knew that Greg had no business getting behind the wheel and driving on that twisty highway into the mountains. She should have stopped him. She should never have buckled Justin into his car seat that rainy night.

Even now, six years later, she could not forgive herself. Even now, after Justin had been allowed to come through the veil and let her see that he was happy, getting older in the spirit world. If only—

"Good morning."

Yelping in surprise, Jessica dropped her bunch of wildflowers, gawking at the man who blocked her path. Fiftyish, with a deeply tanned face, he was tall—though most adult males were taller than her—and in good shape. He wore an outdoorsy fisherman-knit sweater and Levi's. His wavy grey hair was streaked so artfully with silver that once she had regained her poise, she wondered whether he'd had it professionally done.

The man bent and deftly scooped up the flowers. "You're one of the sisters," he said, handing Jessica her bedraggled bouquet. "You looked deep in thought, there, young lady."

Young lady?

A moniker that never failed to ignite her ire. "Uh, who are you?" she demanded.

"Name's Darryl Andrews." She must have looked blank, as he added, "The estate manager. Dianne Maggio was supposed to let you know."

"Oh. Oh, yes, she did. Excuse me, I should have been looking where I was going. Honestly, I didn't expect to run into anyone; certainly not literally." Jessica took the hand he extended and had to keep from wincing at the bruising grip. Intentional? A powerplay? Showing her that she was in *his* territory? As soon as she could without letting him see that he'd left it throbbing, she freed her hand from his grasp.

"I'm Jessica Mack. My sister had an emergency and had to leave right after we got here."

"I guess that explains why there was no vehicle on the driveway."

Darryl Andrews pointed to the garage, where a late model shiny red Camry sat in front of the closed roll up doors. "That one's mine. I thought I'd drop by and introduce myself; see whether you ladies needed anything."

"Thank you. I guess I have you to thank for the fresh food and 'adult beverages.' Nice choices."

"No problem. Was everything to your liking?"

"Absolutely," she said. "Everything was perfect."

Jessica had the distinct feeling that for some reason, like his too-hard handshake, underneath the bland question Darryl Andrews viewed her with scorn. He reminded her of the actor, Sam Elliott, without the big white moustache. If he'd had a hat, it would have been a Stetson, and she was pretty sure he would have tipped it and called her "ma'am."

"If you want anything that's not here, you can give me a list. I'll call the general store and get it delivered. We don't have many of your big grocery chain stores around here."

"I appreciate the offer but you've supplied everything we could possibly need. I don't expect to be here all that long. My partner is coming to pick me up on the weekend."

Andrews gave a slow nod. "Alrighty, then." He had half-turned away, but spun on his heel. "Hey, look, I realize it's a little soon to bring this up, but—"

"We don't plan to make any changes," Jessica interrupted, intuiting what was on his mind. "I hope you'll go on as you have been." Not knowing an estate manager existed until yesterday, it wasn't something she and Jenna had considered. And he wasn't working for free. "That is," she hastened to add, "I haven't been told about what arrangements Mr. Evanov made for your salary."

"That's taken care of for the rest of this year. If you want me to continue as we are, I'm good with that."

His announcement lifted a burden that would have had to be addressed soon. "Yes, we do want you to continue. Jenna and I know sweet nothing about running a place like this. We'd be grateful if you would stay on."

He gave another short nod. "I suppose you'll be putting it on the market?"

One more presumptuous person. For some reason, Jessica found the question rude, akin to asking someone how much money they made. "At the moment there are no plans to sell," she said coolly. "So far, neither of us has seen the whole house. I'm planning to finish that this morning. And naturally, any decisions about the future will include my sister. As you can imagine, there will be a lot to discuss."

"There's a lot to see."

"I'm sure. How long have you worked here?"

He cocked his head, considering the question. "I guess it's been close to ten years by now." Gesturing at their surroundings, he couldn't hide the pride he felt. "An impressive spread, wouldn't you say?"

"To put it mildly. You've done a spectacular job of keeping it up."

"That's what I get paid for."

"Right." Jessica hesitated, unsure of this man; unsure whether to ask the question that was uppermost on her mind. She was quiet for a second, then thought, *what the hell*. "Do you mind if I ask you something, Darryl?"

"I don't know until I hear it, do I?"

"I assume that after being here so long, you and Mr. Evanov probably got to know each other pretty well."

"You know what they say about assumptions."

"Okay, let me just ask, do you have any idea why he chose my sister and me to be his heirs?"

He appraised her through half-closed hazelnut brown eyes. Judging by the long, unsmiling look he gave her, he did mind. "Now, why would you think I would know anything about that?" he drawled. "We weren't buddies. Mr. Evanov was my employer. Our discussions were limited to household business and any special tasks he had for me to handle. He sure as hell didn't consult me on who he was going to put in his will."

The bitter undertone made Jessica wonder whether he had expected to be a major beneficiary himself. If so, he had to have been disappointed to learn about her and Jenna. Switching topics, she started to ask whether he had met the whispering spirit in the foyer—the ghost of Herron Pond—but changed her mind. She refused to let his gruff retort sting her, but his brusque manner discouraged that kind of question.

Jessica had run out of conversation. Darryl had, too. Unless the taciturn silence was his way of waiting for her to invite him to show her around. She was not about to do any such thing. When the lull began to stretch too long and was starting to feel awkward, the estate manager stuck his hand in his pocket and thrust a business card at her. "I'll be upstairs in the apartment for a while. Got some paperwork to catch up on. Call me if there's anything you need."

With a nod of thanks, Jessica took the card and walked away.

***

While she foraged in the refrigerator for breakfast, Jessica considered the second thoughts she had been harboring about returning to the Victorian side. She reached the conclusion that, despite dealing with spirits most days of her life—not all of them friendly—the cause of her unease and her hesitancy was because the whispered command, *"Go away,"* was personal, aimed directly at her.

Just under the surface, too, was the fact that Darryl Andrews had not been exactly welcoming either. *A disagreeable man,* she thought, spooning herself a bowl of yogurt and granola, and adding fresh blueberries. On the upside, the selection of foods he had left was in happy sync with her tastes. Plus, there was another upside—she was his boss.

She could not deny it, though. Her misgivings notwithstanding, something was pushing her to return to the Victorian side of the house. She dallied for as long as she could, cleaning up and tidying her things. When there was no excuse to put it off any longer, she made her way to the sliding door and passed through the dining room.

In the foyer, Jessica checked the atmosphere. Slowing her mind and her emotions, she detected no spirit activity. No whispered warnings. Nothing creating a disturbance.

Letting her intuition guide her, she walked along the entrance hall and arrived at a wide, arched doorway that opened onto a large room. She stood in the doorway, absorbing the quiet elegance of mushroom-colored walls and decorative crown molding. The subdued tones allowed a visitor to concentrate their attention on the mahogany grand piano that stood in a curved window alcove. The room had been set up with rows of concert chairs and sofas, ready for an audience to enter and enjoy a recital or concert.

She stepped inside. When *Für Elise* began to play, the surprise came from hearing it, not in her head for once, but right in the room. The music was so loud and so real that she could not help looking for the unseen pianist. A profound sense that she had been led to this room—that the spirit musician wanted her here—drew her as though by an invisible string to the piano.

In the same way she had done in her vision at Tanya Stewart's office, Jessica sat on the bench and slid open the fallboard. Without conscious volition she placed her hands on the keys.

Like nerves awakening after being asleep, a prickling sensation ran over her scalp. Pins and needles progressed downward into her neck, her shoulders, her arms, and hands. The next thing that happened was something she had never experienced: a strange feeling of fullness that infused her entire body.

Her first impulse was to resist becoming a channel for the piano-playing spirit, but curiosity won out and she stepped aside in her mind, allowing her body to be occupied by a talented musician. Acting of their own accord, her fingers pressed the piano keys tentatively at first, then moved faster, with increasing confidence.

As a child, Jessica had learned just about enough music theory to pick out the simplest composition on the keyboard. The spirit directing her was a virtuoso. For the next hour they played as one: Debussy's *Clair de Lune,* Chopin's *Raindrop Prelude,* Beethoven's tempestuous *Appassionata Sonata.* Jessica, for whom classical music was often a backdrop when she was creating art, recognized them all as her favorites. They played until her human forearms ached with the unaccustomed effort.

As the last strains of the *Appassionata* died away, the tingling faded. As if the puppet master had released the control bar and let the strings fall, her hands dropped into her lap. The spirit that had merged with her vanished the way it had arrived—without fanfare. She was left breathing as hard as if she had completed a long-distance run.

"Encore."

Jessica leapt off the piano bench, whirling to see Darryl Andrews in the doorway, mocking her with a slow clap. "Nice work," he said, pretending to contradict the mockery, but it was there in his derisive tone.

"That's twice," she snapped. "Would you stop sneaking up on me?"

Inching away from the piano, she thought hard to find a plausible explanation for what was impossible to explain. She could never let Andrews in on the secret that it was not she who had produced the music.

"So sorry to scare you, Ms. Mack." He looked not at all contrite. "I came in to let you know I was leaving. I overheard the music. That wasn't bad. Better than some who came here for the recitals. I have a feeling Mr. Evanov would have liked to hear you play."

"Must be the piano," she said, annoyed by his backhanded compliment. The spirit's brilliant performance was a thousand times better than 'not bad.' He had no ear for music, she decided. Or else he was messing with her.

"Hey, keep going, don't let me stop you."

His vulpine almost-sneer raised her hackles. Why did he look at her as though she was beneath him? If his snotty attitude continued, she would have to remind him that for the time being, she and Jenna were his employers.

"That's okay," she said. "I'm done here. I haven't played in ages. I'm worn out." And the funny thing was, that was the bald truth.

"Well, well, Ms. Jessica, who knew? I figured you were rehearsing to play at Carnegie Hall."

She wondered about the glint of speculation in his eye. *If you only knew.* She regarded him with suspicion, her intuition knocking at her like an irritating noogie to the head: *don't trust him.* "That's not going to happen, I can promise you," she said.

"If you say so. Anyhow, I'm heading over to my place in Carmel. Anything you need from me while I'm here? I don't plan to be back until next week."

"No thanks, everything is in great shape."

"Okay." He started to walk away, reversed direction, and came back, one of his tufted brows quirked upward. "You gonna be okay here on your own?" The way he said it sounded grudging, giving her the impression that he was asking only because he thought he should.

"Why wouldn't I be?" Jessica asked, taking his measure. He was good-looking in a tough, older guy sort of way, but the prickly energy that crackled around him was like barbed wire, warning her to keep her distance. What made him carry such an edge? Sometimes it was hard to separate her psychic sense from her opinions. In any case, he seemed keyed-up, seething irritability just below the surface, ready to pop out at the slightest provocation.

"A big old house like this—"

He said it as if it were a warning. If he had been anyone else, Jessica would have smiled, but Darryl Andrews didn't bring out her friendly side. "I know; Dianne warned me about the strange noises I might hear in the night."

"Is that so?"

Suddenly, she didn't care what he knew or what his opinion was of her. It was more important to smoke out what was going on. "She also warned me off one of the bedrooms in the old wing. She said to stay away from the last door on the second-floor landing. Any idea why she wouldn't want me to go in there, Darryl?"

Something sharpened in his eyes, denied by his casual shrug. "I'll have to ask her. But if that's what she told you, I'd advise you to listen. She wouldn't say such a thing without good reason."

Jessica's look was all wide-eyed innocence. "I would have thought that you, being the estate manager, would be better informed about what's going on in the house than Dianne. She said it's because the room is being used for storage. You weren't aware?"

They looked at each other for a beat. Andrews's lips stretched into more of a sneer than a smile. "Do you think I'm that stupid?" he said, and stalked away, shaking his head.

Busted.

What was that all about? Jessica sat at the piano again, waiting for the buzzy feeling across her scalp, but the keys remained lifeless. The spirit she had channeled was no longer in the room.

One thing she knew; the energy that had controlled her was a polar opposite to the energy she had encountered in the foyer. Unless it was one spirit with a split personality, there were at least *two* very different entities in this house—one that welcomed her and one that did not.

eight

Dear Diary

September 25, 1985

Today was my very first piano lesson with the famous maestro, Vadim Evanov. I can't believe it. I was totally terrified to the point I could barely play. My hands were shaking so badly. He gave me this hard look with his scary grey eyes and it felt like he was staring right inside my head. He didn't say anything mean but I bet he thinks I have no talent. He probably wonders why Mrs. Lawrence would even ask him to teach me.

She keeps on telling me that not everyone gets to study with 'the great Evanov.' Like I don't know that! I've listened to his records since I was a little kid. I try to copy the way he plays. I've seen him on TV, too. I can't believe he would even let me audition for him. He is so amazing. I wonder why he quit giving concerts.

nine

THE DARRYL ANDREWS-SHAPED HOLE in the room quickly filled up, leaving Jessica with the memory of the exhilaration that had poured out of her while the spirit had played the piano using her hands, her body. The feeling was like a drug. She had channeled Spirit on other occasions, but never one that had blended with her so completely. Half-apprehensive, half-hoping it would happen again, she looked down at her hands—hands that had produced concert-worthy music. Hands that were vibrating with delayed adrenaline rush.

And as the adrenaline subsided, she had to admit it. She had been used as a puppet but was no closer to the answers she was seeking. Had it been Vadim's wife, Nika, who had taken possession of her body? A virtuoso's wife might well be a musician, too. But the energy she had channeled had not felt negative. If Nika Evanov was the whispering spirit—

Without warning, something changed in the air. Suddenly, it was drenched it in antagonism. The whisper came the way it had in the foyer.

Get out!

Instinctively, Jessica froze, but this time there was no fear in her. She was ready. "Vadim Evanov wants me here," she said, loud and strong.

And was met with silence.

She tried again. "Who are you?"

The whisper came again, louder, harsher.

I do not want you here.

"Tell me why."

Get out of my house!

Not a very nice response, but any response seemed like progress, even a sharp retort like that. Was it possible to have a dialogue with this entity? "Why don't you want me here?" Jessica kept her voice level, reasonable. "I'm not hurting anything."

Like the rumble of distant thunder warns of a brewing storm, the atmosphere in the recital room crackled with the electricity of spiteful emotions. Perhaps in recognition that this human was not intimidated by the demand to vacate, a sudden putrid smell assaulted Jessica's nostrils. The room began to spin. This was not like the buzzing in her ears that often came as she was slipping into a trance. Pressure was building inside her head, a vise, squeezing her from every direction. She fought the stench and tried to make a connection anyway. "Let me help you."

Go away, Go Away, GO AWAY!

No longer a mere whisper near her ear, the demand intensified to the volume of a hysterical screech. There was a time to stop trying to help someone—or something—who did not want help, and this was the time. There was something intensely personal in this attack on her and Jessica wanted to know why. But this entity was too strong for her to fight on her own. Calling on her angels and guides, she asked them to draw a shield of white light around her and safeguard her from all harmful influences.

All at once, the pressure in her head released like the air from an overinflated balloon. The room stopped spinning.

Jessica raced into the hallway. All her instincts were telling her to run out the front door and keep on going. Instead, she forced herself to stop and think about what she was doing. She was too stubborn to tuck her tail between her legs and run away like a scared puppy. There was no way she was going to put a stop to her explorations of the old house until she had uncovered some satisfactory answers. And having made that decision, Jessica went on her way.

Everywhere she went in the house, she saw evidence of the work of multiple service people and housekeepers in the dust-free, polished surfaces, and fresh flowers that enhanced many of its rooms and the tables in hallways. Herron Pond, when occupied, must require a full-time staff to maintain it, all working at the direction of the estate manager, Darryl Andrews. With its owner interred in the family cemetery for the past six months, the need for such a work force would have dwindled. Now that the twins had inherited the estate, the situation had changed again.

Dianne had mentioned the 'public rooms.' After poking her head into several rooms along a wide corridor adjacent to the salon, Jessica decided that 'public rooms' was an accurate characterization. The static, unlived-in aura of the parlor made her think of a stage set, waiting for someone to enter from the wings and put things into motion—nothing more than a showcase for the individual who had lived there. Built-in curio shelves were painted chalk blue, with a deeper-hued tufted velvet sofa and cream-colored armchairs arranged in a conversational grouping. A formal sitting room that made her think of a scene out of Downton Abbey. There was a notable lack of family photos on shelves and tables. Childhood memories of a similar type of bland home prompted her to go on to the next room.

In one room after another, her mouth gaped open at the framed art on the walls. The crown molding and ornate plaster designs on the ceiling. One of the public rooms echoed the upper classes of long-ago. Like similar settings in old black-and-white movies, it had the tone of an old-fashioned gentlemen's club or smoking room. A deep salmon-colored fabric covered the walls. Leather club chairs and sofas had retained the faint odor of pipe smoke. It reminded her of cherry and vanilla, not at all unpleasant.

All the public rooms were entered through wide elliptical arched doorways off the main hallway. She rounded a corner and opened a door tucked unobtrusively in an alcove off by itself.

Undeniably Vadim Evanov's study. She let out the breath she had been unconsciously holding. The encounter with the spirit in the foyer had left her more deeply shaken than she had realized. She stood in the doorway waiting to see whether she might sense anything left of the former occupant's life force. Had his energy become part of the ambience, the way the pipe smoke had in the previous room? It gave off an aura of heaviness.

The study was a cave-like sanctuary, a windowless private place he might have escaped to when he needed to be alone. Although she had not known him, Jessica had no difficulty picturing her benefactor pouring himself a shot from the bottle of Absolut vodka into the cut crystal tumblers on the sideboard, or stretched out to rest on the chocolate-colored leather sofa.

This room was smaller than any of the other rooms she had set foot in so far, and yet it was far from small. Music scores and folders of sheet music were stacked wherever there was space for them. On three sides, the dark paneled walls were lined with bookshelves crammed with leatherbound volumes. The fourth was a gallery of framed photographs, many autographed. Glittery-gowned women and tuxedoed men, most standing or seated at grand pianos of various design and hue. Most of the photos shared a consistent detail: the same man, aging over the years. They started with youthful 1960s-era black and white glossies and continued to present-day publicity head shots of a distinguished senior gentleman in evening attire. Intuition told Jessica that this was Vadim Evanov.

Through the vision of an artist, she studied his strong Slavic features: the light-colored hooded eyes, reddish-tinged wiry brown hair. The corners of the full lips turned down in what may have been disapproval, or simply a lack of desire to lift them into a more gracious expression. He looked down his autocratic nose at the camera lens, projecting the strong impression that he would not be an easy man to approach.

Something nibbled at the edges of her brain, but when she tried to grab onto it, it slid out of her grasp, as slippery as a greased pole. There was something about him—but not having known his name, she would have had no reason to notice him. Maybe she had seen him on a TV show or in a magazine.

The people in the photographs were unknown to her, and existed in a different universe from the performers she would have recognized, like Bradley Cooper or Lady Gaga.

Jessica got out her phone and Googled some of the legible autographs. She learned that Dame Fanny Waterman was a British pianist who gave up the concert stage to be a stay-at-home mother and highly respected teacher. Dame Fanny and Evanov were pictured seated next to each other in one of many rows of jurors in a Chopin piano competition. She had died in 2020 at 100 years of age.

Some of the artists' names had come up in the conversation with Dianne. Van Cliburn, a great American pianist. Lang Lang—a Chinese pianist who had started to play at the age of three. Jessica pictured her niece, Sophie, taking piano lessons. Imagining the pint-sized four-year-old redhead on the piano bench, trying to reach the pedals, made her chuckle. What if she turned out to be a prodigy, too? Vadim Evanov would probably have liked that.

Yuja Wang, a dazzling Chinese woman not much older than Jessica, was depicted in Google Images seated at the piano clad in sexy dresses and high-heeled shoes. In one startling photo she played the piano while standing on the bench. It appeared that Evanov the teacher had kept up to date with what was going on in the field.

She was brought up short reading the name 'Evgeny Kissin.' Vadim Evanov's presumed grandson, the little boy in the graveyard, had been named Ilya Evgeny. His middle name may well have been given in honor of the famous pianist who had started his career as a Russian child prodigy. Had Vadim held lofty ambitions for his grandson, to train him as a world-famous pianist, too? If so, his hopes had been cruelly crushed early on.

Jessica cleared her head of celebrity musicians and moved on to the bookshelves, browsing the titles of biographies—classical and contemporary composers. Music history. Music theory. The history of the mother country: the tsars, Lenin, Marx, Stalin, the Russian Revolution. Rasputin, the so-called 'Mad Monk.' A person's choice of reading matter said a lot about them.

Jessica visualized Evanov sitting at the ornate antique desk placed at the center of the room. there, writing letters—by hand, of course. He had not wanted WIFI in the house. There was no computer. Impossible to think of him using one in a room that took her to the nineteenth century. He must have had a secretary to handle business correspondence from her own office, offsite.

On the desktop, a framed black and white wedding photo showed a serious-looking young but recognizable Vadim Evanov. He held his bride in his arms in a 'carry her across the threshold' pose. The bride's short veil was topped with a flowered headdress, the lower half of her face obscured by the bouquet she held. Above it, her large eyes were happy.

Mid-60s Russia, Jessica guessed, judging by the smiling, happy wedding guests behind them, dressed in overcoats and scarves, gathered in front of, not a church, but an austere, brick building with a sign in a language too foreign for her to figure out what it might be. She could not imagine the bride in the photograph being the spirit who had ordered her to leave.

Nika Evanov. A name from the family graveyard. Vadim's wife had died in 1982 at age thirty-seven. Was that when his face had settled into the look of perpetual disapproval that he wore in the celebrity photos?

Gingerly approaching the desk, Jessica settled into the imprint left by the maestro's posterior. *Maestro.* Not a word in her everyday vocabulary, yet surely appropriate for a world-renowned pianist and teacher. Her eyes flicked over the items on the desktop: a large, round crystal ashtray and two square ones, an early twentieth century green pushbutton phone. Bookended by the two halves of a china grand piano were five books whose titles were printed in what she took to be Russian. At the left side of the desktop was a leatherbound diary and an assortment of fountain pens in a matching leather pen cup.

This was too voyeuristic for her taste, intruding into this stranger's personal effects. Neither she nor Jenna had asked to be heirs to this man's estate. But she would not be here, poking about the place, if Vadim Evanov had not summoned her and Jenna by means of his last will and testament. With more than a little reluctance, she opened the diary and saw, with a sense of relief, that the dark, strongly sloped handwriting inside was written in a language that she guessed was Russian Cyrillic.

On either side of the knee space under the desk was a locked cabinet. Dianne Maggio had encouraged her to look, yet a strong psychic sense—or was it Vadim Evanov's spirit? — was telling her that he had never intended for her to comb through his most private things.

Jessica rested her head against the back of his chair and began her process of relaxing. Closing her eyes, she inhaled deeply through her nose and held it for several beats. Exhaling slowly through her mouth, she cleared away any negative energy that might be hanging on to her. Aiming her attention at the man in the photographs, she willed the chattering monkey in her brain to be quiet. Silently saying his name three times, she asked for his spirit to come to her. And waited. And waited.

The minutes ticked past.

Maybe Evanov was busy. People in the spirit world didn't lie on clouds playing harps the way they did in Renaissance paintings; they had plenty to keep them busy on the other side. Maybe the simple fact was he did not want to talk to her. Crestfallen, Jessica opened her eyes. Staring to rise, something caught her notice that she had missed before. She dropped back into the chair. In the lower right-hand corner of the green felt desk blotter, written in the same bold hand as the diary entries was her name and Jenna's. And below theirs was written another name; a name that had an X cutting through it: *'Elise.'*

Für Elise

For once, the music did not begin to play in Jessica's head.

Was this a new candidate for the vengeful spirit in the house?

Who is Elise?

ten

I always get really nervous when I have to practice for a recital. Mr. E. says it's normal to be nervous and I have to learn to deal with it because—he actually said I do have talent! I can't believe it! He really said it and he also said he's going to train me as a concert pianist and I have to work super hard. I don't know how I'm ever going to get on a big stage and play in front of hundreds of people, but if that's what he wants me to do, I would do anything to make him proud of me.

He wants me to practice Clair de Lune, *which I have always loved, ever since Grandma used to play it for me when I was little. I thought he was kind of mean cause he made fun of Mom naming me after Beethoven's piece, but it's her favorite composition and I don't think you should laugh at people for stuff like that. It's not my fault she's a fan. Besides, I like my name. And duh! Yes, I'll work my butt off! My dream is finally starting to come true. I've wanted this forever—eight whole years, since we got our piano. I was only four, but I knew what I was supposed to do. The piano is my life. I can't believe this is happening!!!*

eleven

HER MOUTH WENT BONE dry. Why had Vadim Evanov written the three names on the blotter? Who was Elise? And what did it mean that he had scratched out her name? Was she someone he had been thinking of including in his will? Someone instead of the twins, perhaps?

Her thoughts chased in circles, staring at those names until her vision was blurry. Trying to interpret the man's motives was useless. She simply had not had a chance to accumulate enough information to smoke out what had been in this stranger's head.

There was one thing she could do. Taking her phone out of her pocket, Jessica snapped a photo of the short list of names and texted it to her handwriting expert friend, Claudia Rose. If there was anything to learn about the personality of the writer, Claudia would tell her.

Jessica: *What can you tell me about this handwriting?*

Thirty seconds later the response pinged in her phone.

Claudia: *I'm not a magician. Send more writing.*

Starting to reach for Evanov's diary, Jessica quickly pulled back her hand. Handing over someone's most personal thoughts didn't feel right, even if those thoughts were written in a language that neither she nor Claudia spoke.

But the writer was dead and Jessica needed information. She picked up her phone again.

Jessica: *Can you analyze Russian?*

Claudia's response included a smiley face emoji

Is it handwriting? Duh.

Jessica thrust aside her scruples and opened the book. To her untrained eyes, the pages resembled a piece of art—thick black ink, heavy, slashing strokes filled the paper. She photographed one page and tapped Send. The response came quickly.

Claudia: *Check your email in a few. Too much to put in a text.*

The house was utterly quiet and still. Jessica thumbed through her iTunes playlist for something bright and powerful to liven things up while she waited to hear from Claudia, but in the end, she couldn't bring herself to do it. Gwen Stefani singing *Hollaback Girl*, or Beyonce's *Single Ladies* somehow didn't jibe with the oppressive ambience of Vadim Evanov's private study.

It was too early for a drink, though after the morning she'd had, the temptation was—a movement from the corner of her eye made her swivel to the leather sofa. For the merest blink of an eye she thought she saw a male figure reclining there—more a shadowy outline than anything. And then it was gone.

"Is that you, Mr. Evanov?"

The study door, which she had left ajar, gently closed.

"Vadim has left the building," Jessica murmured.

For months now, she had accepted this sort of occurrence as a regular part of her life. It would be foolish to let the activity spook her simply because this was about her own life, not doing mediumship on behalf of someone else. She rose from the desk and wandered casually to the liquor cabinet, pretending to herself until she got there that she wasn't going to pour a healthy splash from the two-thirds full vodka bottle.

She hadn't noticed that her hand was trembling until the mouthful of Absolut she choked down calmed it. She dropped onto the sofa gasping from the burn of the fiery liquid in her throat, and started to laugh. Who would believe her if she described what she had experienced since she had been at Herron Pond?

Her email notification sounded and Claudia's name appeared in the Inbox. She could always count on her friend to tell her the truth. Even when it increased her misgivings, which Claudia's comments about Vadim Evanov's handwriting did.

Who the heck is this guy?! First off, he's brilliant. Also passionate, obsessive, emotional, difficult. Fiercely protective of family and those he loves (even when they don't want him to be. 'Dogmatic' is his middle name). Generous to a fault. He takes care of anyone he's responsible for. You're fine as long as you don't piss him off. If you do, he can be brutal.

Jess, if you're dealing with him you need to be very cautious. On top of what I wrote above, he can be highly controlling, strong-willed, domineering. This is who you call when you need dirty work done. What I mean is, he's not necessarily criminal, although if you told me he was some kind of kingpin or mafia don or a professor, it would be no big surprise. Well, since the writing is Russian, he could be a czar. Putin's boss, lol. Handwriting isn't a crystal ball, so I'm just giving examples. I don't think he's violent, but he definitely needs to call the shots and you'd better do it his way (whatever "it" is), or you'll get the sharp side of his tongue—which can slash you to ribbons. He's a stranger to shame or guilt. In other words, he's willing to do what it takes to get what he wants.

I'm sorry if this isn't the kind of news you were looking for. But you asked, and I have to tell it like it is. Again—who is this guy?

Jessica: "Okay, OMG. Thanks. I think. I'll fill you in later."

She reread the analysis once, twice, a third time. The words Claudia had used to characterize Vadim Evanov did not sound to her like the kind of person who would hand over his entire estate to a pair of strangers. On the other hand, *'passionate, emotional, difficult'* were consistent with what Jessica had perceived in his photographs. Words that could have described her, too, she thought wryly as she left the study thinking about the handwriting analysis and what it meant for her and Jen.

She stopped in the imposing hallway to get her bearings. She had entered all of the public rooms and had come to the end of the hallway. Around the corner, she came to a plain door. Opening it took her to an uncarpeted staircase that led down to a large, old-fashioned kitchen. It wasn't as extravagant as the one in the new wing, but had been modernized with an updated stove and refrigerator. Dianne had said the staff ate here when they were working, Jessica recalled, opening drawers that held cookery tools from the nineteenth century, some she didn't recognize.

Floor to ceiling wood-faced cabinets and drawers took up an entire wall as storage for Brussels lace table linens, elegant stemware, and fine china suitable for entertaining. Tangible reminders that a mere six months ago, Vadim Evanov had been the living, sentient occupant of Herron Pond. Without his death, Jessica would not be here, trying to understand the man he had been.

Claudia had said he could have been some kind of kingpin or czar. *How about a music maestro?*

A mental flash showed her a group of bejeweled guests occupying the rows of chairs in the salon where she had channeled the piano playing spirit. After enjoying the recital, they would file into the dining room for a gourmet feast prepared in this kitchen. She saw them laughing and joking—all with the greatest decorum. Whether the mental image came from her imagination or was a memory impressed on the house, it vanished too fast for her identify the people.

As she made her way around the room, the stunning reality slapped her in the face over and over: It's all ours, Jen's and mine, alternating with the question: *Why?*

Absently, she opened the heavy door of an immense icebox pantry and saw shelves stacked with industrial-sized twenty-first century cans and boxes. Storage for those parties. *as cold as a grave* came to mind. Rubbing warmth into her arms, she moved on to the wide workstation that commanded the center of the kitchen. Cooks would have stood there in times gone by, dressing meat for a banquet, using the lethal-looking boning knives that stood in the wooden knife block at one end.

It was the sight of those knives, not the temperature, that chilled her. Rageful ghosts had been known to summon the power to move physical objects. It would take the kind of chaotic fury she had experienced in the salon. The thought sent a sharp spike of dread up her spine. She had survived that close encounter in one piece, but it was too soon to shrug it off.

A vein began to throb, pulsing from her right temple to the base of her skull. The day's events caught up and hit her with the force of a hammer blow. Her encounter with Darryl Andrews, the strange experience of channeling music, and then having to defend herself against the unwelcoming entity afterwards, had exacted a toll, and a migraine was the payment.

She needed to get to her overnight bag in the new wing, and she needed to do it without crossing paths with the entity. To face that kind of rage again would take more energy than she could dredge up when an iron spike seemed to be stabbing her eyeball.

By forcing herself to move one foot ahead of the other, then the next one, and the next, Jessica made it across the kitchen and up the stairs until the empty hallway yawned endlessly ahead of her.

She stood in front of the keypad to the new wing, straining to remember the code. If only she knew of a secret passage that could have taken her instantly from the old kitchen to the new one. But if Herron Pond had any secret passages, she had yet to find one. Pushing its way through the pounding in her head, the panel code slunk back. She punched it in, doing her best to ignore the wavy lines that were rippling at the left edge of her darkening vision. All that mattered was reaching the vial of prescription painkillers that waited in her overnight bag.

The dividing door slid silently aside and Jessica lurched through it. With her head ready to burst open and hands that shook like a drunk on a toot, she rummaged in her bag for the amber-colored medicine vial. Dry-swallowing two pills with a moan of relief, she fell onto the soft leather cushions of the sofa. Within seconds, she was asleep.

twelve

December 18, 1985

Oh. My. God. I met the maestro's son and his name is Ilya—isn't that a cool name? It's so Russian or something like that. Like the guy on that old TV show Dad watches on some funky channel. It's called The Man from U.N.C.L.E. It's about these secret agent guys and one is named Ilya Kuryakin (I hope I spelled it right). He has these really amazing super long eyelashes and gorgeous blue eyes and black hair (the real Ilya, not the TV guy). I've never seen anyone with blue eyes and black hair. He's so cute, I almost passed out.

He came into the practice room when I was there and introduced himself to me. Mr. E. had to go downstairs and talk to someone who came to see him, so I was just practicing this week's pieces by myself. I don't even know what he was doing there, but it made me tons more nervous knowing he was watching me. He is <u>sooo</u> incredibly cute and he was super nice to me. He gave me a lot of compliments about my playing. My face got all hot, so I probably looked like a dork, all red and blushing.

Mr. E. came back and yelled at him to get out. Why did he have to be so mean about it? Ilya just smiled at me like it didn't bother him to get yelled at, but he left. He's the cutest boy I've ever seen. I bet he's a lot older than me, maybe 15 or 16. But I don't care that he's older, I got a vibe that he likes me, too. I'm almost thirteen anyway. I'm not going to tell anyone. It's my secret.

thirteen

Für Elise WAS PLAYING again, faintly. As she had experienced it this morning, the music was outside Jessica's head. It was coming from somewhere below her. Snuggling into the cushions with her eyes closed, a little woozy from the pills and still coming out of sleep, she pretended to herself there was no ghostly piano playing in the house. The spirit world had claimed enough of her attention for one day.

As her head began to clear, she recognized that something was off. Her last coherent memory was of collapsing onto the sofa in the new wing—an overstuffed leather sofa—not the velvety fabric that was rubbing against her cheek now. She opened her eyes and squinted in confusion at high ceilings and eight-foot windows. This was a room she had not seen before. Its curved wood-paneled walls and bulky furniture pointed to her being on the Victorian side of the mansion.

The ambient light in the oak-wainscoted room was considerably dimmer than she remembered when she had lain down. What time of day was it? The heavily frosted glass of the leaded window panes made it impossible to see out.

She stuck a hand in her jeans pocket, nearly nauseous with relief that her phone was there. With a sense of shock, she saw when she checked the screen that more than three hours had passed since she had closed her eyes in the new wing. The medication had never knocked her out that way before. Nor had it made her sleepwalk to another floor in another place. Surely one swallow of vodka had not been the kicker.

Waking up in an unfamiliar room in an unfamiliar house was not outside her realm of experience. In the years since her head injury, she had once woken on a speeding train, not knowing where she was going or where the journey had originated. On another occasion, she woke in her pajamas at dawn on her patio, not knowing how she had got there, or why. One thing was the same, though—every time she awoke in an unexpected place it was as jarring and unnerving as the first.

In search of a memory of how she had moved from one side of the house to the other, Jessica plopped back onto the cushions and closed her eyes.

How did I get here? And where, exactly, is here?

She slowed her breathing the way she did when she was channeling spirit, focusing on taking long inhalations and longer exhalations, and made her mind a blank canvas. After a dozen or so slow, steady inhales and exhales, a hazy scene began to drift into her consciousness that she recognized as fragments of a dream or possibly a vision.

As the minutes passed, she relaxed deeper and deeper into a trance state. The blank canvas acquired the silvery sheen of a movie screen. The hazy contours sharpened. She saw a petite teenaged girl with a sweet, heart-shaped face and long, bushy blonde hair not unlike Jessica's own. There was a boy, too, whose pensive dark looks were typical of film tropes about good girls and bad boys. All that was missing was the overpriced bucket of popcorn and gigantic Coke.

It was a lot like watching a silent movie. No sound, just action. The young couple set out a picnic on the beach, ran into the waves and splashed each other, laughing and playing, as blissfully happy as Jessica and Sage. There were long drives up the coast in a 1980s-era Mustang convertible and, wedged into the tiny backseat, they coupled with the desperate intensity of youth.

Suddenly, in the maddening way of dreams, the girl disappeared from the story with no explanation. Bereft, her young lover's misery was plain. What had happened to her? Had the boy betrayed her? *Killed* her? Jessica knew as well as if she had written their story herself that the girl was not the flighty sort who would have dumped him and taken off with someone else. Something tragic had removed her from the picture, she was certain of it.

The vision went on, but all the pleasure had been sucked out of it. The boy got older and the girl was replaced by a strikingly beautiful young woman with sharp blue eyes and glossy black hair against pale, smooth skin. She did everything she could to please him, but her lover's eyes looked past her, into the distance until the depth of his sadness became etched on his face, the pain of rejection on hers.

Jessica knew he was looking for the blonde girl, who had been so full of fun and laughter, and she wanted to know where she was. But the vision faded, leaving her on the edge of her seat. She could not have been more disappointed if she had paid big bucks at the IMAX and the movie ended with a vital piece missing. If there was any kind of happy ending to this story, she had either forgotten it while she had slept on, or had woken up too soon.

As she began to prepare herself for a return to full wakefulness, somewhere in her consciousness, Jessica recognized that the music she had heard coming from below the round room had stopped. The silence was complete.

Desperate to know what happened next in the vision, and what had brought her here while she was as dead to the world as Sleeping Beauty, with a final deep inhale, she opened her eyes.

On the coffee table was a small photograph that had not been there when she had closed her eyes a few minutes ago. *Or had it?* As confused as she had been by the change in location, it was quite possible that she had missed seeing it.

She picked it up. The teased, feathery hairdo and a fuzzy blue backdrop suggested a high school senior class photo taken in the late 1980s. Her stomach did a somersault. She was looking at the smiling face of the girl who had disappeared from her vision. On the reverse, a small, neat hand had written:

Darling Ilya, I will love you with all my heart forever, Elise

Elise. Ilya.

Für Elise.

The somersault turned into a cartwheel as she put it all together. Vadim Evanov's middle name was Ilya, and so was the name of the little boy in the cemetery. According to his gravestone, the younger Ilya was born in 1992. So, she reasoned, the Ilya to whom Elise had signed her photo must be the younger one's father, Vadim's son.

Vadim, Ilya, and little Ilya.

Whatever had torn the young couple apart in the vision must have been resolved. The spurt of excitement Jessica felt was short-lived. The little boy had died at seven years of age and was buried on the grounds of Herron Pond. Had Elise died, too? Did their story have a tragic ending after all, with Ilya left alone and vulnerable to the raven-haired beauty? That these people were all strangers to her did not stop her from feeling a deep sadness for them. Gazing at Elise's photo, they did not feel like strangers.

The music started up again. The sounds of the piano penetrated the floor and Jessica felt the vibration in her feet. At the same moment, she sensed a spirit enter the room and hover near her left side. And she became aware that the presence was the same one that had assumed her body this morning at the piano. She sent it a barrage of questions:

Are you Elise? If you are, what happened to you and Ilya and little Ilya? And what about the black-haired woman? Who is she?

Without giving her any answers, the presence faded as rapidly as it had arrived, leaving Jessica with a strong impression that it wanted her to follow. She opened the single door in the round room and found herself on a small landing at the top of a circular staircase. Her sleepwalk had taken her from downstairs in the new wing to a turret room at the top of the old side of the house.

Numbly, she descended to the second-floor, which felt familiar from her tour of the bedrooms with Dianne the day before. The sound of the piano grew louder.

The handsome old grandfather clock continued to tick loudly in its corner on the landing. The same vase of flowers, a little less fresh today, stood on a small reception table. For a microsecond, as she passed by the huge pier mirror, Jessica startled, thinking that the girl from the photo—Elise—was looking back at her. Her nervous laugh echoed along the landing as a second glance showed that what she had seen was no ghostly form in the mirror, but herself in the waning afternoon light filtering through the stained-glass wall.

Dampened behind thick walls, the music continued to play. Recognizing a Chopin Nocturne, Jessica knew exactly where the spirit was leading her.

Feel free to go anywhere, except the last door.

The estate attorney's admonition had bothered Jessica from the moment she heard it. Whatever her reason for warning Jessica off that room, it was not sitting well.

If Dianne knew what it was like to have her body inhabited by an unknown spirit—one that was now playing Rachmaninoff's hauntingly beautiful *Prelude in C-Sharp Minor*—maybe she would better understand that Jessica's lifelong habit of making up her own mind was not about to change just because someone told her she could not do something. Her independent streak had been with her from birth and was big enough for both her and Jenna, and something told her that no pile of old furniture was waiting to fall on her when she opened that door.

With her pulse galloping in time to the music, Jessica followed the thunderous crashing chords of Rachmaninoff's *Prelude*. As she reached the last door, the agitato section's passionate crescendo fell to its contradictory soft ending. After the intense performance, the silence echoed along the corridor.

Jessica knocked on the door. "Elise, I'm here."

She tried the handle, not surprised to find it locked; she had expected it. But why had Elise brought her here if she was unable to open the door? A nudge from the spirit told her to look up. A padlock had been installed near the top of the door, another tucked inconspicuously near the floor.

What the hell was kept in that room, that Dianne Maggio and Darryl Andrews had conspired to keep it padlocked? As if locks presented a barrier to the spirit world.

The sudden blare of the *Game of Thrones* theme nearly launched Jessica through the ceiling.

fourteen

JANUARY 3, 1988

Dear Diary,

School is such a drag, so boring. Everyone is so immature. I asked Mom if I could do home schooling but she said no because I need to be 'socialized.' Why? All the other girls talk about is going to parties and their stupid makeup and how obsessed they are with Rob Lowe and Tom Cruise. They're so immature. They don't like me anyway. When they all start gossiping and their childish crap I tune out and think about Ilya.

He says that since he's turned 18 we have to be even more careful not to get caught together. He could get into a lot of trouble for being with me because I'm 'underage.' How dumb is that?! I'll be 16 in June. We've been in love since the day we met. I can't believe I was only 12, but I knew right away that he's my soulmate, and he knew it, too. It was like we already knew each other. There will never ever be anyone else for me and he feels the same.

I guess keeping our love a secret is actually kind of romantic. The big problem is, I can tell the maestro is suspicious. But we're always careful to act like we're just friendly when he's around.

I wish I could sneak out and meet him tonight, but I can't until after the concert. I can't let myself be distracted from my music, even though I can hardly wait to be with him.

January 12, 1988

Dear Diary,

My big performance is this Saturday. I'm crazy nervous, but it's also exciting to play for all those people. This concert is the biggest audience I've ever had. I've been practicing and practicing for months. I think I'm ready but Mr. E. keeps nitpicking the Liszt until I'm starting to hate it. Plus, La Campanella *is one of the trickiest pieces ever. I've been working on it every day for it feels like forever. I'm sitting at the piano for five or six hours every day and it sounds good to me.*

P.S. I don't really *hate the Liszt piece, it's just that Mr. E is so hyper critical about it. Mom says that's why teachers like him have such successful students. I guess she's right, but I'm glad Ilya isn't like him. He's so gentle and sensitive. How can Mr. E. be Ilya's father?*

fifteen

Jessica stared at the phone's screen.

She circled around to the head of the staircase, forcing herself to take a mental step away from the padlocked door and what it implied.

"Hello?"

"Hi, is this Jessica Mack?" said a lively female voice.

"Yes, who's this?"

"It's Amy Herron, the realtor? I got your voicemail from last night. I'm so sorry I couldn't get back to you sooner. You're staying at the Pond?"

It took a moment to re-orient herself from her discovery of the padlocked door to the animated caller. She did her best to sound enthusiastic. "Amy. Thanks for calling. Yes, I'm here on a short visit. I'll be here through the weekend. I was hoping you might be free for coffee and a chat."

"I'd love to. I could meet you down at Java Jake's, or I can come to you at the house. It's totally up to you."

Even over the phone, the vitality Amy exuded made Jessica feel slow and dull-witted. If her energy could be bottled, the realtor would make megabucks. "Now works fine for me. I'm new to the area, so if it's okay with you, if you come here, I'll have coffee ready."

"Awesome. I'll pick up some goodies. See you in thirty."

"You don't have to—" Jessica was talking to dead air. As she clicked off, she realized the music down the hall had stopped.

***

Amy Herron was not Jessica's idea of a realtor, which she pictured as someone with a used car salesman vibe. She greeted Amy at the front door beginning to feel as if she did, in fact, own the place. *Half of it, anyway.*

In skinny jeans and a camel-colored turtleneck under a blazer, Amy was as low-key and nice as she appeared in her LinkedIn photo. As she entered the foyer, she gave an appraising glance at the décor and nodded with approval. If she was aware of either the piano-playing spirit or the surly one, she gave no indication.

"Thanks so much for calling me," she said. "I haven't been here in quite a while. It's beautiful, and it's been so well kept up. Nothing faded or threadbare." She caught herself. "Sorry, valuing everything is a rude habit of the trade. I need to learn to keep it to myself."

"It's my first time here, so I'm seeing what you're seeing," Jessica said. "Dianne Maggio mentioned that your family were the ones who built the house?"

"Oh, that was eons ago—over a hundred years. The name seems to have stuck, though. You'd think Mr. Evanov would have changed it to something—I don't know—more European, I guess. But it's still good old Herron Pond."

"Herron Pond works for me, though I think the pond looks more like a lake." Jessica accepted the paper sack Amy handed her. Printed on the side was 'Café Bellisimo' with a sketched logo of a steaming cup of coffee. "Thanks for this," she said. "I'm starving—slept through lunch." *And woke up in another part of the house to a music-playing ghost.* Amy would think she was nuts if she told her that. She led her through the dining room.

Amy's eyes lit up as Jessica tapped the code on the panel to access the hidden sliding door. "It's like a secret passage. How fun."

"It's just the way to the new wing, which is totally different from the old side—did you know that? Get ready for culture shock."

They stepped through into the passageway, Amy following behind. "I guess after the fire Mr. Evanov—"

Jessica stopped in her tracks and swung around so fast that Amy ran into her. "What fire?"

The realtor's fair skin reddened. "Shoot, you weren't told about it." She gave herself a face-palm. "I thought Dianne—I should have kept my big mouth shut."

"No, no, it's fine." Jessica started moving again towards the kitchen, her mind flying wildly in several directions.

Amy surveyed the kitchen and its high-end appliances. "You weren't kidding about the culture shock, were you?"

Jessica set the pastries on a plate and poured the fresh coffee she had brewed. "If my sister and I own the place, don't you think a fire big enough to burn down half the house is something we should know about? Please clue me in."

Amy looked distinctly uncomfortable. "It happened long enough ago that I don't think it affects you in any way. It's not like you're buying it, is it? I mean, it was left to you as-is. If there had been any legal requirement to let you know—"

Jessica put up her hand to stop the spate of defenses. "Relax, Amy, I'm not talking about legalese. I want to learn about the house we've inherited. Wouldn't you?" She handed her guest a mug and offered cream and sugar.

Declining the accoutrements, Amy took the coffee with a sheepish smile. "Am I overreacting?"

Jessica hiked a brow. "Maybe a little."

"It's just that I'm very careful to tell clients when there's anything concerning in a house I'm showing them."

"I'm sure you are, and this isn't that, all right?"

"Right." Amy looked abashed. She took a sip from her mug and said brightly, "This is really delicious coffee."

Jessica knew she was looking for a way out of answering the question, and that was not going to happen. "It's the water. So, go on, tell me about the fire."

Amy frowned as if searching her memory, then let out a long sigh, surrendering. "Okay, but I don't know all that much. I think it must have been eight or nine years ago. It's the reason they built this new side of the house. There was too much that was unsalvageable. Lots of smoke damage, too." She folded her arms across her body, leaving Jessica to consider whether the body language was signaling that she was withholding information.

"A house this old, they're lucky the whole thing wasn't destroyed," she said. "I bet it cost the insurance company a small fortune to rebuild and to get everything restored that could be saved. I heard there were some valuable musical artifacts and artwork that were lost."

An image of the magnificent house in flames rose in Jessica's mind and left her breathless with dismay. For a moment, she could not speak. Finally, she managed to ask, "What started it?"

Amy's apologetic shrug promised disappointment. "It happened when I was traveling in Europe, so like I said, I don't know much. It was ages later that I heard about it from my dad. From what I can remember, I don't think they were ever able to pin down the actual cause. The fire department said it probably started in one of the bedrooms. Might have been a candle or something like that."

"A candle? I wonder what happened."

"It was in the middle of the night," Amy said, proving that she knew more than she had let on. "The staff had all gone home, of course. All but Darryl, that is. He's the boss—the guy who manages everything. He lived here until Mr. Evanov—"

"I know," Jessica interrupted. "I met him this morning."

"He's the one who called it in to the fire department. He said the glow from the flames woke him up; he saw them from his window over the garage. He ran over but he was too late to do anything much. At that time there no sprinklers in the house. By the time he got here the fire was too big for the garden hose to do any good. The fire trucks got here fast enough to save most of the front half of the house, but the rest was a total loss. It took over a year to rebuild."

"Jesus, Amy," Jessica said, stunned. "What about Mr. Evanov?"

"He was recovering from major heart surgery; had to be re-admitted to the hospital afterwards with smoke inhalation. He was there for a while, as you can imagine."

"It must have been a mess. Thank goodness nobody was hurt."

"I didn't say that," Amy said.

"But you said the staff had gone home."

"That's true. But there was a couple staying here, taking care of him while he recuperated from the surgery." As if someone might overhear and criticize her for telling the story, she lowered her voice to a conspiratorial stage whisper. "Not everyone got out."

Jessica's blood turned to ice. Her eyes drilled into the realtor's, demanding answers. "Are you saying someone—died?"

Amy nodded somberly. "One of the people taking care of him, a woman. Seriously, Jessica, that's all I know about it."

"You know quite a bit." Jessica looked down at the remaining pastry on her plate, no longer hungry. Thoughts of the woman who had lost her life here sickened her. Was the entity that had stayed glued to the house the spirit of the woman who had perished in the fire? Who could blame her for being angry if it was her? What an appalling way to exit this life.

Even so, it did not explain why she would resent Jessica's presence so deeply and angrily.

Evidently done with the topic of the housefire, Amy brought up the earlier subject again. "So, have you found any actual secret passages? This is the perfect place for them, don't you think? It'd be so much fun if there was one."

"I'm not so sure about that," Jessica said, still consumed by thoughts of the deadly fire and its victim. Her mind was half on Darryl Andrews. Aside from the firefighters and the police, he was the one person who was an eyewitness to the tragedy. Would he talk to her about it?

"You could find a copy of the original construction plans at the Building Inspector's office," Amy was saying.

Jessica nodded absently with zero intention of following through. After having met two other-worldly beings in the house, secret passages held little allure. Over Amy's shoulder, through the windows that surrounded the breakfast room, she could see the outdoor barbecue kitchen and the palatial gardens and lake that spread beyond it. The untidy thicket that hid the five graves was invisible from this vantage point.

"By the way, Amy," she said, changing topics again. "When I was exploring the grounds this morning, I came across the family graveyard. Are those your grandparents buried there—Hannah and Thomas Herron?"

"Great-grandparents. Does it bother you, having them buried so close to the house?"

"No. It's not all that close. This place is huge."

"That's the truth. My greats loved the place so much that they wanted to be here forever together when they had passed on. I suppose that's why they're buried here."

"So romantic," Jessica said, although she would rather talk about the Evanov family.

"You'd think. Their kids didn't love it at all. Dad used to talk about how they all hated the isolation up here. There were no other houses close by, so they didn't have anyone else to play or hang out with when they got older. Even now, there aren't that many. He told me his sisters couldn't wait to grow up and move away. When the grandparents died, their parents sold the place faster than you could spit." She chuckled. "Not that my dad moved very far. He married a local girl and I was born in Monterey County. Except for the time I was traveling the world, I stuck around the area, too." She paused for a bite of pastry and a sip of coffee. "And how about you, Jessica? I heard that you live down south in the L.A. area, but are you a native daughter of the golden west, too?"

That was a slippery slope she would prefer to avoid. "My sister and I were indeed raised in Southern California," Jessica said. "We were adopted."

A series of expressions chased across Amy's face and Jessica could see she wanted to ask questions. In the end Amy said, "Oh, adopted. I hope you had a happy childhood."

A question that begged an answer. Jessica's lips twisted. "*Happy?*" her sardonic smile said. *Not so much.* Their mother had trotted out the adorable twins dressed up in frilly dresses and bows for her girlfriends when she was in the mood. Most of the time, she wasn't. The twins had spent their pre-school days in a locked playroom, suffering the company of an indifferent au pair who was more interested in chatting on the phone to her boyfriend.

It was too soon in their acquaintance to unload that mess on Amy. She settled for the basic truth. "We had everything material we could possibly want." As soon as she said it a bud of shame bloomed in her chest, familiar enough to call it a frenemy. She recognized the unwelcome leftover from parents who had drilled into her and Jen what lucky little girls they were. They should be grateful they were given so much more than most children—especially considering that their birth mother had given them away—the offhand comment had been repeated often and burned deeper every time Jessica was forced to hear it. She would gladly have exchanged the closetful of expensive toys, books, and cute outfits for a mother who loved the tempestuous, creative girl she had been.

No. She could not bring herself to be the tiniest bit grateful to the Marcotts.

Amy, unaware of the emotional churning going on in her host's head, went on, "And I heard you have a twin sister. How awesome is that?"

That was Jessica's cue to show photos of her and Jenna together as teens, when they had dressed alike, and a more recent one where they did not. "It was more awesome when we were younger."

Nibbling on her pastry, Amy's eyes went from the phone screen to the live Jessica. "It's incredible. I swear, you two really are identical. I'd never be able to tell you apart." She giggled. "Isn't it kind of strange when you look at your sister? Is it like looking in a mirror?"

Jessica had to grin at her frank curiosity. "We've been looking at each other all our lives. The weirdness has worn off."

"But isn't it fun to have an identical twin?"

"It can be. Sometimes. Or not. When we would switch off at school or on dates and got away with it, that was definitely fun."

There were other times, too. Like the weeks when Jessica was suffering from memory loss and lived Jenna's life, believing it was her own. That was nothing approaching fun. Something else Amy didn't need to hear about.

"I could have used a twin to switch some of my dates," Amy said, unaware of the odd little breeze that ruffled through Jessica's hair as though a shadow had passed over her.

"Twinship sometimes can definitely have its advantages." Jessica dug deep for a smile and changed the subject again. "Hey, Amy, I wanted to ask you something about the little graveyard."

"The graveyard? I've never actually seen it. What do you want to know? I wouldn't even know how to find it."

"That's okay, I know where it is. My question is about the little boy who's buried there."

"A little boy?" Amy frowned. "That's so sad. Who was he?"

Jessica hid her disappointment. "I was hoping you could tell me something about him. He died in the early 90s."

"The 1890s?"

"Sorry, no, the 1990s. The name on his gravestone is Ilya Evanov. He was seven years old."

"That's news to me. I guess he must have been the son of Mr. Evanov. I'm sorry, Jessica, I've never heard of him. But like I said, I haven't been up here in eons, and, well, the 90s is a long time ago. I was a kid myself."

"I think it's more likely he was a grandchild. I think his father was Mr. Evanov's son, whose name was also Ilya."

"I never heard of him having a son *or* a grandson. All I ever knew was, he was a widower. You know, I actually met him once, when I was too young to be interested in his family history. I was about ten. My mom brought me here. She wanted me to take piano lessons from him, but I was too intimidated to say boo, let alone audition for the 'great man.' He was way too scary."

"He was scary?" Jessica thought of Dianne's description of Vadim Evanov's temperament. She had called him 'testy' when he had stubbornly refused to share with her the reasoning behind changing his will. There was Claudia's handwriting analysis, too. Both matched the man Jessica believed she had identified in the photos in his study.

"One thing I've never forgotten—he had these piercing eyes. Like knife-points." Amy scrunched up her eyes and gave Jessica what was meant to be an intimidating glare, but her dismal attempt to imitate the maestro made Jessica laugh.

"No, seriously," Amy said. "He scared the crud out of me. He had an accent, which also made him kinda scary."

"His name sounds Russian." Jessica got up and went to fetch the coffee pot for refills, trying to think of a way she could ask the question she most wanted answered. Jenna was forever telling her she was too blunt when she wanted to know something, rushing right in without softening up her listener with a little polite conversation first. She knew she had irked Darryl Andrews when she asked if he knew why the estate had been left to them. Not that she cared about his opinion, but she didn't want to make that mistake with Amy, who she liked.

Jessica was forming her question when Amy spoke first.

"I'm so happy you called me," she said. "Dianne told me she wanted to introduce us, so we're skipping a step." What she'd said seemed genuine, but there was hesitation in the way she said it. Jessica waited, watching her fingertip trace the rim of the mug as if she, too, was looking for a way to phrase what she wanted to say.

"I've been wondering whether you're thinking of selling the estate. Of course, you don't have to use me—but the thing is, I have a client—"

A pulse of distress began to throb in Jessica's throat. Tanya Stewart had raised the idea of selling Herron Pond, and so had Dianne Maggio and Darryl Andrews, but hearing it from the realtor herself made her feel physically ill. She set the coffee pot down. "Hold up, Amy. We found out about the inheritance less than a week ago. My sister had to leave an hour after we arrived yesterday. All she got to see was the entry hall and the dining room, and this kitchen. It's way too soon to have decided what we are going to do." She had not intended to raise her voice, but the words flew out too fast, too loud, and she couldn't claw them back.

Amy's face paled. Seeing her push her chair away from the table, as if she felt the need to create some physical distance between them, made Jessica pause. She softened her tone and started over. "Look, Amy, I didn't mean to jump all over you. If we do end up deciding to sell, I would have no problem having you represent us, and Jenna will feel the same. But frankly, I'm not excited about the idea of selling. I fell in love with the place the minute I saw it. Mr. Evanov left money for us to take care of it, so if we can just figure out how..."

"Sure." Amy cleared her throat nervously. "I get it. It's a fabulous property, and the house—well, it's amazing, but—" With a tremulous smile, she dropped a bombshell almost as big as the news of the inheritance "I need to tell you, Jessica, my client is prepared to make an offer of eighteen million."

Eighteen million dollars?

The number echoed in Jessica's head but she could not get the words out of her mouth. She had been so busy wondering *why* they had inherited it that it had not occurred to her that the estate might be worth that kind of money. Perhaps it should not have come as such a shock, but the figure left her slack-jawed. The mansion sat on acres of Big Sur land, plus the private beach, she thought. *Of course* Herron Pond was worth a lot. Stupid of her to be surprised.

She recovered from the surprise. "Does your client have a big family?"

"It's a small corporation," Amy said, bursting the bubble of a happy family tearing around the property, maybe installing a playground for the kids. "There's been talk about possibly repurposing it as a retreat. I don't know if you're aware, retreats are big around here. You might have heard of the Esalen Institute and Nepenthe and the Camaldoli Hermitage."

Upon learning of their inheritance, Jessica had Googled the area and read about the famous holistic and religious centers in Big Sur. "All I know about them is, they've been here for a long time."

"Some of them since the 1940's. Herron Pond has everything they need to develop that kind of place—the house, the pond, the land, the ocean." Amy was looking at her with earnest anticipation, but the prospect of strangers traipsing through the house and grounds, seeking spa treatments, had hit Jessica's gut like corrosive acid. She frowned. "I can't imagine seeing it converted, or torn down for some kind of camp site. Even if they were to use only the new wing—" She broke off, unable to bear the thought.

"It all depends on how it was done." Amy gave her a significant look. "Eighteen million bucks can ease a lot of pain. And you could make a counteroffer. They might go a little higher. They're very motivated."

"You're assuming money is the most important thing," Jessica retorted. The realtor's expectation had rattled her. She could well imagine Jenna going for such an arrangement. Her sister had not had a chance to form a relationship with the house the way she had. Even after her short occupancy, Jessica no longer considered herself a stranger at Herron Pond. She knew she belonged there—ghosts notwithstanding.

Ghosts.

"There's something about this place that might not be so attractive to a buyer," she said impulsively.

"Like what?"

"Have you ever heard anyone talk about it being haunted?"

At first, Amy looked puzzled. Her face cleared and she rolled her eyes. "Oh, the 'ghost of Herron Pond?'" She put air quotes around the word. "I didn't realize you'd heard about that."

"You don't think it's real?"

"Nah, I don't believe in that stuff. There have been rumors swirling for years, but I don't think I've ever heard of anyone actually *seeing* any uh, spectral activity, or whatever you want to call it."

"They'd have to be here to see anything. Wasn't Mr. Evanov supposedly reclusive?"

"Well, yeah, but people work here and they tend to talk. I'm sure it's just a bunch of made-up stories. Nothing to worry about."

"People who work here talk about there being ghosts, but nobody ever saw any?"

Amy shifted uncomfortably in her chair. She glanced at her purse on the floor, as though she wished she could pick it up and charge right out the door. She raised her hands, backing down. "Okay, look. My friend's mom used to be a cleaner here."

"And?" Jessica prompted when she fell silent.

"Carmela—my friend's mom—said that in certain parts of the house she would get a feeling like—well, like someone was watching her. And sometimes she would think someone had spoken to her, but there was no one there. That's why she eventually quit. As far as I know, she never actually saw anything, though."

"What parts of the house?"

"Excuse me?"

"You said there were parts of the house where she felt uncomfortable. Where? Which parts?"

"I have no idea."

Jessica's brain was spinning. "Could I talk to her?"

"Oh, no, no, I don't think so. Why would you want to do that?"

"Why shouldn't I?"

"I'd rather not give credence to the whole 'ghost' thing."

"Why? Because you think that kind of talk would chill a sale?"

Amy's thoughtful gaze rested on Jessica's face for a long time. While she was reading Amy, Amy was trying to read her, too. "Not if it was sold to the right person," the realtor said at length.

"And you have that person—the corporation?"

"I think I might."

"You don't think these people believe in ghosts?"

"There are some people who would come here for that very reason," she said, making Jessica wonder whether that was what she had intended from the beginning.

"So, it's a marketing ploy?" Jessica didn't bother to hide her revulsion.

"Marketing is what sells properties."

"To ghost hunters, you mean?"

Amy shrugged. "To people who love that kind of stuff, who enjoy being scared, thinking something might jump out at them."

Having had that very experience at Herron Pond, Jessica looked at her with fake wide-eyed innocence. "And who is this ghost supposed to be? How did she die?"

Amy's eyebrows rose. "Did I say 'she?'"

"Whatever. He or she."

"That, I don't know. As I said, I don't believe in all that voodoo hoodoo myself."

"What about 'no smoke without fire?'" Jessica pressed, which made her think of the actual fire Amy had said happened here. A fire in which a woman had died. "If there is a ghost, as people believe, the ghost would have a reason for staying around after they died."

Amy's sidelong glance confirmed her skepticism. "What about that little boy you said is in the graveyard? Maybe they think it's him."

"It's not him," Jessica said with a firm shake of her head.

"How do you know that? You sound very sure." Amy's tone was tinged with suspicion. Her attention sharpened, laser focused. "Don't tell me you've seen something while you've been here?"

It was Jessica's turn to shrug. "You said you don't believe in ghosts, so would you believe me if I said I did?"

"Try me."

Jessica had spent five years denying that she saw and heard Spirit. She'd had a scarce few months to practice and was gradually learning to accept it. Few in her small circle knew about her gift. Or curse. She had not decided which it was. Anticipating Amy trading skepticism for a scornful laugh, her first urge was to tell her to forget she'd said anything. But instinct told her that Amy was not the kind of person who would laugh at someone—even if she was not a believer. And she was waiting for a response.

"Do you know what a medium is?" Jessica asked.

"Isn't that someone who sits around a table and holds hands with a bunch of people asking the dead to talk to them?"

Amy was not all that far from the truth. Nevertheless, Jessica had to prevent herself from rolling her eyes at the generalization. "You're talking about a seance, and yes, the person who conducts it is a medium, but not all mediums hold seances."

"And you're telling me this, why?"

"Because I am a medium."

"What?"

"I don't hold seances myself, but I do have a bad habit of seeing and hearing dead people. Most of the time they are earthbound spirits that aren't ready to leave their old lives on earth behind." Jessica paused. Amy's face had drained of color. Her eyes were nervously jumping around the room as if an apparition might jump out at her from a corner.

"I haven't had anything like that happen on this side of the house," Jessica assured her. "But I have experienced some strange things on the Victorian side. The stories your friend's mom told you are totally true."

Amy's mouth dropped. "Wait. Wait. You actually see—*ghosts?*"

"Mostly, I just hear them. And most of the time they're really nice. They usually want me to give messages to—" Jessica interrupted herself, drawn to a gauzy male figure that had appeared behind Amy. He was more of an outline than a full body, and was standing to her right. Raising a finger to put Amy on hold so she could listen, Jessica said, "Believe it or not, there's someone here, and he's here for you."

"Here for me?" Amy's voice came out a squeak. "What does that mean, he's here for me?"

"Not to get you! He has a message for you. I can't see a lot of detail yet, but I can tell you it's a male spirit and he's on the same level as you. That means he was a brother, brother-in-law, cousin, or friend. In other words, it's someone in your age range who crossed over a while ago, not too recently."

"What are you *talking* about?" Amy's face had paled. She snatched her jacket from the chair where she had tossed it, fumbling her arms into the sleeves. "You're pranking me, right?"

"Honestly, I'm not. Look, I get it if you don't want me to give you the message and that's okay. I won't say anything else. It's just, this guy is being insistent that he wants to talk to you."

"But I—I don't believe—who the *hell* is this person claiming to be and why would they want to talk to me?"

In her thoughts, Jessica asked the spirit to provide some specific information—evidence that Amy would understand. If he wanted her to pass along a message, she told him, he was going to have to help her. She asked how he had died. He impressed his answer on her and she looked straight into Amy's frightened eyes. "He says he crossed over in a motorcycle accident and it was his own fault." Jessica asked him his name. "He's drawing the letter 'M' over his head. His name must start with the letter 'M'. He's smiling at you. He seems to be a super-nice guy. Does this mean anything to you? Do you know an 'M' name who crossed in a motorcycle accident?"

Tears brimmed in Amy's eyes and slid down her face. "Omigod, Jessica, it's Matt. His name is Matt." She grabbed a napkin that Jessica had put in front of her and dabbed at her eyes. "You're kidding me, right?"

"No, I'm not kidding. And yes, he's nodding that he *is* Matt. Did he have a motorcycle accident?"

"Yes, yes. He's my friend's brother—the one whose mom worked here. He was riding in the canyons with a group of friends. Later, they said he was going too fast on a corner and—"

Those mountain corners were treacherous. On the drive up to Big Sur, Jessica's heart had been in her mouth more than once. She waited for Amy to settle. "Did you and Matt date for a while?"

Amy's mouth fell open. "I can't believe this."

Spirits said a lot of things that Jessica wasn't sure she wanted to 'translate,' and Matt had joined that crew. "Okay, I'm blushing, but I have to repeat what he tells me. He says you were hot then and you haven't changed a bit."

Amy burst out laughing. "That was eons ago in high school. Omigod, Jessica!"

"Matt wants you to know he's fine, and—" The man in spirit pantomimed the act of rocking a baby. "Did someone in that family have a baby soon after he crossed? It's not his, it's the child of someone close to him. There's the letter 'R' in someone's name." Jessica formed the capital letter in the air. "R. Ronnie or Rocky or Rosie—"

"This is incredible," Amy broke in excitedly. "His sister, *Rosie*—my friend—her baby was born two months after Matt died. It's been three years."

"Well, Matt wants his family to know that he was there at the party for the baby, and no one should feel guilty for celebrating the birth just because he was stupid enough to cross himself over—that's what he said." Jessica assured her. "It's not me calling him stupid. It was a wonderful event and he was happy to be there, too. He says even though nobody saw him there, it was a blast." It would be easier if she could just show Amy the party she was seeing. All she could do was try and share the feeling of it. "He's laughing. Oh, he's showing me that it was him making the lights flicker. Rosie will remember that. He wants you to tell Rosie that he loves her and he's often with her and his little niece. He says tell mom and dad, too. He loves you all."

Tears streamed down Amy's cheeks, and she was smiling, too. "You'd better believe I'll tell her. Do you think it was Matt that Rosie's mom heard talking to her when she was working here?"

"I don't know." Jessica was not willing to burst that bubble. It was more likely that Rosie's mom had heard the entity from the foyer.

Amy kept shaking her head, as if trying to deny the message Jessica had delivered. Finally, she gave up. "You had absolutely no way of knowing any of that. It's nothing you could have Googled before I got here. Jessica Mack, you've made a believer out of me."

"Well, that's one way to do it." Jessica had experienced enough rejections that delivering a welcome message and changing the recipient's opinion about the spirit world made her happy.

"Matt is starting to fade," she said. "It takes a lot of energy for them to come through like this. He's happy he was able to get his message to you."

"I don't get it," Amy said, her face a picture of bewilderment. "What is Matt doing *here,* at Herron Pond, when his mom hasn't worked here in years?"

"He's here because you are. Spirit can see what we're doing—I can't tell you how, but they'll use any means they can to contact someone they love. I guess he must have known you were going to be here, even before we knew it. He snagged the chance to use me to bring his message through for you."

Amy held out a trembling hand. "Look at me, I'm shaking all over like a leaf."

"It's a lot," Jessica said.

"No kidding. What about the ghost you said you heard? What did it say to you?"

"It wasn't nice like Matt. It told me to go away."

"And you stayed here all by yourself? I would've run away screaming."

"It's a little different when you're used to talking to Spirit." Jessica wasn't about to let her in on how she had channeled the piano playing spirit. She had a sense that it would be a bridge too far for someone who was just opening up to the possibilities of spirit communication.

"So far, nothing has bothered me on this side of the house. Matt is the first spirit I've felt here. My partner is driving up tomorrow to spend the weekend. I'll go home with him, and I'll talk to my sister about what to do with the place."

"If I were you, I wouldn't be staying here alone for one single minute." Amy gave a delicate shudder. Her shoulders slumped. "I guess I'll have to inform my client about the—you-know-what."

"Yes, I guess you will," Jessica said. Regardless of the talk of people wanting to come to Herron Pond to ghost hunt, it was her fervent hope that Amy's client would be put off by the prospect of a real ghost. She started collecting the mugs and plates, giving herself somewhere to look. "I have a funny feeling that Dianne and Darryl probably know all about it."

"About the ghost? Why would you think that? Of course not. No way. They would have told me."

"Why wouldn't they?"

"Well, because they're—uh, I think they would, that's all."

Something poking at Jessica's psychic sense said that Amy was being evasive. There was more here to unravel. She was trying to figure out what that might be when Amy pressed on. "If my client is interested, ghost and all, how do you feel about their offer?"

Jessica could feel her face get hot and she was sure it was red. She struggled to keep her temper down, "It's a lot of money, but I have no idea what the estate is actually worth. It must have been appraised during probate."

"I thought I'd to talk to you first and get an idea of your level of interest. I'll check some of the comps in the area if it's okay with you."

"I'll need to do some investigating myself," Jessica said. "And talk to my sister. And our attorney, of course."

"Oh. Of course." Amy groped in her purse and came out with a business card, which she handed over. "We should touch base soon, okay?"

"Does Dianne know about your client's offer?"

The question seemed to fluster the other woman. "Uh, well, yes, I had told her about it. Since she's the executor of the estate, she needs to be aware of things like that, right?"

"I guess so. I wonder why she didn't mention it to me when she was here yesterday."

"I expect she thought it was appropriate for me to bring it to you first. It's my client, you know."

"If you say so." Jessica carried the dishes into the kitchen and set them in the sink, ready to end the meeting and boot up her computer.

"What about Darryl Andrews? Does he know about the offer, too?"

Amy busied herself picking up her purse, looking everywhere but at Jessica. "You'd need to ask Dianne about that. Look, I've gotta run. It's getting late and these mountain roads are not the best lit. It was so nice to meet you, Jessica. I hope we can get together again soon."

"Please give me a heads up on what your client says when you tell them about the, uh, unseen resident here. I'll be very curious to hear how they take the news."

"Definitely." Unexpectedly, Amy leaned in and gave her a brief hug. "Thank you so much for the message from Matt."

Jessica saw the realtor out to her car and returned to the new wing. She poured a glass of wine and spent some time contemplating the conversation. Something about Amy's reaction when Jessica had asked about Dianne Maggio and Darryl Andrews did not sit quite right. The more she thought about it, the stronger the feeling grew that she should not fully trust at least two of the three.

sixteen

JANUARY 17, 1988

Dear Diary,

I'm so incredibly stoked. The concert was mega dope. Ilya was in the audience—I saw him sitting with his father. I was playing for him, and I totally played my best ever. After it was over, everyone was really nice. My parents had flowers delivered and even Mr. E. said he was pleased with my performance, so I can believe I did well. And I can't believe this—he's entering me in the Malina Castellini International Piano Competition in Portland, Oregon! I qualify in the Youth Artist Competition. I hope it's fun. It would be so cool if I finally met some other girls my age that I can actually talk to who aren't complete dorks. Other pianists. OMG, I can't believe it!

January 25, 1988

Dear Diary,

Mom and dad are going with me to Portland and Grandma Sharpe is coming to stay with the brats. I know I shouldn't call them that. I love my little brothers. But they drive me batshit crazy! I have to keep my diary hidden so they don't get into it and read all my secrets.

Maestro says I'm gonna have to practice more and more so I can be ready in a few months. Beethoven is my most favorite composer. I can't wait to get working on the Appassionata. *That's what he wants me to play. My fingers are itching to get practicing. I wish it wasn't so late at night or I would be sitting at the piano.*

seventeen

Jessica opened a browser on her laptop. The one task she had set herself for today was to call the County Recorder's office and request the names of any previous owners of Herron Pond prior to Vadim Evanov.

Shit. She had allowed herself to become distracted and let the day end without doing it. Armed with that information, she could have researched any deaths that had taken place at the house—people who might not have left the earth plane but who wanted to continue hanging around the mansion for some reason—the entity in the foyer, for instance. But she had waited too long. And it was Friday. Now, it would have to wait until Monday.

Kicking herself for dallying, she spent a while searching various combinations of 'Elise and Ilya Evanov' and got nowhere. 'Elise plus piano' came up with more than six million results, all related to 'Beethoven's *Für Elise*.'

She keyed in "Ilya Evgeny Evanov," the name of the little boy in the cemetery, and "obituary, 1999, California."

A handful of links came up. The most relevant was an article published in a local newspaper. A grainy photograph revealed a fragile child who looked worn out, as though his little shoulders had borne too much. His mouth was open in a gap-toothed grin as if he had been instructed to smile, but his eyes looked empty. Jessica scanned the brief article in horrified disbelief.

The headline read:

"Mother Questioned in Monterey County Boy's Death."

Seven-year-old Ilya Evanov passed away at Community Hospital last Thursday. His mother, Rostya Evanov, was questioned by police after they learned that the boy had been seen in the emergency room there more than twenty times during the year and hospitalized twice.

Hospital records indicated that Mrs. Evanov claimed that her son was suffering from a variety of rare illnesses, none of which was confirmed. When interviewed, the child's pediatrician, Dr. David Malone, said he was un-aware of the mother's claims. Although the child was seriously underweight for his age group, an autopsy failed to reveal evidence of any major illness. Cause of death is pending.

A Russian immigrant and wife of music impresario Ilya Evanov, Mrs. Evanov was released to the custody of her husband, who was called home from a tour in Europe upon his son's death. The district attorney has not filed charges and it is unclear at this juncture whether any action will be taken.

Jessica got up and walked away from the table confused and appalled. She paced the kitchen and the breakfast room, the coffee and pastry roiling in her gut, making her want to puke. A woman named *Rostya*, not Elise, was little Ilya's mother. There was no photograph but she was as certain as she could be that Rostya was the black-haired beauty in her vision. Which meant that, as in the vision, somewhere, sometime, Elise had disappeared from Ilya's life and Rostya had taken her place.

Pacing burned off enough of the energy to let her sit down and reread the article, once again desperate to find out what had happened to Elise. And to Ilya. A quick search of their names turned up no further mention of either Rostya or Ilya Evanov. Presumably, if criminal charges had been filed, it would have been in the public record and the newspaper would have published a follow-up article. Had Evanov money been used to cover up any consequences—or to dodge them? It was a question Jessica could not help asking herself.

The photo of little Ilya on the screen ripped open a fresh hole in her heart. The article had implied that Rostya had been responsible for her son's reported illnesses. There was a name for that kind of parent. Jessica scoured her memory and came up with it: Munchausen's by Proxy. She had once seen a documentary dealing with this mental illness, where mothers either faked their child's illnesses, or made them ill in a bid for attention.

Keying in the search term produced a link to seven cases that had gained national attention, with the families receiving money and trips and other 'rewards' for the child's apparent illnesses. One victim had finally killed her abusive mother and gone to prison for it. Another mother was found guilty of second-degree murder when she poisoned her five-year-old son with a chemical delivered though a feeding tube.

Reading each of the highly publicized cases, a savage kind of anger boiled up in her, burning her face and leaving her throat dry. Jessica would have willingly given her own life to save her son's without a second thought. And yet, here was evidence of parents who had deliberately harmed their children to get attention for themselves. She wanted to punch something; throw something across the room.

Ilya Evgeny.

Painful personal experience had taught her that the media regularly bloated and misrepresented the truth. That made it impossible to know for sure. She wanted to push away the repulsive implication, unable to bear it. She had to find out whether what the newspaper article said was true. Her head throbbed with the question. And something else.

The child had two parents. Where did the grownup Ilya—the boy's father—figure in this scenario?

eighteen

October 2, 1988

Dear Diary,

I'm completely and totally devastated. Ilya's father caught us kissing. We were hiding in the little graveyard, but he found us. I think one of the gardeners must have seen us and reported to him. He probably told them to spy on us. He was beyond furious. He said he was going to stop teaching me and he threatened to send Ilya to live in Russia.

My dad would never yell and scream at me the way Mr. E. did—most of it was in Russian, so I don't have any idea what he was saying, which is a good thing because it couldn't be anything I would want to hear. Dad would be so pissed if he knew Mr. E treated me like that. Obviously I can't tell him though. If I did, Ilya would get in even more trouble because I'm supposedly too young to be in love with him. As if! I don't care. I'll always love him.

When Maestro yelled at me I couldn't stop crying. Ilya got all quiet like he does when he's upset about something. He doesn't yell back at his father or curse at him, he just kind of goes inside himself. I was so hurt that he didn't say anything or try to protect me, but I guess he couldn't. He wouldn't even look at me, probably because he knew it would make things worse. I know he's afraid of his father. I sure am. What if Mr. E. beats him up? Or worse, what if he really does send him away? I would have to kill myself.

I couldn't stand it if he was thousands of miles away in some foreign country. What would he do there? Of course he would never forget me. Omigod, what is going to happen to us? I won't be 18 for two and a half more years.

nineteen

HER PLATE SAT UNTOUCHED on the table. She had been too upset to eat. After a brief conversation with Sage—she could not bring herself to talk about little Ilya and what had happened to him—Jessica went around picking up her clothes and clearing away the food she had prepared.

Sleep was impossible. She stood in the hot shower and scrubbed her head as vigorously as if it, rather than what she had read in the article about the little boy, had offended her. As if scrubbing could get rid of the sense of moral outrage that persisted like the sting of a slap across the face.

The article she had read said that the boy's father had been in Europe at the time of his death. Did that excuse him? Should he have known what was going on at home in his absence? And what about little Ilya's grandfather, Vadim—the twins' benefactor? Had he not been present to see what his daughter-in-law was doing to her child? He was not mentioned, so it was possible that he had not been present either. If he had been here, would he have interfered; done something to stop it?

Jessica got out her phone and reread once more Claudia's analysis of Vadim Evanov's handwriting. Claudia had written that he was someone who would fiercely protect his family. Had he not loved his grandson? She had also written that he would do 'the dirty work,' and Jessica wondered afresh whether he had somehow greased the wheels to make the investigation into little Ilya's death go away. What had really happened here at Herron Pond?

"Unforgiveable," she hissed through clenched teeth. Unable to stop thinking about the child in the photograph, she pulled on PJs and socks and went to the den. Perhaps Rostya deserved the benefit of the doubt, she told herself as she burrowed under her blanket on the sofa. But there *was* no doubt in Jessica's mind. Even if the woman had not intended to kill her little boy, she had murdered him as surely as if she had driven a knife into his undernourished seven-year-old ribs. And if she had deliberately starved her child or otherwise made him sick, there was no reason good enough to excuse her actions. What she deserved was to burn in hell.

Except Jessica had learned from her mediumship that there was no such fiery place, only of one's own making. Wishing retribution on someone was not spiritual, but in her gut, Jessica wanted Rostya Evanov to suffer the way her child had.

A sudden draft penetrated the thick wool. A child's voice spoke in her head. *"Mama."*

"Justin!"

In an instant, Rostya Evanov and her evil deeds were forgotten. There was only room left for a swell of love and happiness. It had been months since her son in spirit had last come to her.

"I'm 'posed to show you, mama."

The words were not spoken; they were impressed upon her brain. She closed her eyes and began her process of breathing slowly and deeply, opening herself to Justin's vibration, mentally welcoming him into her aura. She could feel his energy move closer, meld with her as one spirit.

A series of images began to flitter across Jessica's closed eyelids: Justin and another child whom she recognized as Ilya Evanov. She recognized, too, the shore of Herron Pond behind this very house. The two boys played, laughing and digging with spades and buckets, filling them with sand. She wanted to run to them and gather them both in her arms.

"I'm so happy to see you, baby," she told her son through her mind.

Justin beamed. "I'm happy, too, mama. This is my friend. His name is Ilya."

The last time Justin had showed up with another child it was to ask Jessica to pass along a message to the boy's family. On that occasion he had appealed to her, asking her to assure his friend's parents that he was safe and happy growing up on the Other Side.

"Does Ilya have a message for me?" Jessica asked. Ilya's head popped up from the sandcastle he was building. Contradicting the newspaper photo, the deep sadness she had seen in him was erased. His little boy grin was radiant with robust health and vitality.

Ilya sent her a mental message: *"Papa says it's okay to look."*

"Papa? Your daddy, Ilya?"

"Yes, I am Ilya."

"I know you are, sweetheart. I meant, do you mean the grown-up Ilya, your father?"

"I am Ilya. Papa says you can look."

Does a seven-year-old understand the difference between junior and senior with the same name? Jessica reframed the question. "Ilya, is your daddy with you?"

The boy shook his head and spoke with unusual formality for such a young child. *"He is not with me."*

"Is 'Papa' your grandfather?"

"You can look," said Ilya. *"It's okay to look."*

Jessica was beginning to feel like Bud Abbott playing, *Who's on first?* She chewed on her lip, thinking how frustrating it all was. If she'd had some cold water, she would have splashed it on her face to rid herself of the negativity. It wasn't little Ilya's fault that the information 'Papa' wanted him to impart was not detailed enough for her to understand what he wanted.

Centering herself, she wondered whether Ilya had called Vadim 'Papa.' If his father had been absent a great deal, traveling, and his grandfather was on hand, it was plausible.

If his grandfather wanted her to look for something, what was it? And where? And if Vadim had a message for her, why not deliver it himself?

She knew the answer: that was the way Spirit worked. She might not like it, but there was seldom anything straightforward in the way the Other Side communicated. It was all too often an aggravating game of charades, where she was expected to puzzle out symbols the spirits transmitted and guess what they meant. Over the past months of her spiritual development, Jessica had been creating a mental 'dictionary' of symbols, which was far from complete and failed to include what Ilya was trying to tell her.

She tried again. "Ilya, do you know what it is that Papa wants me to look for?"

The boy looked behind him and cocked his head, listening to something Jessica could not hear. He dropped his bucket and spade in the sand. *"I have to go,"* he said with a cheery wave.

"Wait a minute, Ilya."

"Bye, mama," said Justin.

Both boys faded and disappeared like the early morning mist, leaving the shore deserted.

Jessica waved with a resigned smile, grateful to have had a moment with her boy, despite not being any closer to understanding the message. The scene had been so real that when she opened her eyes, she was startled to see the den and not the pond in front of her. Moving once again into the physical world and reorienting herself from the relatively short visit, she got up from her chair and shuffled to the kitchen for a glass of water, which seemed to help replenish her energy after these visits.

Now that she had witnessed little Ilya healthy and happy, she felt immeasurably better. Not that her antipathy towards his mother had diminished a speck. Ilya should be alive on earth, a healthy thirty-year-old adult, possibly heir to his grandfather's estate, rather than her and Jenna.

What the hell had happened in this house all those years ago? Why hadn't Vadim's son, Ilya Senior, inherited Herron Pond upon the death of his father?

Analyzing what Ilya had said to her: *Papa says it's okay to look,* Jessica was convinced he was talking about the cabinets under Vadim's desk. That seemed like the logical place to look for whatever it was she was supposed to find.

She was itching to explore, but it was late in the evening and his desk was on the Victorian side. She was not ready to risk running into any unpleasant entities alone in the dark of night.

Something else interesting had come from the visit from the two little boys. She had developed a strong feeling—or perhaps a *recognition*—of who the entity was that had peremptorily ordered her to leave the house.

twenty

Dear Diary,

Thank God. Ilya finally wrote to me, a real letter in the mail. He said he was taking a big risk and I should burn it. I'm not going to do that. I'll put it in a really safe place where my bratty little brothers will never find it.

He said he's basically under house arrest and has no freedom, but he promised to find a way to call me. He said if I stay chill everything will be okay, and that he's sorry he didn't keep me out of the way of his father's rage. I completely trust him. It feels so awful. I miss him so much. In eleven days he'll be nineteen. I don't understand why he can't just leave that house. If he goes away to school it will be hard, but at least I know he'll come back to me eventually. He keeps promising me we'll be together, but when???

When will he ever get out from under his father's thumb? What if the maestro really does make him go to Russia? I can't stand thinking about it.

He was super harsh at my piano lesson today. He made me so nervous that I kept making mistakes and that made him yell at me again. I was shaking so hard I could hardly hit the right notes. I'm learning Beethoven's Silence.

It makes me cry whenever I play it. It feels like it was written for a ghost story. Sometimes I feel like a ghost.

Maestro never said anything about Ilya, but he was in the house. I could feel *him.*

twenty-one

IMPATIENT TO JUMPSTART HER investigation in Vadim Evanov's desk, Jessica dressed in jeans and sweatshirt. She downed a slice of toast and coffee strong enough to walk on its own, and at the first sign of light sent a text to Amy Herron. Over a long, restless night, an idea had emerged and taken shape.

Overlooking the realtor's misgivings, she requested Amy to arrange a meeting with her friend's mother—the woman who had worked at Herron Pond and quit because she had been spooked by ghostly energies. If Amy had delivered the message from the woman's deceased son, it should have convinced her that Jessica was on the up-and-up. Assuming she was willing to accept the message at all. Not everyone was open to communication from the spirit world.

The response that pinged in her phone a short while later lifted her spirits. Amy was not promising that Carmela Durrell, her friend Rosie's mother, would meet with Jessica, but she had agreed, notably reluctant, to ask.

She was sending a fervent 'thank you' when a text arrived from Sage. The Tesla was chewing up the miles and he was north of San Simeon, passing the Inn at Ragged Point on his way to Herron Pond. Jessica's heart did a little happy dance, as it always did when she knew they would be together soon. He expected to be with her in under an hour.

Meanwhile, she had some investigating to do. If she was correct in her assumption that the 'consent to look message' little Ilya had delivered *was* from Vadim and that it referred to his study, which seemed the logical place to look for personal papers, she might as well get started.

At the entry to the Victorian wing, as she started to tap in the code, she hesitated. Her terrifying encounter with the angry entity flashed back, leaving her less sure of what she was about to do. Her hand hovered in front of the panel, a pulse beating in her throat. Maybe she should wait for Sage to go with her.

This is nuts.

She was a spiritual medium in training, not some scared little kid who needed to be saved by her boyfriend from a whispering ghost. As long as she called on her guides and angels for strength, she would be safe.

Jessica lifted her hand and tapped in the code.

***

With the morning sun pouring through the two-story stained-glass wall in the foyer, no visitor would have believed that a ghostly presence had ever occupied such a brilliant, peaceful space. If it had not been for what she had experienced in the recital room, Jessica herself might have laughed off the entity. But that experience had been too real, too personal. Today, she was prepared for it.

Hoping the entity would show up, she paced the wide hallway. As she paced, Jenna sent her a text, asking how everything was going. She wanted to let Jessica know that she had made an appointment with a piano tuner. She was researching teachers, too. Jessica smirked. Her twin antenna told her that the message was prompted by a twinge of conscience for 'abandoning' her at Herron Pond.

As she put the phone back in her pocket. Suddenly, the energy shifted. The light in the foyer dimmed. Jessica's skin began to tingle and the fine hairs on her arms stood on end as if an electrical charge had passed over them. The entity she had been waiting for had arrived.

"Good morning, Rostya," she said aloud without hesitating. "I know it's you."

A rush of hostility hit her like a closed fist. Jessica moved to the foot of the staircase, listening to what felt like a held breath. The most powerful energy seemed to be emanating from the area near the stained-glass window.

"There's help for you on the other side, Rostya," she said. "The Light is waiting for you if you'll just go there."

Jessica's glance swept every part of the entry hall. She knew what she had said was right, but the strain of holding in her animosity towards little Ilya's mother hurt her throat.

Herron Pond had been the home of Rostya's father-in-law, where she had lived with his son and their child. Vadim Evanov had been a widower. It was likely that Rostya had taken the role of the lady of the house, running the household. Making her son sick. Taking him to the hospital countless times with made-up diseases. Putting him in harm's—

Jessica gave her head a sharp shake, cutting off the negative thoughts. Those sentiments were not going to persuade Rostya to listen to what she needed to hear. Regardless of her personal feelings about the child, Jessica had to acknowledge that leaving this home must have been difficult, even after death.

She gave it another try. "Let me help you, Rostya. You don't have to—"

"You do not belong here."

It came as a low hiss close to Jessica's ear, frosty enough to form icicles. She jerked away, resisting the urge to rub warmth back into her flesh.

"So you say. Yet, your father-in-law wanted me here, so I guess I do belong."

The words came louder. *"This is not your house."*

A misty cloud formed on Jessica's exhalation. "Whatever happened here, Rostya, you don't have to stay. Ilya's not here anymore—neither of them."

Why am I baiting the spirit of a woman who killed her child? Angry that she knew the truth was in the question—that she was taunting herself, too—Jessica had not expected to feel this level of responsibility for a boy who was not her child. It didn't require a Freudian scholar to understand what was going on. She had failed her own child. If she was honest with herself, she would admit that despite the fact that little Ilya was long past needing her help, Justin was why she refused to fail him now.

"All you have to do ask Spirit for help. You *will* get it," Jessica said, praying the entity would listen.

But the very atmosphere seemed to pulsate. It radiated in waves from the top of the staircase all the way to the bottom where Jessica stood. It pumped into her head, filling it like a bag of cotton balls, injecting bitter poison into her sinuses, swelling against her cheekbones until it felt as though they wanted to burst right through her skin.

"You can't get rid of me, Rostya," she gasped. "I have the protection of the Light."

"Go! Leave! Get out!"

Hatred churned from the entity like a pot boiling on the stove, ready to belch its contents onto anyone unlucky enough to be close by. All at once, a torrent of angry Russian spewed at her. It ended on a phrase in English, leaving Jessica perplexed.

"—the filth he played with."

The phrase drummed in her head, repeating again and again. Rostya must have wanted Jessica to understand. *What is she talking about?* An image blazed across her mind. The blonde girl and her lover from the vision. They had been so happy together until outside forces had torn them apart. With a suddenness that kicked her in the teeth, Jessica understood.

What was a woman capable of doing to a rival when she was willing to deliberately harm her child?

"What did you do to Elise?" Jessica shouted, shocked by the harshness of her own voice. Her body vibrated with anger and she realized that she wanted to do violence to the unseen entity. "Rostya! *What did you do?*"

Above her, the chandelier began to sway. It swung to and fro, its tiny crystals crashing against each other, threatening to explode and rain a million lethal shards down on her.

Jessica's muscles no longer responded to the commands she sent them. The arc of quivering lights swung wider. Gathering all her strength she scooted as far away from the lights as she could. Movement drew her eyes to the stained-glass. High up, past the second-floor landing, a wispy fog appeared. Jessica stared, transfixed, as the life-size figure of a woman materialized like a photograph developing in a darkroom—the woman in the vision who had replaced Elise.

The figure, floating in mid-air, appearing as solid as a mortal being. Malice glowed in ice-blue eyes. Her hair, as black as a raven's wing, whipped about her as if she were in the midst of a gale. A ghastly wail came from the blood-red lips, a shriek as powerful as a banshee, piercing the marrow. Jessica clapped her hands over her ears, but the sound would not be blocked. The entity began to float down the staircase, feeding off the dark forces building and swelling around her.

Jessica opened her mouth to call on her spirit guides and angels. A gentle voice inside her head spoke.

The light must always win.

A second spirit had materialized behind Rostya; one Jessica recognized as an older version of Elise, the girl in the high school photo. Elise, the sweet, heart-shaped face of the blonde girl who had disappeared from the love story of her vision, now, much, much stronger.

Extending both arms, fingers splayed outward, Elise propelled a bolt of energy that arrested Rostya's movement as abruptly as if she had run into a glass shield. Eyes widening in surprise, Rostya twirled to face her adversary.

The two spirits faced each other as Jessica watched the scene play out, locked in a silent war of energy and will. Like a pair of cymbals clashing, waves of energy rebounded through the foyer, hitting her with a force powerful enough to take her breath away. Abruptly, the shrieking stopped and a stillness descended so complete that it hurt.

The force that had held her paralyzed evaporated like manacles suddenly unlocked. Her body freed, her legs gave way and she slid down the wall to the floor.

Minutes, or it may have been just seconds, later—a sound came like the roar of a freight train. And out of the roar a swirl of grey-black smoke manifested. It spiraled and whirled, a vortex that spun around Rostya until she could no longer be seen. A thunderclap split the air and the smoke was gone, taking the entity with it. Whether by her own design or some stronger force, she was gone. At least, for now.

The temperature, which had dropped to an arctic freeze, returned to normal. Jessica sucked in a big gulp of air. She had not been aware that she had stopped breathing.

Elise, smiling gently at her, glided up the staircase, pausing at the junction that made the turn to the second-floor landing. There, she waited, looking back directly at Jessica, sending a message.

She wants me to follow her.

Shaken, but no longer afraid, Jessica scrambled to her feet and ran up the stairs after her. She knew where Elise was taking her. For the second time she followed the spirit, arriving at the door at the end of the hallway in time to see her dissolve in a greyish puff.

This was the door Dianne Maggio had warned her not to open. The door that was locked, top and bottom. As she stood there wondering again how she was supposed to get inside, Jessica heard a soft click. And another. The padlocks at the top and bottom of the door dropped open.

twenty-two

MAY 5, 1989

Dear Diary,

This is the one place where I can tell the whole entire truth. I am so scared and I don't know what to do. I'm almost sure I'm pregnant. We've been sneaking out and meeting at his friend's apartment on the weekends. We were always careful except for that one time. We hadn't seen each other in so long. I've been so happy being with him but I just don't know what to do. I can't tell my parents. They'll be so disappointed in me. And what is going to happen my career?

I haven't said anything to Ilya, but I can see in the way he looks at me that he knows something is up. What's going to happen to us? I won't be 18 until July. I don't think I can keep it secret that long.

twenty-three

Not bothering to shield herself from what she was certain was a product of Dianne's creative imaginings—a precarious mountain of furniture or sports equipment waiting to topple and injure her—Jessica cautiously pushed the door open a few inches. Cobwebs festooned the jamb, their dusty strings drifting to the floor. The spiders who had woven them had abandoned the web long ago, moving on to other homes, or dying.

Using her foot to open the door the rest of the way, she saw nothing that at first glance appeared to require padlocks. The cobwebs, and the dust motes dancing in the air, disturbed by her entrance, told her that she was the first to see this room in a very long time. Certainly, no staff had been in here to clean. Or to store attic-bound junk.

Raindrops pattered on grime-caked windows and the lowering clouds cast it in somber shadows, but in contrast to what had just happened downstairs in the foyer, there was nothing dangerous or frightening to see.

Dianne had lied when she claimed this room was used for storage. But lied for what purpose? The downstairs salon was dignified and elegant with its impressive grand piano. This was a room where a student might spend hours practicing on the old upright that stood against the rear wall, an empty music stand nearby, and an armchair whose seat cushion bore a shiny indent.

She let her imagination run wild, picturing Evanov the teacher sitting in the armchair, patiently, or more likely *im*patiently, listening to his students and instructing them. "You need to practice your trills," he might say kindly. Or, perhaps issuing a stern warning. "How much time did you spend on this piece in the last week? You have made absolutely no progress. If you expect me to continue teaching you, you must do better."

She could easily picture him intimidating a young student into submission. A heavy Russian accent would be a bonus. With a name like his, he would have one, wouldn't he?

Like a czar, Claudia had said. It seemed to fit.

Jessica dusted off the piano bench with her hand and wiped her hand on her jeans. An old metronome stood on top of the piano. Unlatching the cover, she set the pendulum rod at a slow tempo and sat down. With her eyes following the steady back and forth of the tick-tick-tick of the pendulum, she placed her hands over the keys and waited to move into a trance state.

It did not take long for pesky thoughts to intrude. *Why couldn't we play on the more impressive grand piano in the salon? Is it because of what happened with Rostya?*

For some reason of her own, Elise had led Jessica up here. If she did not want to play the piano, what were they here for?

Jessica, irked by her inability to concentrate, shoved away the noise in her mind and refocused her attention, poised for the spirit to take control of her body and play her favorite pieces.

Ten minutes later, when she was as fully present as when she started, she stopped the metronome with a sigh and gave up on the idea of going into trance. She swung her gaze around the room again, seeing nothing special or noteworthy in the Victorian-era rug, woven in a pattern of red roses, or the pink brocade wallcoverings. Rising from the bench, she went to a tall bookcase in the corner and browsed the books of music. Collections by Chopin, Beethoven, Shubert, Haydn, Debussy, Rachmaninoff, Tchaikovsky. Books of finger exercises by Hanon and Czerny.

"Why did you bring me here, Elise?" Jessica asked aloud.

The response came in a ripple of energy that ran through the atmosphere. Suddenly, it was as though she was looking through an eddy of swirling water.

Without warning, she is thrown into another time. She is in this room, and she is in the mind of Elise.

She is seated at the practice piano playing Beethoven's Silence *when the door opens behind her. Spinning around on the piano bench, her gasp of fright changes to one of pleasure. It's her darling Ilya who is entering the room. As he takes her into his arms and holds her, she is fully aware that he can feel her desperation and her love.*

"What's wrong?" he asks.

Why does he bother asking, when he knows the answer? She says it anyway. "She's at it again. She's trying to kill me. We have to get away from here."

"My sweetest love, how can she do anything to you?"

"I don't know *how she can, but I'm telling you, she's pure evil. She hates me and she won't stop until she's destroyed me."*

Ilya gives her a look of concern, but he doesn't ask for details, just strokes her hair to reassure her. "We'll leave the minute he's well enough to be on his own."

"Why do we have to stay? He's well enough now. He's got people to take care of him."

"It was a serious surgery. He nearly died. I can't go while he's bedridden. Whether he likes it or not, I'm all he's got left."

"And you're all I've got left. I hate it here. I hate him for what he did; what she did. It's all his fault. How can you stand to be here?" Elise presses her face into the soft cashmere of his sweater and Ilya lays his cheek against the top of her head, murmuring to her as if she is a child.

"I know, I know." His shoulders sag. "Believe me, baby, nobody could be sorrier than I am that we're here."

Elise jerks away from him, heartsick that she had forgotten for even an instant the loss he suffered at the hands of his first wife. "Oh, God, Ilya, I'm such a jerk. I'm sorry. Can you forgive me?"

"There's nothing to forgive, my sweet Elise. You have every right to feel the way you do. The minute he can be left alone I'll take you away from here." Ilya hesitates. "Or, you can leave right now, today. I'll follow as soon as I can."

Her eyes blaze. "There's no way I'm leaving you here alone. Knowing him, he would find a way to keep you forever."

Ilya considers her with a serious gaze. He nods. "You're absolutely right, and I don't want you to be anywhere that you have to be afraid, even for a minute. He should be well enough in a few days. Why don't you make reservations for next Monday. We'll fly home then."

A long sigh of relief escapes her and for the first time, Elise smiles, her pretty face lighting up with the love she feels for him; has felt from the moment they met.

Once again, there came the ripple. Troubled by what she had just witnessed, Jessica struggled to reestablish herself in the present. What was she was meant to do with the information?

Elise and Ilya had aged quite a bit since the first vision where they had been teenagers. This time, she guessed, she had seen them in their forties.

It struck her that while in trance she had moved to the teacher's chair. Beside her, the piano bench began to vibrate. As if a giant hand had picked it up and was shaking it like a salt cellar, it jumped up and down, moving faster and faster. Jessica watched in disbelief. She had heard of table-tipping at *seances*, but this was no *seance*.

As abruptly as it had started, the bench stopped moving. The lid popped up.

Was she supposed to find something in the storage compartment? She began to sift through the untidy array of sheet music. Handwritten scribbles appeared between the lines and in the margins—notations of chords; of when to slow down a passage or speed it up.

She was no handwriting expert like Claudia, but she believed she recognized this as a more mature version of the handwriting on Elise's high school photo that she had found in the turret room. Okay, fine. But there had to be a better reason than this for Elise to animate the piano bench.

Jessica gathered the sheets into a pile and started to pick it up. She could feel something thicker and heavier than sheet music underneath the papers.

At the bottom of the pile was a well-worn leather diary. Jessica set the stack of music on the floor and removed the booklight blue. Its corners were embossed in a flowery vintage design, the cover secured by a wide leather strap with a combination lock.

She was lifting the diary into her hands when a text came from Sage. He was at the gates of Herron Pond.

By the time Sage had driven to the front of the mansion Jessica was waiting at the bottom of the steps, her heart bumping like a teenager on a first date. The quiver of pure joy that came with seeing him climb out of his SUV and stretch his long legs made her forget about the wintry weather.

"You're here," she said, giddy with happiness.

Her feelings were reflected in his face. He picked her up and swung her around as though she weighed nothing. "I couldn't wait another minute to see you."

"I'm so glad you're here."

Sage was close to a foot taller than the diminutive Jessica. Although he was, like her, an artist, he had an athletic build. Mixed-race heritage had favored him with a golden complexion, full lips, and curly black hair that he kept cropped close to his head. He had not taken the time to shave and dark stubble powdered his chin. Add startling the sapphire-blue eyes and he was, in short, the hottest guy she had ever met. But it was not his sexiness that most attracted her. They were soulmates, pure and simple. And here he was, at Herron Pond, ready to share her excitement.

A few months ago, when she was still drifting through life believing that she was destined to be alone, Jessica's friend, Claudia Rose, had introduced them. Claudia had sent Sage to pick up a sculpture she had commissioned from Jessica. A shock of recognition had passed between them that penetrated to the depths of Jessica's soul, and Sage's, too. That moment had brought them together in a way neither had dreamed possible.

Tasting the sweet familiarity of his lips, she closed her eyes and let his kiss consume her, melting into him with a murmur of contentment. Finally, when they let go, he gaped at the house with the same kind of astonishment Jessica had felt—continued to feel.

"This is incredible." He shook his head as if he could not believe what he was seeing. "It's friggin' amazing—even bigger than my aunt's house. Those photos don't begin to do it justice. The size of it—and it's absolutely gorgeous."

"I'm glad we agree," Jessica said, laughing at his enthusiasm. "It's freezing out here. Come inside and I'll give you the tour."

She had left the house without stopping to put on a jacket. Sage took off his coat and draped it across her shoulders. He grabbed his overnight bag and followed her up the steps to the front door. Jessica half-expected it to slam in their faces the way it had on her first day at Herron Pond, but the door behaved as any door should and they entered without any ghostly interference.

There had been no time to tell Sage about the latest events. She brought him up to date.

The space between his brows creased into a worried frown. "Are you serious? You forced a confrontation with an entity that you knew was spiteful and nasty?"

"Well, yeah, I guess I did," she said sheepishly. "But I never meant for it to get *that* heavy. And who knew that Elise would show up and save the day? Yay for that."

"What the hell were you thinking, angel?"

Jessica shrugged. "I was thinking that I could encourage Rostya to leave here and finish her journey on the other side. Her attachment to the house is unhealthy for all of us. Unfortunately, she wasn't in the mood to hear it."

"Thank goodness for Elise's intervention. God only knows what she might have done otherwise."

"It was pretty scary and unpleasant, but I don't think she would be able to actually harm me." Even as she said it, she heard the doubt creep in. "And this is where it all happened."

Sage set down his bag and gazed around the foyer, taking in the main focal points—the grand staircase and the stained-glass wall. "The 'battle of the spirits?'"

She nodded. "I don't know what happened to Rostya, but I get the feeling that she probably isn't going to show up anytime soon. I hope not anyway. The air feels clear now. No scary spirits."

"Fine with me." Sage's grin had a devilish glint. "These spirit ladies sound too powerful for me to want to mess with."

"I admit, I preferred it when we were playing the piano."

"Elise likes having you channel her music."

Reminded of the elation she had experienced, being the vessel that carried the music, Jessica had to admit, "I don't have a scintilla of the talent she did. I can barely play a scale on my own."

"I hope she'll let me hear her play," Sage said. "Do you think she'll show up while I'm here?"

"Maybe." Jessica grinned. "Not many guys are as tolerant as you. How many of your friends could hold a conversation like this without getting spooked?"

"I find it fascinating. When are you going to show me where you played like you were at Carnegie Hall?"

"Later. Right now, I just want to look at you and make sure you're really here." She showed him through the dining room and to the sliding door panel.

"This is so cool," Sage said, as excited as a kid. "I feel like I'm in a museum. Or a palace."

"Yeah, the Victorian side has that effect. It's a lot more formal than the other wing. We can stay in one of the guest rooms over there. Let's put your bag in one of them, then I'll show you everything."

"I'll hold you to that," he said, his eyes twinkling.

Collecting a bottle of wine and glasses from the kitchen, they chose the upstairs room where they would stay. Jessica made a pile of the luxurious down bed pillows and poured wine while Sage lit a fire in the fireplace, which had been set and readied by the hands of an invisible work force.

Since his arrival, the skies had opened again and a steady downpour pounded at the windows. Great peals of thunder crashed in the distance. Lightning strikes burnished the sky. Jessica crawled across the duvet and arranged herself against the pillows. "It couldn't get any cozier, could it?"

"Omar Khayyam got it right," Sage agreed. "But the 'jug of wine and thou' are all I need. The loaf of bread and spreading chestnut bough can wait."

"You're making me hungry. We should have brought some cheese and crackers."

The sapphire eyes flashed wolfishly. "All I'm hungry for, angel, is you."

***

They spent the afternoon getting reacquainted, leaving the bed in sensual disarray. After Jessica's two nights on the sofa, it was a wonderful luxury. They fell asleep in each other's arms and woke in the afternoon, content. The rain had ceased. A rainbow shone through the bedroom window like a good omen.

Sage rolled over with a big yawn. Jessica stretched and sat up in bed. Elise's diary had been on her mind and in her dreams. She took it from the nightstand where she had left it. "Since she didn't tell me the combination, we need to find some other way to open the book. I have to find out what she wanted me to see."

Sage reached for her. "Ah, I knew your mind wasn't totally on what we were doing," he said, and ran his slender fingertips all the way down her bare back, making her shiver with pleasure.

"Not so," she protested. "You had my full attention. It was later that my mind started wandering a teeny bit. When you were snoring." She leaped out of bed, laughing as he stretched his long body to try to hold her there. "Come on, let's find some scissors."

It didn't take much rummaging in the kitchen to locate a pair of scissors. Jessica handed them to Sage along with the journal. "Be careful, they're as sharp as a scalpel."

"You want me to do the honors? Elise showed it to you."

"I don't want to be the one. I think she'd be okay with you doing it."

"Anything for you, angel." His smile made her sweat, but this was no time to be distracted.

The strap quickly yielded to the blade, rendering the combination lock moot. "All yours." Sage handed the diary to her with all the solemnity of a ceremonial rite.

She held it close to her chest, making no move to open the cover.

"I thought you were so hot to read it."

"I am, but..." Jessica spoke haltingly, gathering the courage to verbalize her hesitance so that it might make sense to someone else. "When I lost my memory...on the day Claudia and Joel came over and told me they knew who I was, it was like a door had cracked open to my past. I was afraid to open it all the way. I was afraid of what I would find if I remembered what was there."

"I get it," he said, and she knew that he did. "When you remembered, was it better than being in the dark, or worse?"

"Eventually it was better, though it didn't stop being excruciating. It took a while to assimilate it all, and maybe I'm still processing it." She felt the pain she could never forget wanting to force its way through. She pushed it back down and faced the facts. "It's true, I am a little worried about what's in the diary but it's pretty clear I need to do this."

"Because Elise wants you to read it."

"Yeah. It's just, something tells me I'm not going to like what I read. In that dream, or vision, that I had about her and Ilya being in love as teenagers—they're happy together, then poof! Suddenly, she's gone from the picture. Something happened to Elise, Sage, and I have a strong feeling it was something really bad."

"Something that happened here, at Herron Pond, you mean?"

"Maybe. Probably. This morning, in the vision she showed me in the practice room, she and Ilya were there, in that room. I don't know why the journal was in the piano bench, but what I do know is she was afraid in this house. More than that—she was terrified."

"She wouldn't have led you there if she didn't want to let you in on what really happened," Sage said. "You need to read what she wrote. C'mon, Jess, she gave it you. It has to be you."

She knew he was right, but she wasn't quite ready to let go of her romantic hopes for the young couple. She cradled the book against her, steeling herself to open the cover. At last, she did.

Inside, written in a girlish hand was the name 'Elise Sharpe.'

"A last name," Sage exclaimed, "That should make it easier to track her down."

Jessica flipped through the pages. "She dated every entry. It starts in January of 1985." On some pages Elise had written no more than a line or two. On others, entire pages were filled with the details of a pre-teen's daily thoughts about school and homework, her younger siblings, and most of all, her love for the piano.

After perusing the first quarter of the book, she looked at Sage in puzzlement. "This is what she wanted me to read? It's all so childish."

Sage shook a finger at her in mock admonition. "Keep going, oh impatient one. We've only just begun."

"It's so irritating that you're always right." Giving him a little push for emphasis she resumed reading. "Hey, look at this entry in September of 1985. She was twelve when she started taking piano lessons with the maestro, Vadim Evanov. That's interesting. She'd been playing since she was a small child, but she was excited and nervous about it. She stopped making daily entries after that. When she does, it's mostly about the piano pieces she was studying and what 'Mr. E' had to say about her progress." Jessica skimmed through pages. "Here, she skipped to December." Her eyes met Sage's, "Oh, look! This is where she met Ilya." She read a passage aloud:

He has amazing super long eyelashes and gorgeous blue eyes and black hair...

"Ilya sounds a lot like you," Jessica said, calling up the memory of the young man from her vision. He and Sage might share similar coloring, but that was where the similarity ended. Ilya's face had the Slavic angled planes of his father's. Sage had an oval face and sensitive features. "I wonder why there are no photos of him in the house," she said, amending it to, "None that I've seen."

"I was a month old in December, 1985."

"Elise thought Ilya was about sixteen, but she could tell he liked her. Aw, Sage, they were so young and in love." Jessica pictured the couple as they must have been in those days. Elise on the brink of adolescence, dreaming of a musical career, falling in love with her piano teacher's son. And Ilya, that pensive broodiness transformed when he looked at her.

"They were older in my vision, driving all over hell and creation in his Mustang. I'd guess she was maybe sixteen or seventeen. That would put Ilya in his early twenties."

"They cared for each other for a long time."

"She writes a lot about her love for him. She was so young, but she sounds mature for her age." Jessica continued reading. "I'm up to 1988. She starts calling him her soulmate. He'd turned eighteen and they had to keep their love a secret because she was underage."

"Was she still taking piano lessons from his father?"

"That's the other thing she talks about constantly—the recitals and concerts she had to practice for, and 'Mr. E's' criticisms. According to Elise, he was a tough taskmaster."

"That's how world-class students are made."

"That's what her mother said." Jessica tapped the book. "It must have worked. She got into an international piano competition."

"How did she do?"

"I haven't got that far. You should hear her play, Sage. She's *superb*, even when she's playing through me. I don't know much about the piano, but even I can tell she had enormous talent."

Sage took one of her hands in his. "These magic fingers can play all kinds of instruments."

Jessica laughed and pulled her hand away. "Don't try to distract me." She read on to the last quarter of 1988. At the October 2nd entry, she paused in dismay. "Oh, no."

Sage moved behind her chair and leaned over her shoulder. "What happened?"

"They got caught. Mr. Evanov caught them making out in the little graveyard behind the house. Elise thought he had one of the workers spying on them. He threatened to send Ilya away to Russia. I wonder if that's what happened." Jessica frowned. "Why was he so against the two of them being together? Because she was his pupil? She was a few years younger than him, but—"

"Think about it, angel. We know from your vision—and from her telling you to get out of the house—that he ended up with Rostya, had a child with her."

"Who died," Jessica said bitterly. "Probably at her hands."

Sage went to the fridge and got out two beers, continuing to mull it over aloud. "It sounds to me like the maestro had other plans for his son than to marry his star pupil." He handed Jessica a bottle.

"What other plans? You mean an arranged marriage? In the *1980s?* You can't be serious?"

"He lived in a Victorian house. From the way you described him, plus he wasn't from here, maybe he *was* that old-fashioned. You just read in the diary that he threatened to send Ilya to Russia. Believe it or not, in some European cultures, arranged marriages were a thing into the twentieth century. We can't count it out."

"Poor Elise," Jessica said, dismayed on behalf of the girl she was coming to know. She read further. "She finally heard from him," she said, glancing up. "He wrote her an actual letter."

Sage chuckled. "No text messages or email in those days."

"He was trying to reassure her, but she was scared of his father."

He stroked her cheek, cupping it in his hand. "Can you imagine having to sneak around the way they must have?"

She put her hand over his, holding it there. It was these moments with Sage that were the most precious to her; when they connected in a way that went far beyond words or sex. Sometimes when she looked at him, she wanted to sob with thanks that he had come into her life. An image came to her of Elise and Ilya, caught by his father in the graveyard. "It must have been awful."

Over the next year and a half Elise had filled her diary with entries about her music, about the secret rendezvous that had continued with Ilya, and about her mounting fear of his father's wrath. And then, confirmation that Sage had guessed correctly about Vadim Evanov's intentions for his son.

"Omigod, Sage, you called it. Evanov had plans to marry him off to the daughter of a Russian oligarch. He told him the two families had been allied for generations and that it would settle his future. What's an oligarch?"

"Basically, a very wealthy businessman. Possibly someone high up in politics."

"What did he think? He was going to start a dynasty?"

"An oligarch's daughter," Sage mused. "That had to be Rostya."

"How could he force his son into a marriage he didn't want?"

Jessica's look of outrage put an amused grin on Sage's face, which he quickly wiped away. "I'm sorry, angel, I know it's not funny. It's just, you're the size of a mouse—an adorable mouse—and when you get upset, you puff up so fierce, you could scare a lion."

"Yeah, yeah, I get it. I've had a lot of practice finding ways to make up for being the size I am. But what about Ilya? It doesn't sound as if he fought for Elise."

"Think about how young they were. His father was a controlling bastard—isn't that what Claudia was saying in her handwriting analysis? After growing up under that iron thumb, it wouldn't be easy for him to break away. I doubt Ilya would have the resources to leave home and take Elise with him. Plus, she was just beginning her career as a concert pianist and after all those years of slaving at it, she might not have wanted to give that up. That's my guess."

Jessica was adamant. "There's no way she would give up Ilya, even for her music. I just know she wouldn't." As Sage was sharing his theory, Jessica had continued to riffle through the pages. Coming to an entry in May, 1989, what she read made her stomach drop. "Oh no, no, no."

"What happened?"

She handed the journal for Sage to read from the entry she indicated.

'I'm almost sure I'm pregnant.'

"Oh, shit. Pregnant. What the hell happened after that?"

"She didn't write anything after that, dammit. How could she stop like that, right there? I need to know what happened!" Jessica felt as though she had read a novel three-quarters through, only to find the last quarter of the pages ripped out. "What the hell? First, I thought Elise was little Ilya's mother, then it was Rostya—that's what the newspaper article said. I guess it would have said so if she was his stepmother. I mean, if Elise gave birth to little Ilya and then she died and then Ilya married Rostya. But that doesn't work with the whole 'oligarch's daughter' scenario. I am so frigging confused."

Sage got up from the table, where they had sat reading the journal, and went to the computer bag he had brought in from his truck. "I think it's time we Googled Ms. Elise Sharpe."

twenty-four

SAGE INPUT ELISE'S FIRST and last name and 'pianist,' which produced references in musical publications of the late 1980s and early 1990. Jessica read out the first headline:

Teen piano prodigy Elise Sharpe stuns audience with her powerful rendition of Chopin's Ballade *in G minor.*

"The *Ballade* is one of my favorite pieces," she said.

Sage registered mild surprise. "I didn't know you were into classical music."

"I listen to it while I'm working."

At that point, Sage insisted on going to YouTube to hear the *Ballade* for himself. They spent the next ten minutes listening to Yuja Wang's interpretation of the Chopin composition. When the video ended, he said, "I can see why you love it. That middle part made my heart hurt. Damn, I nearly cried."

"I truly love that you're a romantic," Jessica said. "But can we please see what the article says?"

"Your wish is my command, and so on." He clicked to the article and they read it together. Elise was mentioned in the first paragraph.

At the tender age of 15, Ms. Sharpe is the youngest pianist to win the 1988 International Piano Competition held in Paso Robles, California. The competition sets the highest artistic standards and offers a platform for pianists between 12–25 years old around the world. In addition to cash prizes, winners receive support in starting their careers on the concert stage.

"I told you she was good," Jessica said with a swell of pride that she might have felt if Elise was her best friend.

"To win that kind of competition, you would have to be more than good." Sage went to the next article, dated the next year. "Look, she did it again, even bigger."

After winning the prestigious 1989 Malina Castellini International Piano Competition in Portland, Oregon, teen prodigy Elise Sharpe will perform concerts throughout Europe this summer. Her program will include compositions by Beethoven, Liszt, and Rachmaninoff. Ms. Sharpe prevailed against 60 competitors from 15 countries. Her teacher, the renowned Vadim Evanov, is reported to be fielding offers from a number of classical record companies vying to produce her first album.

"Okay, that's weird. When I googled Vadim Evanov, I didn't find anything. What's up with that?"

"Could be that because it's an article about Elise, and when you searched on him his name was further down in the results. How many pages did you go through?"

"Just the first one," Jessica admitted. "It's so cool that they wanted to do a recording with her," She was thrilled beyond anything that made sense on behalf of the young Elise. She leaned over Sage's shoulder to click to the final link that mentioned Elise Sharpe. The brief citation appeared in a music publication dated June 6, 1990:

The promising young pianist, Elise Sharpe, left for an extended tour of Europe, where she will celebrate her eighteenth birthday, July 15th.

"That's all. There's nothing else about her. What happened to her? It says she went to Europe. Was she pregnant when she left? It was in May that she wrote about it, so she must have been a couple of months along, if not further. By July she would start showing a baby bump." She sighed, disappointed. "Could be it was a false alarm and she wasn't pregnant after all. I mean, this article says she left the US, so—"

"Maybe she terminated the pregnancy."

Sage keyed in, *'What happened to Elise Sharpe?'* Scanning the results, he slowly shook his head, disappointed. "There's an obituary for an 88-year-old woman with the same name. That's much too old to be 'our' Elise." He added the phrase, 'concert pianist' to the search terms. Shook his head again. "Nope. Nothing. Nada."

"In the vision she showed me today, Ilya was talking about them flying home. I wonder where home was. Elise could have stayed in Europe and had the baby. It could have been adopted. That might make sense if she wanted to take up her career again. And if she did, we would find *something* about her online. Except if it was in another language, it wouldn't come up on our search." Knowing how their story turned out wouldn't explain why Jessica was now at Herron Pond, but she had become deeply invested in it. Not knowing the ending was a bitter pill. "She and Ilya must have eventually married. They were probably around our age in the vision, so that's long, long after the diary entries."

"It would be interesting to know whether her mother went with her to Europe," Sage said. "Too bad they didn't have social media in those days. It's so much easier to dig things up now."

"You're as into this as I am," Jessica said, reading his intent expression as he tapped on the keyboard. "I wonder whether she ever made any recordings. Is there a discography for her?"

Sage tried varying his search terms, finally shaking his head. "It's a fascinating mystery. She had such a promising start to a career. Why would she give it up and disappear like that?"

"She could have given up her career to raise her child."

"That begs the question of where Ilya was in all this."

"Doing what his father wanted and marrying the oligarch's daughter?"

"Even though Elise was pregnant with his child?" Sage's lip curled in disgust. "That would make him a real rat bastard."

"Yeah, it would." For a queasy moment, Jessica relived the morning sickness she had experienced daily during her pregnancy with Justin. Was Elise sending her the feeling, trying to tell her something?

Sage was looking at her with questioning eyes. "Are you okay, angel?"

"I can't stop thinking about her having that baby. We know she didn't die in childbirth because she came back here with Ilya to Herron Pond years later."

"She was eighteen when she was pregnant," Sage said thoughtfully. "How old does she look in spirit? Would that be the age she crossed over?"

"It's a good thought, but not necessarily. Spirits usually show themselves at the age they want you to remember them, which could be older or younger. You have to be able to either recognize them, or, for me as a medium, describe them to someone else so they can identify who it is. In Elise's high school photo, she was around the same age as in my dream—mid-teens. The spirit who went up against Rostya was recognizably Elise, but older. I'd say close to my age now—early to mid-thirties."

The spirit image of Elise reconstructed itself in her head. "Her clothes could have been from anytime this century. I didn't think about it at the time—I was a mite distracted by the 'battle of the spirits.'"

"What's funny?"

"I just remembered what she was wearing. Denims and white sneakers with an off-the shoulder top—it was red, a sort of Chinese print, with a handkerchief hem—cut on a slant."

"What about Rostya?"

"Some kind of black robe, which is fitting."

"Fashionable ghosts?" Sage shrugged. "Well, why not? I guess she didn't cross over while performing a concert or she would have been wearing a formal gown, wouldn't she?"

"In the 90s? Yeah, probably a gown. These days concert pianists tend to be hipper. And hot. Maksim Mrvica, for example." Jessica took over the laptop and brought up Google Images to show the sexy Croatian pianist in leather pants and vest at the piano.

"Should I be jealous?"

Jessica laughed and tapped a few more keys. "Let's make it even. Here's Yuja Wang dressing sexy for her concerts, too. And Ladyva. She's a Swiss pianist who plays boogie woogie in miniskirts. My point being, Elise wouldn't have been so 'out there' when she was performing at her young age. She's a totally different type of person than they are."

Sage glanced up from the screen. "How do you know what her type was, angel?"

Jessica's brow wrinkled. Coming up with a good response wasn't as easy as she wished it was. She shrugged. "Dunno. Maybe after blending with her energy? Anyway. She was dressed casually both times she showed herself to me. I wonder whether that's the outfit she was wearing when she crossed over." She shivered. "I'm getting that prickle across my scalp. I think she's telling me that I'm right."

"Too bad you can't just ask what happened to her."

"I wish it was that easy. I can try."

Closing her eyes, Jessica started with one of the deep, calming breaths that helped her get into a meditative state. Exhaling long and slow, she repeated the process over and over until, eventually, reaching out with her thoughts, she asked Elise if there was anything she could tell them about how she crossed over. Minutes passed. Finally, Jessica huffed a long *giving up* breath. "I get the feeling that she might not be able to come through fully right away. She must have used a lot of energy shielding me from Rostya. She needs to recharge her batteries—so to speak."

"What about Ilya? What else do we know about him?"

"The older Ilya? Nothing other than what that article said—that he was a music impresario and he got called home from Europe when his son died."

"Maybe he lives overseas," Sage said.

"True. He might be living—or dead—in Europe, or somewhere else. He could be in Russia for all we know. Okay, so we don't know what happened to either Elise or Rostya, but we do know that both of them died. We also don't know why Ilya didn't inherit Herron Pond when he was the obvious heir."

"I wonder whether he was mentioned in the will at all."

Jessica perked up. "We should be able to see a copy at the county courthouse. Dianne Maggio had to have filed it and had it probated."

"The county seat for Big Sur is Salinas."

"That's about an hour drive from here."

"Why not have Dianne show it to you and save us the trip?"

Jessica rose and stretched, stiff from sitting at the table. "She's supposed to get us a copy, but so far, I haven't seen one. There's something about her that I don't trust. I'd rather she didn't know about our 'investigations.'"

"The courthouse won't be open until Monday," Sage said. "We'll be staying here longer than we expected."

"If you need to get back to work, I can stay here and use one of the cars in the garage. They must be missing you after the two days you were away at that seminar."

As she suspected he would, he flapped a dismissive hand. "If they can't do without me for a few days, I haven't done my job properly in training my assistant. I'll call the doc in residence tomorrow. It's easy enough to conduct business remotely. Besides, I can stand a few days alone with you."

Jessica leaned over to drop a kiss on him. "You are the very best person in the world, Sage Boles. At first, I was totally loving it here, but since I met up with Rostya, not so much."

He gave her a wry smile. "I can see how she could throw ice water on a party."

"With you here, it's all good again."

She texted Jenna to let her know they were staying in Big Sur for another couple of days. A response pinged back shortly afterwards with some unexpected news.

Jessica read the screen. "Roland wants to see Herron Pond. I can't believe it. They're driving up tomorrow. So much for us having time alone together. They'll be here by midday."

Sage, ever the optimist, tapped her affectionately under the chin. "Never mind. It could be fun. We can play host and make brunch for them."

"We're certainly stocked to the gills with food." Realizing that a visit meant she would get to see her two young nieces, Jessica let his mood infect her. "Rostya had better not show up while they're here. Jenna would freak if she knew the place is 'haunted.'"

"We won't tell her. By the way, where do you think Rostya went?"

"I wish I knew." She folded her hands in prayer mode. "Please God, may she be prevented from showing up here again."

"Ghost jail?"

"She deserves a life sentence for what she did to her little boy."

"I thought you didn't believe in eternal damnation."

"It's true that I don't believe there's an old man with a beard who sends you to burn in hell if you were bad. Everything I've learned from Bella tells me that whatever punishment or reward there is comes from our facing up to what we've done in this life, good or bad. We punish or reward ourselves. If and when she decides to go into the Light—and that's up to her—Rostya will have to deal with what she did. She'll have to experience the kind of pain she inflicted on little Ilya."

"That sounds like my personal idea of hell."

"Mine, too."

"You did say you hadn't noticed anything 'spooky' on this side, didn't you?"

Jessica gave him a cryptic smile. "Not so far."

twenty-five

THE SPARKS FAMILY BROUGHT the Southern California sunshine north with them. The rain of yesterday had vanished, leaving marshmallow clouds in a luminous bluish-violet sky. There could not have been a more picture-perfect introduction to Herron Pond.

Sage and Jessica descended the front steps together, welcoming the new arrivals like the lord and lady of the manor, laughing at Roland's reaction, which mirrored Sage's own.

Roland climbed out of his vehicle, shaking his head in awe. "This is completely nuts. What a fantastic house." Gazing up at the turrets, he corrected himself. "Mansion. It's nothing less."

Sage shook hands with Jessica's brother-in-law. "Not too shabby, is it?"

Roland clapped him on the shoulder. "Bro. It's friggin' amazing."

"Wait till you see the lake. And the grounds go all the way to the ocean. It's incredible."

"Can't wait."

Roland went to free the four-year-old twins who were clamoring to be released from their car seats. All anyone had to do was compare Roland's neatly trimmed rust-colored hair and theirs to know their genetic heritage.

The twins' feet hit the driveway and two little pairs of arms wrapped themselves around Jessica's legs. Crouching to eye level, she folded her nieces in a big hug that encompassed both of them. "How are my girls?"

"We love you, Aunty Jess," the girls chorused. "We love you a lot and a lot and a lot."

Emily was first to pull away. "We drived a long, long way," she exclaimed, jumping up and down. "It was too much sitting. I'm so happy we got out."

"It was dark and we were asleep," Sophie added. "And we woke up and ate pancakes."

"Yum, pancakes. That sounds like so much fun." Jessica seized hold of Emily, whose bouncing was a fair imitation of Winnie the Pooh's Tigger. "Let me see where you hurt your forehead, Em."

"Don't encourage her," Jenna said. "There's abrasion *and* a laceration. Thank heavens it's not going to scar. She kept ripping off the Band-Aid, so I gave up."

"She needs one of those cones of shame like they put on dogs after surgery," Jessica joked.

Jenna made a rueful face. "Don't tempt me."

Emily pushed her bangs away from the injury with chubby fingers and displayed the wound on her forehead. "I falled down, Aunty Jess, and there was soooo much bleeding."

"I heard you were a very brave girl at the hospital."

Her niece nodded vigorously. "And I got ice cream and a new baby doll." She twirled around and tugged on Roland's trouser leg. "Daddy, can you get my baby, please? She stayed in the car." To Jessica: "Sophie didn't get a new baby 'cause she didn't get hurt. But *I* did."

"We're happy Sophie didn't get hurt, aren't we?" Jessica said. Emily nodded, but looked as though she was not sure.

"Daddy, I want my kitty," Sophie said.

"You know what?" Jessica said. "We have lots of ice cream, and you can both have some after we eat lunch." With that promise, the little girls hugged each other and started a game of tag, hiding behind the vehicles on the driveway.

Roland and Sage unloaded the suitcases. As they carried them into the house, Jenna spoke to her twin. "We thought that since it's such a long drive we'd stay overnight and leave first thing in the morning. Is that okay with you?"

"Why wouldn't it be okay with me?" Jessica swept her hand dramatically at the Victorian mansion. "It's as much your house as it is mine, dear twin. And it's as big as a hotel. And you're right, that's a crazy long drive."

"The other day when we got here, I—I'm not sure what it was, but...I got this funny feeling; didn't you?"

"Funny, like what?"

Jenna gave her a squinty-eyed look. "When we were looking at that stained-glass window in the front hallway—" she broke off.

"What about it?"

"It felt like someone was watching us."

"What, do you mean, like a spirit?"

Jenna shuddered. "Spirit stuff is your thing, not mine. All I can tell you is, I didn't like it, whatever it was. It was totally creepy."

"And yet, here you are. With your kids, too."

"We're here because Roland wanted to come. and, well, frankly, I feel safer with him here."

"Why?" Jessica snorted. "Is it that big gun he carries?"

Jenna shuddered again. "I don't think a gun would be effective against whatever it was that I felt."

"Don't tell me you're getting psychic?"

"Don't even joke about that! I don't want to be psychic."

"Neither did I. But I didn't have a choice." Jessica gave her a sister-ly nudge. "I do understand what you mean about the house. It's the old-timey Victorian vibe on this side. It feels like you're living in history. Stick to the new wing and you won't even think about it. Guess what I found out about why the two sides are so different."

"After that drive, I'm too tired to guess. Just tell me already."

"There was a bad fire here a few years ago. When he rebuilt the house, Mr. Evanov made the new wing modern."

"A fire? Was it the Victorian wiring?"

"They don't know what caused it—" Jessica repeated the information she had gleaned from Amy Herron. Anything to distract Jenna from thinking about spirits in the foyer.

They ate lunch at the marble table in the formal dining room. The little girls sat boosted on cushions, behaving themselves under the nervous watch of their mother, whose eyes jumped from one vintage heirloom to another, making sure nothing got damaged.

Emily kept her new doll on her lap. She had named it Heidi after a friend at her preschool. Not to be outdone, Sophie had brought her life-size furry white cat, Lexie, to sit with her.

"This is all very nice, not to mention delicious," Roland said. He board-inghouse reached for a casserole dish further down the table. "You guys did a superb job with the food."

"Sage gets all the kitchen creds." Jessica beamed at him proudly. "He knows it's not a good idea to leave the cooking to me. I make a better sous-chef."

"You're great at salad-making and baked potatoes," Sage said, managing to sound supportive and not patronizing.

"I chopped the mushrooms and grated the cheese for the casserole." It sounded like a confession.

From the other side of the expanse of table Jenna grinned at them. "You two are such a pair of lovebirds."

"You say that like it's a bad thing," Jessica grinned back.

"I think it's adorable." Jenna rescued Emily's fork, which she was using to stab a mushroom. "That guy, the estate manager, really knows how to provision a pantry. I can't believe how much great food is in there, presumably brought in for us."

"Darryl Andrews. He wasn't very welcoming, but you're right, he's done an impeccable job of managing the place. He said he's been here ten years. Sage and I were wondering whether his rotten attitude is because he expected to inherit, since there were no apparent heirs."

"Or heirs apparent," Sage quipped. "We don't know for sure that he *didn't* inherit something, do we?"

"No. Dianne didn't tell us about any other bequests in the will."

"Have you come up with any interesting reasons for *your* bequest?" Roland asked.

"Not so far. We're going to the courthouse in Salinas to look at the will." Catching her sister's sharp glance, Jessica could have kicked herself. She knew as well as if Jenna had said it out loud that she was wondering, as Sage had, *why not ask Dianne Maggio?* There was no easy way for Jessica to explain her mistrust of the attorney, which had started with the unexplained caution to stay away from what she had discovered was simply a music room. Nor could she tell her and Roland about Elise and Rostya without sharing the supernatural happenings since their arrival. Jenna would lose it if she knew about that.

"The will is the right place to start," Roland said.

"That's what we thought." The conversation was headed down a path Jessica would rather not travel. Her relief to have her brother-in-law run interference was short-lived.

"A place like this, in this location, is worth mega millions." Roland continued, "If it all had been left to the estate manager, I would consider that suspicious. Though you do sometimes hear of old ladies leaving their millions to the cat."

"That's no more shocking than having him leave it to us," Jenna said.

"True. Either Evanov came from big family money or he was super-successful. Or both."

Or married his son off to an oligarch's daughter.

Another piece of information Jessica had to keep to herself, or explain she knew because a spirit had told her, which was not happening. "Being a world-famous pianist could explain it," she said.

"And if he bought the property at the right time, which he seems to have done—"

"Amy Herron, the realtor, has a client who wants to make Herron Pond into a health spa for the wealthy," Jessica blurted without thinking it through. "They've offered eighteen million."

Jenna's jaw dropped. *"Eighteen million*—and this is the first I'm hearing about it?"

"We haven't had much time to talk," Jessica said, shamefaced and regretting having spilled the beans that way. "You were down on the place from the get-go. I wanted you to have a chance to see it properly before we started talking about offers. I wanted you to fall in love with it. Who knows if her client is even serious? I think it's a horrible idea."

Her twin's accusing glare told Jessica that her argument had fallen flat.

"It's not horrible at all. You can't make that kind of unilateral decision. There are two of—"

"Mommy, why are you mad at Aunty Jess?" Emily tugged on her mother's arm. Jenna pasted on a big fake grin, but her eyes burned with anger.

"I'm not mad, sweetie. Finish your lunch and you can have some ice cream."

Roland, with six years of experience in heading off the twins' quarrels, spoke calmly. "That's a very interesting offer, and here we are, ready to see the whole enchilada. We can talk about what the realtor said later." He reached across the table to spoon second helpings of casserole and salad onto his plate. Addressing Sage, he said, "Hey, are there fish in that lake behind the house? I can't wait to get out there and have a look."

Sage picked up the conversation and for the next little while, the talk was of rods and reels and boats. Finally, with the ice cream consumed, the dishes in the dishwasher, everyone dressed in warm gear and went outside.

The men exclaimed over the outdoor kitchen as though it was more fun than their favorite video game. And, just as Jessica had envisioned, the little twins played on the lakeshore.

Once the girls had exhausted themselves, Jessica and Sage took Roland on the Victorian wing tour. Jenna, using the twins as an excuse, sat it out with them in the new wing.

They showed him everything—the public rooms on the ground floor, the turret room, all of the bedrooms, and the practice room whose door now stood open. But they did not share with him what had happened there. Roland was aware of Jessica's skills as a medium—had used them privately in his cases—but it would do no good to put him in the middle of Jenna's objections.

It was impossible not to be impressed with the mansion. It was plain on Roland's usually impassive face. Jessica wondered whether he was quietly calculating a counteroffer to the eighteen million dollar offer.

Back in the new wing, Jenna had selected a bedroom for her and Roland, settling Sophie and Emily in the king-size bed next door. Worn out from the long day, the little girls were soon asleep, leaving the grownups free.

Darryl Andrews had stocked the wine fridge with some delicious reds, which the adults opened in front of the fireplace in the room Jessica thought of as the library-slash-den.

Tacitly agreeing to leave the topic of a sale as the silent elephant in the corner of the room, they talked about the wine and the food and the Victorian décor in the other side of the mansion, until Roland yawned and set his glass down.

He leaned over to kiss Jenna on the forehead and stood. "That's enough wine for me. I can use some shut-eye. You can stay and talk some more if you want, hon, but we have to be up at o'dark-thirty and get out ahead of traffic. I'm gonna hit the sheets."

Droopy-eyed herself, Jenna stretched out a hand for him to pull her up, too. "I'll come with you. I'm feeling a little tipsy." On their way across the room, she stopped to give Jessica a hug. Her words were a little slurred. "Remember, twin, don't go making any big decisions without me. We have to talk."

Jessica returned the hug, for once not having the desire to engage. "Love you, twin."

"Love you more."

Sage switched off the light. Jessica snuggled next to his warm body, drowsy with wine and content with his arm around her shoulders, her cheek on his chest. They lay together quietly for a while, not needing to talk, absorbing the sweetness of each other's essence.

"What's on your mind, angel?" Sage murmured in the dark, his fingertips finding and gently caressing her cheek, her chin, the hollow of her neck. "I feel you wandering.

As usual, he could read her. Why couldn't she keep her mind quiet? "Do you think Jen will make me sell my share?"

"She's your twin, angel face. What do *you* think?"

Jessica puffed out a sigh. "That I should think about more important things." She brought his face down to meet her lips.

***

Jessica jerked upright from a deep sleep, for a moment not sure where she was. "What was that?"

"One of the kids." Sage was out of bed and climbing into his clothes.

A second shrill scream sounded through the walls.

"Mommy, mommy, mommy!"

They arrived outside the twins' room at the same time as Jenna and Roland. Jessica found the light switch and followed them inside. Little Sophie leapt from the bed into her father's arms, sobbing. Her little fists clung together around his neck. Emily, lying in bed, sleepily rubbed her eyes.

"Did you have a bad dream, baby girl?" Roland rocked his daughter like a baby. "Tell daddy what scared you."

Sophie kept her face pressed into his shoulder. "Somebody was right there." Without looking, she pointed behind her to the foot of the bed. "There was a lady sitting there."

"You don't have to be scared," Emily chirped, all at once wide awake. "She was a nice lady. She was singing a pretty song."

Jenna whirled on her twin with a jaw set like iron. "What is she talking about, Jess?"

"How would I know? I was asleep, just like you were." Jessica sat on the bed next to Emily. "Sweetie, can you tell me what the lady looked like?"

The child sat up, nodding vigorously. "She had long yellow hair like you. She was pretty. She didn't want to hurt us. Sophie's just being a baby."

"I'm not a baby," Sophie wailed. "I was scared."

Jenna made to take her from Roland, but Sophie wouldn't budge. From where Jessica sat, she could see that her brother-in-law's neck was wet with tears.

"I want my Lexie," Sophie sobbed. "Where's my kitty cat?"

"She had it with her when they went to bed," Jenna said, seizing the bedcovers. She wrenched them to the end of the bed more forcefully than she needed to, exposing the bottom sheet. While she was doing that, Jessica got on her knees to look under the bed and Sage checked the rest of the room. The toy cat had not made its way to the foot of the bed, nor underneath it, nor was it anywhere else they looked.

Gently, Jenna stroked her daughter's hair. "Did you take it outside and leave it there, sweetie?"

"No, mommy, she was right here. I want my Lexie. Where is she?" The questioned ended on a long wail that threatened to spin into a meltdown.

Emily, who was eyeballing her sister with interest, made her an offer. "You can share Heidi." She picked up her new baby doll, which was lying next to her on the pillow, and offered it to her twin.

To Jessica's relief, Sophie took the doll and hugged it close with a whispered, "Thank you" to her sister. Roland set her on the bed and Jenna rounded on her husband as if this was all his fault. "We need to leave, Ro. We need to leave this minute."

His eyebrow quirked up. "We're not leaving at three o'clock in the morning, hon. She had a nightmare. What do—"

"Are you *sure* that's what it was?" Jenna pointed an accusing scowl on her twin. "Is that all it was, Jess?"

"What are you suggesting, Jen?" Roland asked. "What else do you think it was?"

"Never mind." For a minute, Jenna sat there holding her child in the circle of her arms and glowering at Jessica. She told Sophie to lie down and slid under the covers between the two little girls. "If we have to stay, we're sleeping in here with them. And the lights stay on."

She might as well have stomped her foot.

Sage and Jessica drifted back to their own room and climbed into bed. Was her brother-in-law right and Sophie had experienced a scary dream? Or had one of the spirits crossed through to the new wing and made herself known? Unease held her in its grip and refused to let go. Scaring four-year-olds was outside the bounds of what was acceptable, especially when the four-year-olds in question were her nieces. Jessica had read plenty of autobiographies by mediums who had been terrified as young children when spirit people appeared to them. Even when there was nothing menacing about them, as Emily had indicated, what child would not find a gauzy-looking stranger appearing in their bedroom in the middle of the night terrifying?

"Do you think it was Rostya?" Sage asked.

The very thought left her momentarily speechless. "Rostya? She'd better not get near my nieces—"

"That doesn't make sense, though," he interrupted. "Emily wasn't scared. If there *was* a spirit, wouldn't it more likely have been Elise?"

"Rostya has black hair. Em said the 'lady' they saw was blonde, so...yeah."

Jessica scooted close to him. As he wrapped his arms around her, she asked the question that was bothering her. "Why would Elise go to the twins' room?" Sage had no to time offer an answer. Her intuition—or perhaps her psychic sense—provided one. "Because she lost her own baby and she couldn't resist visiting while there were kids here." And even though she had no evidence to support it, Jessica knew in the peculiar way that another heartbroken mother knows that Elise had suffered that loss. "The way Em described her sounded like Elise as I've experienced her. That is, unless there's a third spirit we haven't met."

Sage's eyebrows shot up. "Do you think there is?"

"Not really."

"I thought they didn't come to the new wing."

"Surprise," Jessica said. "I think it'll be quiet for the rest of the night." She crossed her fingers, just to seal the wish.

"Hey, you know that question you had about whether Jen will want to sell?" Sage said. "I have a feeling you just got your answer."

"I know," she muttered. "I know."

In the morning, Sage was the first down in the kitchen making coffee. He came back to their room as Jessica was dressing, and beckoned her to follow him downstairs.

"There's something you need to see," he said, leading her to the breakfast room.

Sophie's plush toy cat, Lexie, sat on the middle of the table. Jessica looked at him in amazement. "Where did you find it?"

"I didn't. It was sitting there just like that when I came down."

Her eyes welled up. "I asked her to help. I guess she heard me."

"You asked—"

"Elise. I asked Elise to help us find the cat."

Sage raised a quizzical brow. "So, did Sophie leave it here and Elise led me to it? Or did Elise somehow put it there?"

"I wish I—"

"Where the hell did you find the damn thing?"

Roland, speaking from the doorway, went straight to the toy cat and picked it up. "I was looking for it in the dining room—thought it might have been left there after lunch. I was going to look under the table to see if Sophie had dropped it there—I didn't really think so because she never goes to bed without it. But when I got near to where she had been sitting it felt like I was walking into an ice cave—I mean, *goddamn,* it was as cold as a witch's butt. Just in that one spot. When I moved away from that area, the temperature was normal. It was the eeriest thing."

Jessica and Sage exchanged a quick look. "That's weird for sure," Sage said. "But hey, we found the cat."

"Yeah, but *where* did you find it? I'm as close to positive as I can be that she took it to bed with her last night."

"Don't let Jen spook you," Jessica said, sidestepping the question. "Did she get any sleep?"

"Not much. She flopped around for the rest of the night." Roland made a droll face. "Trust me, I know. She made sure I didn't get much sleep, either. And we have a five-hour drive ahead of us." He leveled a serious look at Jessica. "My wife is convinced that the girls saw a ghost. Is that what this weird shit is? Disappearing toys and cold spots in the dining room? Is she right, Jessica? Have you been experiencing supernatural phenomena here? I need you to tell me the truth."

She was saved from having to fumble for an answer. Jenna swept into the room with the two little twins in tow, dressed for the outdoors in their warm coats and hats and gloves. The dark, puffy flesh under Jenna's eyes bore mute testimony to her lack of sleep. "Ro, would you get our bags? I want to get out of here. This minute."

"It's barely seven o'clock," Sage protested. "How about some breakfast before you get on the road?"

Jenna ignored him and swung a blame-filled glare on her sister. "I'm so done with this place. I knew from the start there was something wrong here. As soon as we get home, I'm calling Amy Herron about that offer."

twenty-six

JESSICA COULD UNDERSTAND HER twin being upset about the spirit visitation to her children, but Jenna's attitude angered her, too. It was not up to her to make a decision on selling the house by herself any more than it was up to Jessica. But if she aligned herself with Amy, Jessica would be outnumbered and that would make it all the harder to argue her side.

After the Sparks family had left Herron Pond with terse goodbyes, Amy herself sent a text message to arrange a meeting that day on Carmela Durrell's lunch break.

The wintry weather had returned to match Jessica's mood. Heavy steel-wool clouds scowled overhead, reflecting the way she felt. Observing Sage's relaxed hands on the steering wheel, she was thankful that he was the one driving the treacherous winding roads that were a feature of Big Sur, not her. He moved with such confidence and grace; it was impossible not to trust that he would get them to their destination safely.

Amy met them outside Java Jake's, a rustic roadside coffeehouse down the mountain road from Herron Pond. They had decided in advance that Sage would not intrude on the meeting with Carmela, who, Amy had indicated, was decidedly skittish about it. Leaving Jessica with a kiss and a promise to keep his phone handy, he went to check out the shops and services of Big Sur Village.

Seated at a table in a far corner of the café, Jessica thought that Carmela Durrell appeared nervous. Amy had said that she was currently working at a retirement home in the area. That explained the former Herron Pond employee's royal blue uniform with its snowy shirt and apron. A small, squarish woman with grey-streaked hair and deep lines at the corners of her mouth, she looked to be in her early fifties. Her deep brown eyes skipped anxiously around the coffeehouse, finally settling on Jessica, who approached her with an outstretched hand. "Thank you so much for meeting with me, Carmela. May I buy you something to eat? I don't want you to miss your lunch."

Carmela declined with a head shake. "Coffee is fine. Black, please."

"Got it. I'll be right back." With Amy trailing her, Jessica went to the counter and pointedly placed an order for two black coffees. "Unless you'd like one to go?" she asked the realtor.

"No thanks. I need you to understand that the only reason she agreed to come today is because of what you said about Matt. She isn't thrilled about talking about the—" She paused and got quieter. "the *you-know-what* at the house."

They stepped away from the counter and went to the waiting area.

"I get it, and I'll be respectful. But if you wouldn't mind, I'd prefer to speak with her alone." Jessica strained to keep her patience. Amy had previously explained Carmela's objections more than once.

"Are you sure that's a good idea?" Amy said. "She might be more comfortable having someone there that she knows."

"Or, she might feel freer to speak without someone she knows listening in. Especially if this is stuff she hasn't talked to you about already. Which is what you said, right?"

Amy looked unhappy, but in the end, she didn't put up any further argument. "If that's what you want." She threw Jessica a sidelong glance. "Where's that hunky boyfriend of yours gone?"

Jessica, accustomed to women swooning over Sage's looks, had learned to take it in stride. "He's gone to explore. I'll call him to pick me up when I'm done here."

"I don't suppose he has a brother?" Amy said hopefully.

"He does. Jade is a happily married new daddy, so don't bother."

"Jade? I love their names. Is he as smokin' hot as Sage?"

Jessica grinned. "Is that even possible? Of course, I'm prejudiced."

The barista called Jessica's name and Amy grudgingly took her leave. Carmela was looking at her phone screen when Jessica carried the cups to the table. As she took her seat and set one of the cups in front of her, the other woman turned the screen to face her.

The image Jessica saw brought a lump to her throat. A laughing young man dressed in motorcycle leathers. A helmet under one arm, he had leaned down to kiss his mother on the cheek. "This is Matt?" she asked gently.

Carmela's eyes brimmed with unshed tears. "Yes, my son; my baby."

"I'm so very sorry. I can see from his photo that he was a wonderful guy."

"Yes, he was. Rosie, my daughter, told me what you said to Amy about him talking to you." Hope lit her face. "Is he here with us? Can you see him now?"

Jessica had guessed this was the real reason for Carmela's agreeing to the meeting. She regarded the other woman with genuine regret. "I wish I could, but I don't have any control over when spirits come to me." Disappointment creased Carmela's face, and Jessica added, "It's not easy for them to come through."

The housekeeper's grief was plain in her bowed head. "But he came when Amy was with you."

"I know. People in spirit sometimes manage to communicate with someone other than family when they believe they can get a message through. I promise, if I hear anything from Matt, I'll let you know. But in the meantime, you can always talk to him directly. He is listening to you."

"Really?" Carmela sounded incredulous.

"Yes, really."

"How do I do that?"

"One way is to ask him to send you signs that he's around you. He will, I guarantee it." Jessica studied the housekeeper, gauging her receptiveness to what she had to say next. It was always agonizing to utter, but sensing this woman's need for comfort, she made herself say it. "I lost a son, too."

She watched the empathy ripple across Carmela's face as she took in what she had just heard. People didn't expect it. Carmela reached out and touched her arm. "But you're so young."

"As you know, death doesn't respect age. It happened about six years ago. We were in a car accident. Justin was just shy of three." It was hard not to choke on the words. "He's been growing up in the spirit world. So, you can trust me to be truthful with you."

"Oh my God, Jessica, that's too sad—a baby. My Matteo would have had his thirtieth birthday the next week."

"It doesn't matter how old they are when it's your child."

"That's true. I will pray for your son." Carmela crossed herself. "Okay, go ahead," she said, as if Jessica's revelation had allowed her to pass some kind of unspoken test. "Ask me your questions. What do you want to know?"

Reaching over, Jessica squeezed her hand. "Thank you, Carmela. Amy probably told you I'm staying at Herron Pond. I have some questions about when you worked there."

"Even after all these years, thinking about that place makes me break out in a cold sweat." Carmela made the sign of the cross again.

"I understand. We don't have to talk about anything that scares you. When did you work there?"

"It was a long time ago. I left in 2004. My husband was out of work and the kids were little. I needed the job. It was fine until—" Carmela hesitated. "You know, it's because I felt sorry for the little boy. I stayed on too long for his sake. I mean, not that I had anything to do with him. I just—" She broke off.

"The little boy?" This was what she was here for, and she hadn't even had to ask. Could it be that easy?

"Mr. Evanov's grandson."

"You mean Ilya?"

Carmela eyebrows rose. "Yes, little Ilya. There were two of them. His father—Mr. Evanov's son—was Ilya, too. How did you—?"

"I saw his grave when I was exploring the grounds."

For just a moment, Carmela buried her face in her hands. "That poor little guy. When I started working there, he was five years old. That was in 1997. I remember it because my Matteo was the same age as Ilya. Rosie was three."

"I heard that Ilya was sick a lot," Jessica said tentatively.

"She *claimed* he was sick." Her curled lip said a lot.

"She? You mean his mother?"

"Yes. Mrs. Evanov."

And there it was, confirmation that Rostya, not Elise, was Ilya's mother. Jessica was torn between feeling comforted and disappointed. Either way, the appalling fact was, the boy was dead and according to the article, for no legitimate medical cause.

"It sounds like you didn't believe her," she said.

"There was never anything wrong with him until Mr. Ilya and his father would go away on a trip. That's when the little one always got sick. She was constantly rushing him to the hospital." Her focus softened and she seemed to gaze into an unpleasant past. "He was such a quiet little kid, always playing by himself. Some days I brought Matty to work with me so the boy could learn how to be with other kids."

"Was Mrs. Evanov okay with that?"

"She never noticed, that woman."

"It sounds like he didn't go to school."

"She didn't want him to go to kindergarten. She kept saying the other kids would make him sick. But he would get sick a lot at home without other kids."

"What kind of illnesses did he have, do you know?"

"*She* said it was seizures, but from what I heard about it, she never took him to his doctor, just the urgent care, or the emergency room. As a good Christian, I should give her the benefit of the doubt. She didn't speak a lot of English, so maybe she didn't know what to do or how to get help."

For Jessica, a language barrier was no excuse for a woman who had all the advantages and resources Rostya Evanov had that could have gotten help for her son. She said nothing, and Carmela continued.

"The other staff whispered about it all the time. We were all worried, but there was nothing we could do. I heard that the head housekeeper tried to talk to Mr. Andrews about it more than once, but he told her to keep her nose out of the Evanovs' business."

The apparent callous attitude of the estate manager made Jessica curious whether, the harsh rebuke notwithstanding, knowing of the housekeeper's concern, he had tried to intervene on little Ilya's behalf. If he had not, in her mind, he was culpable, too.

"It was a monstrous thing that the boy died," Carmela continued. "He was so young, so vulnerable. Something like that is always a shock, but I don't think anyone at the house was exactly surprised." She paused for a beat and Jessica waited, not daring to interrupt. "When the police came, we were all hoping they would take her away and lock her up."

"But they didn't?"

The housekeeper's bitter laugh was all the answer Jessica needed. "Was she a bad employer?" She wished she could take back the stupid question as soon as it was in the air. "I mean, well, aside from what happened with her son."

"Mr. Evanov was our employer, not her," Carmela said emphatically. "Considering the way she did her poor boy, do you expect she would treat *us* like human beings?"

"Got it. Could we back up a little bit? You said the police came—"

"They came and they all talked for a long time. Both misters—they had to fly home from Italy or Greece or somewhere like that. Europe. They were always going to those countries. Something to do with music; the piano. Missus Evanov was hysterical. We could hear her screaming to the detectives over and over that she never did nothing wrong. Hah. Kind of funny how she knew English when she wanted to say she was innocent. We all knew she was doing *something*, maybe feeding him something to make him sick." The anguish on her face twisted Jessica's gut, for the child, not for the employees who had stood by and watched it happen. Carmela hiccupped a little sob. "You see there was nothing we could do, don't you?"

You could at least have called social services anonymously.

"So, she got away with it?"

"Rich people," Carmela said with a look of loathing. "That's how it goes for them, you know? I don't know if they couldn't prove it, but she didn't go to jail like she should. She didn't exactly get away with it, though. Like I said, when the boy died, the missus was yelling and screaming all the time. I mean, you and me, we know what it feels like to have your son die. But it wasn't like that with her. You could tell it was a big act, like she was acting and saying things she thought she was supposed to. She would be 'crying' but you never, ever saw her squeeze out a single drop. What do they call it? Alligator tears?"

"Crocodile tears."

"Yeah." Carmela got quiet, as if someone might overhear the repulsive tale. "She must have acted too good. They finally put her in a hospital." She twirled a finger next to her ear. "Not a regular hospital—"

"She was admitted to a mental facility?"

"Uh huh, that's right. One of those expensive, fancy kinds, like where the movie stars go when they have drug problems. Money talks. Missus was there for a long time. Months. Close to a year, I think. Mr. Ilya left right away to go out of town. The staff gossiped all the time about how it was like he couldn't even look at her."

"Because he blamed her for his son's death?"

"No, no. I'm talking about a long time before that happened. When I worked there, he always went away a lot. But even when he was home, except for dinner, he never was in the same room with her. I mean, when the staff was there. Who knows what they did when we weren't there? We all thought it was kind of strange. If he didn't even like her, how come they got married? He barely was polite, didn't talk much. To her, I mean. He was very nice to us. Mr. Ilya always gave us a big Christmas bonus and ordered cake for our birthdays. I mean, he had an assistant to keep the dates for him, but he took good care of the staff."

Carmela paused to drain her coffee cup. She put it down and reached for her keyring. "After that, the other bad thing happened and it got worse."

Jessica leaned forward in her seat, unwilling to lose her so soon. "What? What bad thing?"

"I gotta get to work," she said uneasily shifting in her chair.

"Wait, Carmela, how did it get worse? You can't say something like that and leave me hanging. Please tell me what happened."

"Mrs. Evanov passed away."

Jessica knew that, of course. Rostya had died and her spirit was inhabiting the house. Nevertheless, to hear it from someone who was there when it happened gave it a new impact. And there was one question she had not raised, even to herself.

"How did she die?"

"She had a lot of pills. You know, for the depression. There was talk that after she got home from the hospital, she saved them up and took a lot of them all at once."

"Suicide," Jessica muttered.

For the third time, Carmela crossed herself. She raised her eyes heavenward. "Life is the property of God. To take your own life is to steal from God."

"Was Ilya out of town?" Jessica asked, not wanting to get off onto a theological tangent.

"No, Mr. Ilya was home, but they stayed in different bedrooms, different parts of the house, so she could do what she wanted. That was before the fire. There was just one big house. She had rooms on one side and he stayed on the other."

The fire. Jessica knew she had to move quickly to get what she needed. "When did the fire happen? Were you working there then?"

Carmela grabbed hold of the crucifix she wore around her neck. "No. Thank you, God, that wasn't until years after I quit." She stopped and did the math in her head. "Maybe ten years. When I heard that it burned, I felt like it was the Devil finally claiming it for himself."

Jessica could see that she was ready to cut and run. "Why did you quit, Carmela?" she pressed.

The former housekeeper's convulsive shudder spoke more exquisitely than words. "I started hearing people talking—something whispering in my ear, but there was nobody in the room. I was so scared, I nearly peed myself. Like I said, the Devil wanted that place for his own."

"What did the voices say?"

"I couldn't hear what they said, and I didn't care. Look, I'd been working there for a lot of years by then. After that started, they couldn't pay me enough to stay. It wasn't only the whispers. I could walk into a room to clean and I would get this feeling like someone threw a heavy cover over me. Like a big blanket or something? I couldn't hardly breathe. It felt like I was smothering. But other times, it would feel like I walking through an ice cave."

Carmela had described the same experience as Roland. Jessica didn't have to force an empathetic response. She had lived it, too. "I can't blame you for wanting to leave," she said. "Did all of this happen after Mrs. Evanov died, or—?"

"Yes, it was after." Carmela's eyes popped open wide in alarm. "Do you think it was her? You think she's haunting the house?"

Let's not give that particular rumor any additional fuel.

"Was there any particular room where you heard the whispering?" Jessica asked.

"Not really. It happened in different rooms, different times. It was all so freaky. The baby, little Ilya, had died. His father was crazy with grief, you know? Can you imagine how he must have felt? You sure can. And so can I. But he got married again, so I hope he got some happiness."

Jessica's heart leapt painfully in her chest. "He got remarried?"

"That's what I heard. After the first Mrs. Evanov did what she did; after she—passed away—Mr. Ilya left. For good. I heard he was living in Europe and got married again."

"What about Mr. Evanov senior—Vadim? How did he take the death of his grandson?"

Carmela stood and shoved her chair to the table. "I don't like talking about this stuff, and I have to go. Thanks for the coffee. Good luck, staying there. You'll need it."

Jessica stood, too, and squeezed her hand again. "Thank you so much for coming, Carmela. I can see why it's tough for you to talk about it. I hope you understand, since I'm staying at Herron Pond, I want to learn everything I can. You have no idea how much I appreciate all you've told me."

It was never easy for a bereaved parent to open themselves to the pain talking about their loss brought. Initiating physical contact didn't come naturally to Jessica, but she took a chance and gave the other woman a brief hug. "Please believe me when I say that Matt wants you to know that he loves you very much and always will."

Carmela nodded once and with a whispered 'thank you' took a step away, in a hurry to leave Herron Pond behind and resume her current, ghost-free, life.

The housekeeper sped through the coffee house and out the front door. Too late, Jessica realized she had missed the opportunity to ask an important question: how had the fire at Herron Pond started?

twenty-seven

Tuesday morning at seven-thirty, Sage circled the blocks surrounding Church Street, looking for an open slot to park his truck near the Monterey County Courthouse. After two circuits, and Jessica assuring him that the parking gods were on their side, a beat-up old Chevy pulled out and they replaced it.

The Art Deco court building had undergone a forty-million-dollar renovation, but the crowd waiting outside in a dank drizzle didn't care about that. People dressed in torn jeans and wifebeater t-shirts waited. People in business attire waited. People in soggy house slippers waited. Family groups and solo gangstas. Lawyers in cheap suits, looking as though they could use a week's sleep. The court system attracted a wide spectrum of the population, most of them—except for the lawyers, who were getting paid—wishing they were elsewhere.

Jessica tugged her hood close around her face, holding off the moisture as best she could. She leaned close to Sage and spoke quietly. "I thank God I'm not here as a defendant."

Sage, who had spent some unjust days in a jail cell, tucked her cold hand through his arm. "You have no idea how thankful you should be."

On the dot of eight o'clock and not a second sooner, someone inside the building unlocked the doors. The line started moving, first pushing to get beneath the portico where it was slightly drier. Next, shuffling through the courthouse doors. One at a time, they shook off the raindrops and dropped phones and pocket change into small plastic trays. There had been no shootings at this location and the courthouse administrators intended to keep it that way.

Once they made it through heavy-duty metal detectors, Sage asked for directions to the probate office. The early hour did not stop the uniformed officers who beckoned them through from looking bored. "Third floor," one of them responded.

"Is that where we go to see a will?"

"Nope," another said. "That's probate *court*. You want to look at a will, go to the clerk's office." He gave them the room number and they headed in that direction.

A flock of butterflies woke up in Jessica's stomach without warning and started fluttering. She had not been able to make herself eat breakfast and her head was pounding. She wasn't sure what she was expecting, but whatever was in the will, there was no question that it had already changed both her and Jenna's lives.

"You really think they'll let us see it?" she asked.

"That's the ninety-fifth time you've asked me that," Sage said mildly. "I told you, angel, I looked it up. In California, anyone can see a will that's been filed with the court. *And* we can buy a certified copy to take with us."

Pushing through the doors designated 'Court Clerk,' they were first in line at the counter. A dour-faced woman looked out from behind a plexiglass screen. Jessica recited Vadim Evanov's name and made her request for a copy of his will.

"Date of death?" The woman's attitude blared as loud as a howling monkey perched on her shoulder.

"I don't have the exact date. He died last October, if that helps."

"A lot of people died last October, ma'am."

Jessica decided that she was probably already screwed, but she arranged her mouth in what was intended to be a disarming smile. "I'm sure that's true, and I don't mean to be difficult, but 'Vadim Evanov' isn't exactly a common name." She spelled it out. "Would you look it up, please?"

The woman stayed pokerfaced. "I need the date."

She's been at work for about five minutes. What's the big deal?

Sage, who had been standing off to the side, stepped forward and leaned close to the glass, favoring her with one of his dazzling smiles. "We drove all the way up here from Ojai. It's a really long way to go for nothing. Is there anything at all you could do help us?" His long, penetrating look ensured she could see the sincerity in the unusual blue eyes.

The clerk visibly thawed under his gaze. She would be dripping all over the floor in about ten seconds, Jessica thought with a mixture of amusement and annoyance. She had seen it more than once—Sage looking into someone's eyes and mesmerizing them in a way that came naturally to him; something she instinctively knew that she couldn't learn if she tried for a thousand years. How the hell did he do that?

The clerk heaved a tortured sigh "That *is* a long drive. Okay, gimme a minute and I'll see what I can do."

"All I ask is that you give it a try," Sage said with a little nod of encouragement.

"No promises," she said, but her coy upward glance said otherwise. Tap-tap-tap on her keyboard and she found what she was looking for. Ignoring Jessica and asking Sage nicely to please wait, the woman got up from her station. Annoying though it was, observing the little performance, Jessica was glad to have him as her secret weapon.

The clerk disappeared for nearly ten minutes and returned to her counter with a sheaf of papers in her hand. "Here you go. It's forty dollars to certify a record. Copies are fifty cents a page, and there's twenty pages here. Total, fifty dollars."

Sage thanked her profusely and passed his debit card through the security drawer. Jessica swallowed the retort she would like to have made in response to his *I told you so* smirk. With the pages of the will in hand, they left the courthouse.

The rain was falling heavier than when they had entered, making it less appealing to step outside. "As long as we're here, we should get a copy of the marriage certificate for Ilya and Rostya, and a death certificate," Jessica said as they approached the front doors.

"I thought you were in a rush to read the will."

The butterflies were flying again, wreaking havoc in her stomach. With the document in her hands, she felt a reluctance to look at it, the same way she had felt with Elise's diary.

"A marriage certificate might add something to what we know. We've got the will, so there's no big rush."

"Well, angel face, I hate to break it to you, but I looked it up. In California, only certain people are permitted to request a copy of a death certificate."

"You're kidding. What people?"

Sage thumbed a query into Google, giving her the eye once he found what he was looking for. "Are you the deceased person's parent or legal guardian?"

"No."

"Are you their child, grandparent, grandchild, sibling, spouse, domestic partner?"

"No."

"Are you in law enforcement, an attorney, or a funeral director?"

"No."

"Then, dearest angel, you don't qualify."

Jessica could feel her shoulders droop with each denial. "Don't tell me it's the same with birth certificates?"

"Yep."

"Death certificates?"

"Uh huh." He put an arm around her shoulders as they exited the courthouse and gave her a consoling squeeze. "We've got a copy of the will. Doesn't that make you happy?"

"Yes, it does. Let's go get some breakfast and see what it says. I'm starving."

They discovered a restaurant on Main Street with seventy-seven five-star reviews on Yelp.

After their waitress had taken their breakfast order and departed, Sage, who had experience as beneficiary of his aunt's will, unfolded the lengthy document and started skimming it. He stopped almost as soon as he had started reading. "Ilya's the first person mentioned."

"He inherited after all? Then how—"

"Not so fast, angel—"

"What does it say?"

Sage read aloud. "Article One: *I have elected to forego any provisions for my only son, Ilya Evanovich Evanov in the disposition of my estate.*" Jesus, Jess, he makes no bones about deliberately disinheriting his son. There's a *No Contest Clause*, too. If the will is contested by any of the beneficiaries, they get nothing."

"But you just read that Ilya gets nothing. So, who would contest it? Not Jen and me. Are there other beneficiaries?"

"The estate manager, Darryl Andrews. He got $100,000. There are some bequests of $10,000 each to certain house staff, and a couple of music charities. The remainder of the estate goes to you and Jen, including the liquid financial assets, which are considerable."

Sage continued skimming pages. "If we skip most of the boilerplate language, the last clause restates it. *"I have intentionally and with full knowledge omitted to provide for my heir, Ilya Evanovich Evanov. If any person who, if I died intestate, would be entitled to any part of my estate, shall either directly or indirectly, alone or in conjunction with any other person, claim in spite of my Will an intestate share of my estate, I give that person One Dollar ($1.00) and no more, in lieu of any other share or interest in my estate."*

"Who are the witnesses?" Jessica asked.

"Darryl Andrews and Dianne Maggio."

"Is that even legal when she's the executor?" Jessica did a quick search of California law on her phone and confirmed it. "As long as the executor is not a beneficiary, they can be a witness."

"You're not thinking there was some kind of funny business with the will, are you?" Sage said.

"I don't know. That would be something to ask Claudia." A pall of dread crept over her, penetrating deep into her core. "I wonder if Ilya knew about Jen and me inheriting. I mean, if he's alive, he must be furious, and hurt, too." She was speculating, but how could he have felt otherwise? "I haven't seen any photos of him anywhere in the house, or of little Ilya, either. I guess Vadim didn't want to be reminded of his death. But his son—for a father to do something so extreme—giving this huge estate to strangers when he had a son—assuming Ilya is alive—how could he? If it was some crappy little house, it would be no big deal. But Herron Pond—"

"There's someone else to consider," Sage said. "What about the baby Ilya and Elise had together? That wasn't little Ilya. Rostya was his mother."

"Assuming Elise actually gave birth, that's a good question. Somehow, Ilya ends up married to Rostya and Elise seems to have disappeared. She didn't die in childbirth because they got back together later. Carmela said he got married again, so that must have been to Elise. Something must have happened to their baby. Or it was adopted." All of the options sickened her. She so desperately wanted Elise and Ilya to have a happy ending. But there was Rostya...Always Rostya interfering.

"We have way too many unanswered questions," Sage said. He slipped the will into his jacket pocket. "I'd love to know what the hell Ilya did to piss off his father so badly."

A fresh wave of sadness brought tears to Jessica's eyes. She swiped them away with a fingertip. "Whatever it was, it cost him everything."

Sage gave her a stern look. "Don't you dare start looking for him. The way I read this, you wouldn't be able to give him the estate, even if you wanted to."

"What makes you think I would do that?" she protested indignantly.

He tapped her lightly on the nose. "Because, my angel, I know you too well. Can you honestly tell me that it wasn't what you were thinking?"

She couldn't bring herself to look at him. "Okay, fine, I admit it crossed my mind. But as you know, I can't do anything without Jen's consent anyway." She paused to gather her thoughts.

"Here's what bothers me. The Ilya that Elise showed me in the vision loved her so deeply, I could feel it. I believe he would have done anything for her. He wasn't some bad person who deserved to be cut out of his father's will." Jessica picked up her fork and pushed scrambled eggs around on her plate, not really seeing them. "What if Vadim intended to change the will and put Ilya back in it, but he died first?"

"That's something we'll never know. According to this copy, though, if *any* changes are made to the bequests, the entire estate goes to some music conservatory. And if you're wondering whether Dianne Maggio or Darryl Andrews had something to do with Vadim Evanov's car accident, I don't think $100,000 is enough to kill over."

"I swear, Sage Boles, you are a mind reader," Jessica grinned. "It doesn't make any sense, but that thought was sneaking into my mind right when you said it."

He grinned back at her. "Your mind is transparent enough for me to read. So, if you don't want to keep the inheritance, I suggest you accept the terms and after that, if you want to sell or give it away, you can consider the offer from Amy's client."

Jessica stared glumly at her plate. "If Jenna follows through on her threat, I won't have a choice."

twenty-eight

DIRTY GREY CLOUDS FOLLOWED them all the way back to Herron Pond. Conversation in Sage's truck continued to center on Vadim Evanov's will and his puzzling decision to cut out his only son and presumed heir. Without additional information, there were no answers to be had, and once they had exhausted the topic, Sage, who was almost as fascinated with the estate as Jessica, wanted to talk about the mansion. He had visited all of the rooms in the new wing, and the second-floor bedrooms in the Victorian wing—in particular, the practice room where Elise's diary had been hidden. Jessica had yet to show him the salon, or any of the 'public rooms' on the ground floor.

Black clouds were gathering like an angry mob as they arrived at the estate, bringing the imminent threat of thunderstorms.

"How about some coffee before we resume the tour?" Jessica suggested.

"A woman who knows what I want. I'll brew us the old-fashioned kind; no fancy pods for me."

"Looks like the rain could start any minute. I'm glad we're inside where it's toasty."

"Don't speak too soon." Sage was looking out the window that faced out onto Herron Pond. "There's someone down by the lake; a dude."

Jessica followed the jerk of his chin. "That's the estate manager. I wonder what he's up to out there in this weather."

"Andrews? The guy I've heard so much about?" Leaving the coffee maker, Sage shrugged into the jacket he had just removed. "I want to meet him."

Darryl Andrews was crouched over an upended maroon-painted canoe on the shore, poking at something in the craft's bottom. Hearing them coming, he straightened and turned to greet them. The two men shook hands and sized each other up the way men do. Once the introductions were over, Andrews ignored Jessica and directed his attention to Sage. "The fellow who takes care of the maintenance left a few minutes ago. He'd been meaning to repair a rip in this guy for a while."

"What happened to it?" Sage asked, openly curious.

"Some guests last fall—crazy musicians. Got wasted and took it out without knowing what in hell they were doing. Ran into a rock, pushed in this section at the front. Lucky they got it back to shore without sinking it." Andrews indicated the repair, a rough, whitish patch on the hull, approximately the size of a cell phone. "It's been sitting in the boathouse, waiting for Steve to come and patch it up. What with Mr. Evanov passing away and all, not long after that—well, there weren't gonna be any more guests, so we let it go; no big rush to take care of it. When we heard there were new owners coming up to have a look-see." He cut his eyes at Jessica, a disapproving sidelong glance, not directly acknowledging her presence. "Steve was in the neighborhood today, so he stopped by and got it patched before the rain starts up again. He'll have to paint it some other time when the weather's better."

"It's 'seaworthy' now?'" Sage asked.

Andrews gave a short nod. "Not that you'd want to be out on the pond in this weather."

"Not with the storm coming," Sage said. And in her mind, Jessica agreed. She would not want to be on the pond, or lake, or whatever you called it, in *any* weather. Unlike Jenna, who had the instincts of a mermaid. If she ever gave Herron Pond a second chance on a warmer day, it would be Jenna who rowed out onto the lake.

Andrews continued talking to Sage about the grounds and the acreage and the private beach. There was something in his look that bordered on insolence and she wanted to know what was behind his need to slight her. He had received a generous reward for his years of service. Wasn't $100,000 enough for him? Or did his resentful attitude stem from her, a stranger, coming in and taking over, while he had worked at Herron Pond for so long?

Jessica had found that as small as she was, she was often not taken seriously by men of Andrews's ilk. Refusing to let them get in her way, she had grown an attitude of her own. She took a step into his space that demanded his attention. "I didn't expect to see you here today, Mr. Andrews. Where's your car?"

As if she were a normally quiescent pet that had suddenly bitten him, he couldn't have looked more surprised. Extinguishing the look, he took a step away from her. "If it's important that you know, my car is in the garage, out of the weather. I didn't expect to see you either, Ms. Mack. I thought you were supposed to leave last weekend."

Her chin went up. "I wasn't aware there was an expiration date on my visit. My sister and her family decided to come up on Sunday, so we postponed until tomorrow; maybe later. We haven't decided." She tried to hold his eyes, but Andrews looked away and bent over to flip the canoe upright, speaking over his shoulder.

"You didn't say you were staying on, so I had the housekeepers in today."

"It's a lot to keep up," Sage noted, effortlessly defusing the tension he must recognize was building in Jessica like a mini volcano. "The place is amazing. You must have a very well-trained crew, inside and out."

"I won't argue with that," Andrews agreed. "I normally schedule the cleaners when they're not going to bother anyone. You weren't here this morning…" He paused, letting the sentence hang in a question mark.

"We took a drive," Jessica said, refusing him the satisfaction of knowing where they had gone.

His flat brown eyes gave nothing away. "Well, they cleaned up the rooms where you've been staying, so you're all set. They're working on the other side."

"I don't want anyone cleaning up after me," Jessica said, mortified at the thought of someone picking up her lingerie from the bedroom floor.

"It's what they get paid for." Directing a small salute and a nod at Sage, Andrews said, "Unless there's something you need from me, I'll be on my way. The rain is gonna start up again soon enough."

They said their goodbyes and stood on the driveway watching his car disappear through the avenue of trees.

"Dude's all charm," Sage noted with uncharacteristic sarcasm.

"If by 'charm' you mean he's a total ass." Jessica squeezed his hand. "He gives me the willies and pisses me off at the same time—treating me like the hired help. What the hell is up with that? If you weren't here, I might have popped off and slugged him."

That made him chuckle. "He's a jerk. You're his boss and he's trying to intimidate you. Don't let him."

"I won't." Tamping down the spark of antagonism Andrews's behavior had set off in her, she shrugged philosophically. "Do you still want coffee, or should we get on with the tour?"

"Coffee can wait," Sage said. "Lead on, darling."

She took him first to the salon where she had channeled Elise's piano playing. Jessica ran her fingers lightly over the keys, trying to attract the spirit's attention, mildly disappointed when Elise failed to show up. "I was hoping she would want to play for you. I bet you'd be a lot more impressed with her music than Andrews was."

Sage pulled her against him and leaned down to kiss the top of her head. "Like you said, angel, he's an ass. Working for Maestro Evanov doesn't mean the dude has an ear for music."

"Good point," she conceded. "And, speaking of the maestro, I'll show you his study last. We can take our time and look at any papers he kept in his desk. I hope they're not written in Russian, like his diary, or whatever that book was on the desktop. We'll never be able to decipher it."

"Don't give up so fast," Sage said. "I know a Russian guy who could translate."

Jessica couldn't help being amused. "I should've known, Mr. Boles. That's one of a thousand or so things I love about you—you are a man of many solutions." She slipped her arm through his and led him to the next room.

When he'd had his fill of Victorian architecture and formal furnishings and had commented on the smoking room, they descended the flight of back stairs to the old kitchen.

Sage, as Jessica had on her first visit there, prowled around, opening and closing the wide drawers and cupboards, inspecting the vintage appliances and cooking utensils as closely as if they had been visiting a scullery museum.

"Check out all this fancy silverware and linens," he said. "There must have been some happenin' parties in the old homestead."

"Yup, the place is equipped to entertain. Dianne Maggio said famous people came here from all over the world for Mr. Evanov's recitals." As they stood there soaking it all up, a dreamy sensation poured over Jessica like a warm shower. "I'm getting the feeling that he enjoyed the prestige. He would have wanted his events to have all the bells and whistles."

Sage gave her an affectionate elbow bump. "Is that a psychic feeling?"

"Maybe. I think so. It's not just that, though, the photos of him in his study have that kind of vibe. After all, he was 'the Maestro.'" Jessica walked to the one door they had not yet opened. "Last time I was down here was the day there was all that spirit activity—the day I channeled Elise and met our buddy, Darryl Andrews. I got a migraine and went to lie down, and woke up in the turret."

"And here you are again. Let's see what's behind the mysterious door."

As Sage spoke, she felt a chill, and involuntarily shrank from it. "It's probably another pantry," she said.

He snaked an arm past her and twisted the old-fashioned barrel key in the lock beneath the doorknob. "How about we find out?" He pulled the door open.

"Oh!" she exclaimed. This was not what she had expected.

Facing them was a small square landing surrounded by unfinished brick walls. A rough wooden staircase disappeared into murky pitch-darkness below. He pressed a push-button light switch on the wall. A naked light-bulb dangling from the ceiling flickered and blinked on, disturbing a fat brown spider from the string of web it had been lolling on. It scurried up the web and out of sight of the rude human visitors.

"Do you think we've discovered a secret passage?" Sage said.

Jessica could see he was only half-joking. "It's behind a kitchen door, so not exactly secret. I wonder where it leads."

"The cellar would be my guess." He bounced an eyebrow at her. "You're raring to go down there, aren't you?"

"Uh, no, I'm definitely not. There's something fundamentally unpleasant about a dark basement. Especially in an old Victorian mansion."

His low chuckle was intended to sound devilish. "Good thing we're not teens in a movie."

The look she threw him was self-mocking, fully aware that, as little as she wanted to, she was going to descend those stairs. He was aware of it, too. "We don't have to," he said. "Or, do we?"

"You know we do. I wouldn't go alone, but with you to scare the spiders away, what do I have to worry about?"

"To be fair, it's us who disturbed the spider—"

"Hairsplitting. Let's get this over with, Mr. Boles."

"You're the boss, boss." He drew one of the wooden chairs away from the table and jammed its top rail under the door handle.

"Good idea," Jessica said. "You go first. I'll be right behind you."

The lightbulb was connected to a wire strung along the wall and followed the staircase handrail down, terminating at a brick-walled chamber that measured about ten by fifteen feet. Overhead, the lights shone dimly on racks of wine bottles and dingy black and white tile flooring. An arched doorway at the far end appeared to lead to another underground room.

Jessica, who was wearing sweatshirt and jeans, shivered. "It's freezing down here. If I'd known we were going underground I would have worn my outdoor jacket."

"Wine cellars are kept in the mid-50's." Sage's voice sounded hollow in the dreary chamber. "Or maybe it's cold because it's ... a ghost portal."

"Not funny."

"Oh, too soon?"

Jessica wrinkled her nose. "Smells musty."

"Don't be surprised if we run into a dead Victorian rat or two or a bunch."

"Doesn't that sound like fun." She walked over to the wine racks and blew on one of the grimy labels. A cloud of dust rose and made her sneeze. "Oh, man, judging from the dust on these bottles, whoever was last down here, it probably wasn't in this century. Maybe we should take one with us and see if it's any good."

"Sure, let's," he said absently. Sage wasn't looking at the wine bottles. An antiquated electrical panel had captured his attention. The wires terminated on one side and started up on the other. Identical to the one at the top of the stairs, a single lightbulb hung from the ceiling.

"If I'm not wrong, this panel has been here since the turn of the century *before* the last one."

"No wonder your name is Sage, oh wise one. Since when are you up on Victorian wiring?"

"Since I did some reading this morning while you were in slumberland. This is called knob-and-tube. See, there's one black hot wire and one white neutral—"

"Okay, Bob Vila, you are way more interested in wiring than I am." Looking around in the dim light, from where they stood, Jessica could see only the wine racks disappearing into the shadows. "I'm kind of amazed it's so dilapidated down here. Thank God the rest of the house has been updated, even if they didn't bother rewiring the cellar."

They started to move away from the staircase, squinting in the gloom. Something about the old cables clicked in her head. "Do you think it might have been the wiring that started the fire Amy told me about?"

"Bad wiring does often cause house fires, and it doesn't have to be Victorian made. You said the fire was about eight years ago, right? Google should have some reference to it. The local online papers will have covered such a destructive fire; especially since you said someone died in it—Evanov's caregiver."

"Omigod. Sage!"

"What's wrong, angel?"

Jessica gaped at him, stricken. "I can't believe I didn't make the connection until right now. It was Elise. *Elise* and Ilya were the caretakers. *Elise* died in the fire here."

He took her hands in his. "What makes you think it was her?"

"The vision she showed me this morning. Remember, I told you that she and Ilya were talking about being here to take care of his father? She was scared that someone was trying to kill her. What she actually said was, *'She's trying to kill me.'*"

"Rostya," he said. Awareness and distress dawned on his face. "Rostya somehow started the fire that killed her."

"Do you really think it's possible?" she said. "I didn't think a ghost could kill a human, but..." The muscles in her neck and shoulders spasmed painfully. Seeing her reach up to rub them, he stepped behind her and began to massage and knead out the knots.

"I don't know, angel, but it seems to fit."

"Maybe a ghost can't kill a human directly, but can do something that causes their death."

He dropped his hands and they stared at each other, the chilling realization buzzing between them like a horde of angry bees. A feeling of darkness fell over her that had nothing to do with the poor lighting. Were they crazy to think such a thing? It didn't feel crazy.

The idea was too hideous to contemplate for more than a moment. "Let's see what's through that doorway and get out of here," Jessica said. "This place has all the charm of a dungeon." Her shudder was a visceral repudiation. "Can you imagine being left down here to rot in the dark?"

"Now, there's a happy thought."

Sage took her hand and they walked to the archway at the end of the chamber and stepped through into the next one. The dim lighting showed a miscellany of forgotten junk stacked against the walls. A collection of chipped Brown Betty teapots. An empty flowerpot in a rusty saucepan. Piles of old dishes littered on the floor, some broken, others whole and painted with the grime of more than a century. Someone had braced a tall interior door against a wall, the paint cracked and scratched.

At the rear of the chamber was another arched doorway, another corridor, another subterranean room. Sheets of plaster peeled off the walls looking like a three-day-old sunburn. This far into the cellar, the flooring and walls were a rougher brick. And the further into its depths they walked, the more detritus littered the floor—rusty machines and parts of machines from times gone by whose use they could only hazard a guess.

"It's all fascinating," Sage said. "Like walking through a time capsule."

Jessica was not fascinated. The place was giving her the heebie-jeebies. "I just want to leave," she said.

He squeezed her hand. "Okay, angel, let's get out of here."

They turned back and were halfway through the chamber when the distant sound of a slammed door reached them. Three seconds later, the overhead lights went out.

twenty-nine

Jessica's heart lurched into overdrive. She didn't intend to scream; it just came out. She seized hold of Sage's sweatshirt. "The door shut. Who shut the door? Oh, God, do you think it was Rostya?" It all came out in a stream, high-pitched and strained.

His arms encircled her and held her against him. "Don't panic yet, angel."

Too late for that.

He was close enough that she could feel the heat radiating from his body, but though she opened her eyes wider, the inky blackness was blinding. When he said, "Hang on to me," he didn't have to ask twice. She felt him fumbling in his pocket. Something skittered across her foot, making her squeal. Was it her imagination that the temperature seemed to take a sudden dive?

Her dread of cold, dark places grabbed her around the throat and for one terrible moment dragged her right back to the cold, dark basement she had been locked in once before. It had been the night when the impenetrable fog of amnesia had started to lift, tormenting her with flashes of agonizing memories that had no context.

This time, she reminded herself, there was a big difference. This time, she knew who she was, and she was not alone. And yet, those truths did not keep thoughts of Rostya Evanov and the power her spirit had displayed from intruding into her mind and smoldering there. Was Rostya capable of moving the chair Sage had used to prop open the door? Had she been so soon released from the place where she had been banished?

Sage's phone screen winked on, bringing Jessica back from the sneaking suspicion that the entity was plenty capable of causing the cellar door to slam shut. The flashlight app illuminated the chamber better than the electric lights had.

"Is there any reception?" she asked.

"Zero bars."

"Dianne was right. She said the cell service is bad on the old side of the house."

"Let's go." Sage took her hand again. With the flashlight illuminating their way, they hurried back through the chambers, retracing their steps all the way back, past the wine racks. At the foot of the stairs that led up to the kitchen, he handed her his phone so she could shine the light on the door at the top.

Sage ran up the steps. The doorknob was as securely locked as Jessica had intuitively known it would be. They were prisoners in the cellar.

"Fuck. Fuck. Fuck." Each expletive came louder than the last as he delivered a vicious kick at the door, then kicked it again. When that produced no results, he hammered the sturdy wood with the side of his fist "Hey! Open the goddamn door! *Hey!*"

In the months she had known him, anger was one emotion she had rarely heard Sage express. He had confessed to her that it had gotten him into serious trouble more than once, and he had fought a hard-won battle to get it under control. Even so, Jessica was glad for his anger now. They might well need it to get out of here.

Sage backed up to the edge of the small landing. Bringing his knee up and, aiming at the lock area, he smash-kicked the door with the flat of his boot. The sound echoed through the cellar but the move was as effective as kicking a stone wall. In the low light he looked pale and purposeful as he tried again. And again. The door failed to budge and he rammed it with his shoulder.

"It's not working," Jessica said. Her drooping mood told her that this was no random act. "Please stop. You'll hurt yourself."

He rejoined her at the foot of the stairs, rubbing his shoulder. "Maybe there's another way to get out that we didn't see. We might not have gone into all the rooms."

"Some of those alcoves might have led to other rooms or hidden a door." Jessica made herself force an optimism she didn't feel. In reality, she was struggling to keep the tiny flame of hope from flickering out and she didn't want Sage to see how afraid she was.

Looking for anything that could be used to batter the door, they made one more pass through the chambers they had already seen. Old wine bottles and broken china were of no use. Sage grabbed a wooden stud from stack of two-by-fours and hefted it in his hands the way he would a baseball bat. "This might come in handy. Especially if we run into whoever shut us in."

"It'd make some noise against the door," Jessica said. "And save your shoulder."

"Yeah, but as we just learned, noise isn't enough." They were in one of the chambers where they had seen a scattering of tools. Sage's light picked an old crowbar out of the murk. He handed Jessica the two-by-four and grabbed the metal rod with a low growl of satisfaction. "This might do the job."

"I'd like to use that on whoever shut us in here," Jessica said darkly.

"I never knew you had a violent streak." He actually sounded amused.

"Getting locked in a basement mucks up my naturally peaceful nature."

"Can't argue with that. Let's keep looking."

They were in a maze of dank, dark chambers. Coming to one they had not yet entered, they reached a corner that led into another corridor, which led to a final doorway. A dark rectangle of an opening. Shining his light through it, Sage stepped inside and aimed his phone at bare stone walls and a dirt floor with a sound of disgust. "There's nothing in here."

Jessica, unwilling to accept defeat just yet, fished her phone out of her pocket and swung the flashlight around the room, pointing it high up. Her breath caught. "Sage, look, there's a window."

Their flashlight beams joined and lit up a dim oblong shape on one of the walls. Dull greenish light filtered through glass so dirt-crusted it was almost opaque. Sage stood six-three and the bottom of the sash was at chin level for him. Rising on the balls of his feet, he stretched up and ran his fingers along the sill and jamb, looking for a latch.

"Shit, there's no way to open it."

"Are you sure?" Jessica felt her heart sink as low as it could go.

"Yeah, I'm sure. It's fixed in place." He peered through the grimy pane. "We're lucky it's not one of those old glass block windows. That'd be a lot harder to break." He switched off his light to save the battery. "The bottom of the window is at ground level. I don't know what part of the house we're under, but there's a ton of thick plants in front of it. That's what's blocking the light."

Gauging the window size, Jessica judged it to be approximately two and a half feet wide and eighteen inches high. "If you can break it, I can climb out," she said. She didn't have to state the obvious: there was no way Sage would fit through the opening.

There was a moment's hesitation that made it clear he was not happy with her solution. "It may be the only way," he said at last with a sigh. "I'll lift you on my shoulders."

She nearly jumped up and down. "I'll take that over being locked in here any day."

He looked down at her for another long moment, and she knew he was seeing the determination settle on her features. "Once the window is broken and the glass cleared away, getting through that thick growth is going to be the hardest part," he said.

Jessica's mind was buzzing. She had been focused on getting free before their phone batteries started to die. Now that a solution was in sight, a new idea was building up a head of steam.

"We can use that door we saw leaning against the wall in one of the rooms. We can make it a ramp. Wouldn't that be easier than trying to climb out from your shoulders?"

Sage considered it and agreed. "That could work. Once you get out, you'll have to find a way to re-enter the house. Did you lock the patio door after we met up with Andrews? I didn't."

"Maybe. I don't remember. Look, if I have to, I'll break another window and set off the alarm. One way or another, I'll be here to open the door for you. It should only take a few minutes." Jessica tried to block the voice in her head that said, *depending on who shut it. It might not be that easy.*

Regardless, they had a plan and she was ready to implement it.

They went back through the chambers and found the interior door leaning against the wall. It was tall, and heavier than it looked, but they agreed that its weight worked in their favor. Lugging it between them, they maneuvered it around the corners with some difficulty and stood it against the wall. Sage studied the window. "The glass looks thick. I'm gonna guess it's tempered."

"Which means?"

"Which means there are two panes of glass with a small space between them. The bad news is, that makes it harder to break."

"What's the good news?" Jessica asked, longing to hear something that would improve their odds of escape. No one would ever think to look for them down here.

"The *good* news is, it's less likely to break up into big, dangerous pieces and fall on me."

"And me?"

"You, my angel, will be safely on the other side of the room."

"Oh."

Once he had made sure she was out of harm's way, Sage swung the crowbar into a lower corner of the sturdy pane and made a small hole. Two more hard swings and a spiderweb of fractures radiated outward. Before he could swing a third time, a cracking sound echoed across the glass and a fractal pattern of lethal art spread from one edge to the other.

Lifting the crowbar above his head, with a grunt of effort Sage brought it down at the top of the frame. The glass exploded and came apart. Chunks and shards fell to the floor.

The empty frame gaped like a toothless mouth, letting in a rush of frigid air and the burnt wire smell of ozone from the storm. Jessica didn't care that the cold stung her cheeks. They had made a way out of this abominable place. She crossed the room, crunching on broken glass, and held up her light on Sage, who was gingerly patting his face. "Did you get cut?"

"A splinter or two; no big deal."

"Your cheek is bleeding."

Covering his hand with his sweatshirt sleeve, he reached up to dab at the pinpricks of blood on his face. "I'll worry about it when we're out of here."

A sudden flare of lightning lit the chamber. The rumble of thunder boomed through the open window frame. Then the rain came—great sheets of it. Rain like Jessica had never seen in her Southern California life.

After the heavy downpour that had continued on and off throughout the day, the earth outside the window, already saturated, gave up and overflowed. With no glass pane to stop it, a half-dozen rivulets began to pour in through the opening and run down the wall, splashing onto the floor and the shattered glass.

"Let's get the door over here," Jessica said, propelled by an instinctive sense of urgency that was growing stronger with every passing second. "Hurry, we need to make the ramp."

But Sage shook his head. "The storm is too strong right now. We can wait until it calms down. As tiny as you are, that wind will blow you all the way to Kansas."

"In case you hadn't noticed, this is not the Wizard of Oz. The storm could go on for hours." She was as close to yelling at him as she ever had been, and the strength of her reaction left her feeling baffled.

Aiming his light in her direction, Sage looked into her face, as confused as she was. He frowned in disbelief. "We can wait for the worst of it to die down."

"No. I'm not staying down here a minute longer than I have to."

His lips compressed into a thin line, he looked away from her. When he spoke, his had tone cooled. "This isn't a good time to be stubborn, Jess—"

"*Stubborn?* I may be *'tiny'* but I'm not a child. Don't treat me like one." Paradoxically, she wanted to stamp her foot and prove herself wrong. She railed at him, barely holding on to her temper. "As soon as we get that door in place, I'm going. If you won't help me, I'll do it myself."

Sage turned away and began silently to work the crowbar, chiseling away the remains of glass that clung to the edges of the frame. The heavy greenery outside was keeping most of the rain at bay, leaving mini Niagaras streaming down the wall and pooling on the floor.

Disapproval radiated from him like a sore that Jessica had opened and picked at for no good reason. Could she blame Rostya for influencing her emotions? Or was it a case of PTSD from long-past events? Whatever the cause, it was knotting her stomach.

An uncomfortable silence grew between them. When Sage had cleared the sash of as much glass as he could, he pulled off his sweatshirt.

"What are you doing?" Jessica asked.

Sage calmly folded the sweatshirt and laid the thick padding across the lower window ledge, where it quickly sponged up rainwater. "That should keep your knees protected if any fragments are left on the bottom," He said stiffly without looking at her. He sounded unfamiliar, not like the man she loved with all her being. "Keep your hands away from the sides of the frame as much as you can."

"But you'll freeze." She reached out and clutched his arm. "I'm sorry for my stupid attitude. I don't know what got into me. You don't deserve that kind of treatment when you only want what's best for me."

The taut muscles bunched along his jaw immediately unclenched and he grinned. "We're good," he said, and Jessica knew they truly were. "Not being able to go with you is killing me. We don't know what's waiting out there. I want you to be safe."

"I know," she said. And if he could read her as well as she suspected, he would recognize that her agreement did not mean that she had changed her mind.

Together, they positioned the door at a forty-five-degree angle on the wall. When it was firmly in place and there was nothing more to be done,

Jessica flung her arms around his neck and held him. She knew he could feel her heart beating as wildly as she could feel his. Gazing up into his face, she saw the risk she was taking in leaving him there, and his in staying behind. He lifted her up and she wound her legs around his waist, tilting her face for a lingering kiss. And while they kissed, she squeezed her eyes shut and called on her angels and guides. And on Elise, who had stepped in and sheltered her from Rostya's rage before. She asked Elise to protect them both if she could.

Sage's hands, cold against her face, reminded her of the need to hurry. Jessica opened her eyes. "Meet me at the kitchen door. I'll be there as fast as I can."

He kissed her once more and set her on her feet. "Be safe, angel."

"You, too."

With a thumbs up, he gave her a hand as she tested her weight on the door, setting her right foot on it, then the left. As slight as she was, and as heavy as the door was, the wooden panel held without the slightest bowing. She clambered to the top and scrunched herself into the smallest bundle she could manage.

She pushed her head and shoulders through the opening. The bitter cold stole her breath and returned it on clouds of mist. Looking up, she saw that the eaves of the house were shielding her and the cellar window frame from the worst of the rain. Pulling her sweatshirt hood up over her head, she reached for the nearest clump of flattened wet greenery and grabbed hold. Sage gave her a boost from behind and she wriggled the lower half of her body through the opening, keeping a grip on the slippery stalks until she was confident that she had gained enough of a purchase not to slide back down the slight rise.

Sage had been right when he'd warned that getting through the plants would not be easy, Jessica realized. Twigs scratched at her face. Her sweatshirt rode up, smearing her bare midriff with slime and mud as she elbowed her way, snakelike, through the dense shrubbery. Leaves invaded her eyes and mouth.

She emerged on the waterlogged lawn feeling as though she had hauled herself through a jungle. She climbed to her feet on the other side of the hedge and stepped out from under the protection of the eaves, instantly drenched. As if someone had upended a large bucket directly over her head, her hair clung to her neck under the soaked hoodie. She pushed it off her head and turned to look back at the house. Sage was no longer visible through the vegetation.

Jessica was not familiar enough with the grounds of Herron Pond to know with any certainty where in the house she had exited the cellar. The long grey walls of the mansion stretched behind the barrier of shrubbery she had crawled through. Ahead, a flagstone path wound around the corner and disappeared. The disorienting mix of howling wind, driving rain, and roiling sky conspired against her. But Sage would be watching from the empty window frame, freezing cold and naked from the waist up. That was all the impetus she needed to keep moving.

Hunching her shoulders against the onslaught, Jessica lowered her head like a charging bull and stepped into the howling wind. It drove her along the path, as vengeful as Rostya Evanov, and as brutal as a chain gang boss, all the way to the rear of the house.

thirty

THE POND LOOKED EVEN more like a lake than it had that morning. Swollen like a pregnant belly, it had crept closer to the house than it had been hour or so earlier when they had descended to the cellar. The newly repaired canoe that had rested on the shore during their meeting with Darryl Andrews was now in water several inches deep at the bow.

Approaching the French doors, which opened onto the dining room, Jessica was afraid to allow herself the hope that they might be unlocked. When they were, she fell inside nearly sobbing with relief. The wind ripped the door from her hand and slammed it behind her, leaving the storm raging outside.

Everything she wore was caked in mud. Her boots, wet inside and out, were no better. For a nanosecond she stood where she was, wrapped in the welcome warmth of the house, fighting the temptation to run upstairs and change into dry clothes. But Sage was in the cellar and nothing mattered as much as getting him out.

Without a thought to the muck she was tracking across the spotless floors, Jessica ran straight to the foyer. From upstairs, the sounds of a bump, a scrape, a faint whirring brought her to an abrupt standstill. She was not alone in the house. Rostya? Elise? Someone human?

Whoever, or whatever, was upstairs would have to wait. She would not give Rostya, or whoever had locked them in, the opportunity to do worse. The thought of Sage, waiting for her on the small landing behind a locked door, kept her moving to the Victorian kitchen.

She ran down the stairs expecting to find everything the way they had left it when they entered the cellar. Her first glance told her that something was very different.

The chair that Sage had jammed under the door handle to keep it open was in its place at the table. Her mind was already brimming with questions, she ran to the cellar door and reached for the key. Her hand halted midway, her brain struggling to process the sight of an empty keyhole.

Who did this?

He has to be safe. He has to be safe. He has to be safe. It reran in her head like a mantra as Jessica banged on the door with her fists and yelled his name. "Are you there? Are you okay?"

"I'm here, open the damn door!"

"I can't—the key is gone—I heard noises upstairs—I don't know who's there—" The words rushed out and she had to force herself to slow down and take control of the runaway emotions that were tying her stomach in knots. She heard him curse.

Then, "Andrews said he had people cleaning today. Find them. There must be an extra key."

The realization that he was right and what she had heard upstairs was not some diabolical mischief-making entity left her limp with gratitude. A housecleaner was something easily dealt with.

"Hang tight," she called to him, already halfway across the kitchen. "I'm going for help."

Her boots had run out of mud to trail on the pristine carpets as she dashed up the grand staircase to the second floor. Her clothes, as sodden as if they had been removed from the washing machine ahead of the spin cycle, adhered to her body, cold and clammy. She approached the second-floor landing and the whirring, which was still going strong, resolved into the pragmatic earthly sound of a vacuum cleaner.

From the doorway of Vadim Evanov's spacious bedroom, Jessica saw a slender woman dressed in blue scrubs and a sweater, her hair tucked under a bright red bandanna. She was faced away from Jessica, pushing the vacuum in long strokes across the plush carpet, her hips and shoulders gyrating to some inaudible music while she worked—maybe rap, judging by the rhythm.

A yell across the room failed to penetrate her earbuds. Coming up behind her, Jessica tapped the cleaner's shoulder, eliciting an unearthly shriek worthy of any spirit. The young woman—she was not much more than a teenager—dropped the vacuum wand and whirled on her. Her face was drained of color. Pure terror dilated her irises to black saucers.

When it registered that Jessica was a living being, the look of terror shifted to an angry scowl. Ripping out the earbuds, she switched off the vacuum and bent over, hands on knees. One hand was pressed to her heaving chest as if she had run a marathon, and she stayed that way for a good ten seconds. "Oh, my friggin' god, I thought you were the ghost."

"Were you down in the kitchen a while ago?" Jessica demanded, caring less about scaring her than who finding out who had imprisoned her and Sage. "Did you shut the cellar door?"

The cleaner straightened, gaping at her as if she didn't understand the question. "You scared the ever livin' crap outta me. What did you say?"

"Did you shut the cellar door?"

"What? The cellar? I have no idea where it is and I sure as hell wouldn't go there if I did."

"Shit!" Jessica's shivering shoulders sagged. She had known in her gut that it wasn't this girl who had trapped them, but she'd had to ask. For the first time in their brief exchange, the young woman appeared to really look at her and see her filthy clothing and matted hair.

"You're soaking. You were outside in that weather?"

No shit.

She disappeared into the en suite, reappearing with a luxurious Turkish bath sheet, which Jessica took with thanks and wrapped, cape-like, around her shoulders. "Someone's locked in the cellar. I've got to get him out. Where is there a spare key?"

"You're kidding me," The cleaner's eyes grew bigger and rounder with a sick sort of dread. "How does that even happen?"

"I don't know!" Jessica itched to shake a helpful answer out of her. "Who cleans downstairs?"

"Um, that'd be Patty."

"I didn't see anyone. Where can I find her?"

"It's not her day. Anyhow, Mr. Andrews is the only one who has keys."

Frustration was eating an acid crater into Jessica's stomach lining. "Dammit, he left an hour ago."

The cleaner shook her head, denying what Jessica had seen with her own eyes. "No, he didn't. I saw him a little bit ago when I was cleaning the veranda windows. He's gotta be around here somewhere."

Was the woman mistaken or lying? Jessica's eyes narrowed, assessing her demeanor. She and Sage had seen the estate manager drive away. Had he returned while they were exploring the Victorian wing? Had it been Darryl Andrews who shut them in the cellar? She spoke sharply to the cleaner. "How long ago did you see him?"

"Hey, I didn't look at the time. It wasn't all that long ago, though." The careless one-shoulder shrug the house cleaner gave her showed the complete lack of understanding of how important feedback was.

"What's your name?" Jessica asked.

"Eva," she said pertly. "Who the hell are you?"

"One of the new owners."

Leaving Eva with her mouth agape, Jessica bolted down to the kitchen, hell-bent on finding a way to get the cellar door open and releasing Sage.

But that wasn't necessary.

The key had been returned to the lock.

***

In the extravagant Roman-style bathroom in the new wing, wide marble steps led up to a tub flanked by white columns that rose to the ceiling. Wide window walls looked out into the crowns of the leafless trees and cotton puff clouds, making it feel as though they were outdoors. Yet, even in the face of such luxury, as she lay in the hot steam, snug in Sage's embrace, the chill in Jessica's bones had not left her. Nor did it as they fortified themselves afterwards with a bowl of chicken noodle soup. A shot of good whiskey did nothing to warm her soul, either.

The rain had fizzled and the wind died down. They were safe together, and she had not been able to bring herself to talk about what had happened. The events of the afternoon remained unanalyzed until at last they were sitting together on the rug in front of the fire they had built in the library-den.

They looked at each other in unspoken agreement that the time had come. Sage, who had been champing at the bit, was the first to speak. "So, what the hell? Is it Darryl Andrews playing tricks for some reason?"

"You and I both saw Andrews leave long before we went down to the kitchen. Eva the maid must have gotten mixed up on the time."

A hint of skepticism glinted in Sage's eyes. "He could have come back to screw with us for some reason."

"It's a big house," Jessica acknowledged. "But even if he did come back, he wouldn't know where we were going to be."

"Could he have got in and followed us without us knowing?"

Remembering her initial feeling of stepping into a game of Clue upon arriving at Herron Pond, she couldn't help laughing. It felt good to let go of some of the residual tension. "What? A secret passage? He was looking through holes in the eyes of a painting? Colonel Mustard in the library with a candlestick?" The moment of humor passed quickly and the question became serious again. "As huge as this place is, and him having all the keys and codes, I guess he could easily get in and out without us knowing. But *why* would he want to scare us? What would be his motive? I don't think he wants us to sell. He'd lose his cushy job."

"I have no idea, but is the alternative any more palatable?"

Jessica heaved a sigh. "Rostya? I'm not sure which is worse—being locked up by the estate manager or a hateful entity. And, by the way, for about a millisecond Eva thought *I* was a ghost, so I'd say she's experienced something that scared her."

"She could have heard about it from someone," Sage countered.

"Hmm, she could have. She's too young to have been here when Carmela was working, but maybe some of the older staff talk about it—especially if they've run across Rostya, or even Elise. Most people can't handle friendly spirits any easier than—"

Sage held up a restraining hand. "Let's start with the idea of Andrews trying to scare you—or us—away. We need to figure out why."

"And if it was him, why replace the key after we thought we were locked in?"

"That's easy. So that if something happened to us down there, there would be plausible deniability—they could say the door was unlocked; we could have gotten out."

"Say it was Andrews, then. What did he plan to do, leave us down there?"

"Depends on whether he intended to scare us, or..."

Jessica finished the sentence. "Kill us." She shuddered. "I'd rather it was Rostya."

"Killing is as extreme as it gets. What would he have to gain?"

"The terms of the will are clear. He got his hundred-thousand-dollar bequest, plus he was paid his salary for the rest of the year." She saw something flare in Sage's eyes. "What?"

"The offer from Amy's client. Eighteen million dollars would earn her a *huge* commission, and she said the client might go even higher." Sage did a quick reckoning in his head. "Assuming a five percent commission, that's nearly a million bucks. If she brokered both sides of the deal, it could be even more."

"Amy and Andrews are working together to get us to sell?" She felt the jab of disillusionment like a punch to the gut. She liked Amy and believed they had connected as friends. She could not imagine the other woman being capable of the kind of duplicity they were considering.

Sage shrugged. "I don't know, angel, but someone locked us in the cellar. And a plausible reason could be to scare you into selling."

"I can't see Amy being involved in something like that," she insisted.

"Maybe she's not aware of it. Maybe Andrews is using her for his own ends. Look, it's nothing more than a theory."

"Okay, that cheers me up. A tiny bit."

"And what about the other woman—Maggio?"

"You think Dianne is in on it, too?" Jessica thought about her instinctive distrust of the woman. Was this what she had been picking up psychically?

He grabbed a log and tossed it onto the fire, sending a shower of sparks up the chimney. "I have no idea, but we need to consider the possibilities before we start blaming a ghost."

"Okay," she agreed. "I have an idea. I need to let Andrews know there's a broken window in the basement so he can get it fixed. Let's call him and see how he reacts to the fact that we're not locked up."

Sage was quiet for a moment, considering her suggestion. "It'd be a lot better if we could see his face when you tell him."

"Yeah, but I doubt he'll show up here right away. In any event, not where we can see his reaction."

"Which means that if he *is* responsible and there hadn't been a window, we could have been stuck down there for days or worse."

"Oh, thanks for that image."

"Nah. Jenna would be up here in a hot minute if she couldn't get hold of you. You piss each other off every thirty seconds, but you have that twin thing going. And you love each other." He leaned over and kissed the tip of her nose. "Go for it, angel. Call him."

She had programmed the estate manager's number into her phone. He picked up the call straight away. She put him on speaker so Sage could listen in.

Andrews's deep voice boomed over loud background noise. "Ms. Mack?"

Was it consternation she'd heard, or plain old surprise that she would be calling him? She let the silence hang, her ears tuned for any inflection when he spoke next.

"Everything okay up there?" he asked after a pause.

With a significant glance at Sage, she answered, "No, Darryl, everything is not okay. Where are you? How far away?"

He paused again, perhaps out of reluctance to share his location with her. "I'm still in Big Sur. I'm at a restaurant—Nepenthe. Hold on a sec, let me get someplace quieter." He must have held the phone against his chest or otherwise stifled the sound, but Jessica could hear him tell someone that it was her on the phone. A woman responded, and while she could not hear what she said, Jessica could have sworn the voice she heard was Dianne Maggio's.

thirty-one

"So, we're more suspicious but have no more information." Jessica topped up their glasses with what they discovered was a very nice cabernet they had brought up from the cellar. She had stood against the door, making sure it stayed open while Sage retrieved a couple of bottles.

He raised his glass to her. "Suspicions add up."

"Good ol' Darryl didn't sound particularly surprised to hear about our adventures in the cellar."

"He was smooth as honey the way he brushed off the 'mystery of the missing key and the moving chair' as if you'd dreamed it."

"Or I was making it up."

"You didn't accuse him of anything. Maybe you should have."

"He all but accused *me* of it being my imagination." Indignation rose like bile in her throat as she relived the conversation with Darryl Andrews. "He was more upset about the busted window and the rain getting into the cellar than us being locked in there."

Sage regarded her with a sympathetic eye. "Some men feel threatened by a female boss."

"Ya think?" Jessica retorted. "I don't give a good crap if he's threatened. If I get any proof that he locked us up, he's fired."

Sage got to his feet and held out a hand to her. "It's time we did some digging. Carmela said our buddy Darryl was here for the house fire. Let's start there."

A Victorian mansion set on stunning grounds with a sensational ocean view was badly damaged by fire Friday night. The owner, Vadim Evanov, narrowly escaped the conflagration when his son carried him out of the burning house. The elder Mr. Evanov had been recovering at home after recent heart surgery. Tragically, his daughter-in-law, Elise Evanov née Sharpe, was unable to escape and succumbed to smoke inhalation at the site. Her distraught husband had to be forcibly restrained when he attempted to re-enter the home and search for her.

Local residents will recall that this is not the first time tragedy has struck at the property. In 1999, Mr. Evanov's seven-year-old grandson passed away due to an undiagnosed illness, followed a few months later by the suicide of his mother, also a Russian national.

Ms. Sharpe, the younger Mr. Evanov's second wife, and a celebrated former pianist, surprised audiences by disappearing from the US classical music stage in the late 1980s when she relocated to Europe and took a lengthy break from a budding career.

A spokesperson for the Evanov family indicated that the 10,000 square-foot mansion, known as Herron Pond, was originally constructed in 1880 and had been fully restored. According to sources, the multi-million-dollar estate will be rebuilt.

Firefighters were called to the scene by the estate manager, Mr. Darryl Andrews. The cause of the fire has yet to be determined. Ms. Sharpe is survived by her parents and two younger brothers. Private services will be held at an undisclosed location.

Jessica swiped at her eyes, choking away tears that suddenly clogged her throat, embarrassed to be crying for a woman she had never known. Glancing at Sage from under wet lashes, she saw his eyes were glassy, too, and knew he was the last person who would judge her for her compassion.

"So, it really was Elise who died in the fire." Sage said in a subdued tone. "What a godawful thing to happen. How Ilya got through that, especially after losing his first wife and child—it's unimaginable."

"After rescuing his father and losing his wife in the process, Ilya got cut out of the will regardless," Jessica said, anger flooding through her. There was clearly more to Vadim Evanov than a kindly old man who wanted to gift two strangers his estate. "What kind of person could do something like that?"

Chicken soup roiled in her innards, threatening to make an unwelcome reappearance. "I want to know what happened when Elise went to Europe. If Vadim was hateful enough to force Ilya to marry Rostya while she was gone, she would have been devastated. And look how it all ended up with both of them dead. It's tragic and it sucks. And what happened to Ilya?"

Something else hit her. "The fire was only eight years ago. That article—and my vision—said they were here together at Herron Pond, taking care of his father when it happened." Jessica's scalp prickled as if a light electrical charge had touched her. Sage, seeing something change in her face, raised his brow in a question. She signaled him to stay silent while she spoke to the spirit in her mind.

Is that you, Elise?

The prickle came again.

What do you want to tell me?

Rather than impressing words on her mind, Elise sent an image: Jessica in a small boat on a lake. With the meanness of a recurring nightmare, her worst childhood memory burst back and left her shaking. Her mother, pushing her into the deep end of the pool. With it came a feeling of impending doom that wrapped itself around her like a hungry boa constrictor.

thirty-two

COLD WATER HITTING HER skin like needles jerked Jessica awake. Even before she opened her eyes, she knew. Still, it didn't fully sink in until she blinked and blinked again. She was living the vision Elise had showed her. No. Not a vision, a warning. She was in the canoe, surrounded by the black waters of Herron Pond.

Is this real, or am I in a trance?

The boat rocked on the water and drove her racing pulse up to Defcon Five.

It's real.

As slowly and carefully as her quivering body would allow, she clutched onto the fiberglass sides of the canoe, trying, and failing, to remember rising beside Sage's sleeping form—after polishing off the wine, they had fallen asleep fully clothed in front of the fire. There was no memory, either, of leaving the house, or of climbing into the canoe and somehow ending up at the center of the lake in the moonless night. She could feel the dread rising in her, filling every pore, every cell. She was not capable of swimming the fifty feet that would take her to shore. Even if she were to tempt fate and try it, she would certainly drown in the ten-foot depths.

It was raining and the air felt thick, like setting jelly. Although the wind had died down, the wintry air sliced through her fleece sweatshirt like a razor-sharp knife. The sense of a malevolent presence watching, entertained by her terror, poked at her with a bony finger. Rostya, of course. Who else would invade her sleep like a demon torturer and play on her deepest fear, bringing her to the very last place she would choose to be—alone on the water?

As if confirming her conviction, like a klieg light in a prison movie, a colossal fork of lightning split the sky and thunder rolled through the superheated air. Jessica screamed.

The act of releasing emotion seemed to shake loose the neurons in her fear-frozen brain. *"It's my house now,"* she would have shouted if her breaths were not coming so fast and shallow on little sobs of despair. Any other time she might have laughed at the irony of having escaped whatever her fate was supposed to have been in the cellar, only to face drowning or electrocution in Herron Pond.

Think, Jess. You're being hysterical. Just stop it! The thoughts came in her twin's sharp tone, yelling at her with her ever-practical advice. Was Jenna, two-hundred miles south, feeling her distress and responding to it with a message? It wouldn't be the first time one of them had sensed the other's thoughts and feelings.

For once, Jessica made herself listen to her sister. Closing her eyes, she did her relaxation breathing, opening her mouth wide and filling her belly with air, expelling it on a hard exhale. The sound of raindrops plinked on the water all around the canoe. She couldn't see the ripples forming on the surface and traveling away from her to the lake's edge, but she knew they were there. If they had been solid, she would have run across them like a bridge to safety.

Jenna's advice wasn't working. Her heart rate had not slowed.

Be calm. You're safe. The water won't hurt you.

A new voice was speaking inside her head. Not Jenna's, nor was it Jessica's own.

Elise.

There was no conscious decision to loosen tense muscles. The shivering stopped on its own. The hyperventilating slowed. Her chattering teeth quieted. In defiance of the rain, she was as warm as she had been in front of the fireplace with Sage. Gradually, the night air lost its menacing thickness.

Her first thought was that she had died. The sensation was not dissimilar from her experience after the near-fatal car crash. But tonight, she was not rising into the heavens, gazing down at her body as she had six years ago. She was sitting in a canoe, observing a small orb that had appeared a short distance above the bow and hovered there. A gasp caught in her throat as the bluish-white light began to expand and grow until it closed around her and the canoe.

Her mind spun, trying to keep up with what was happening. She was still trying to comprehend it when she realized that Elise was inside the orb with her, and she appeared as real as any living being.

Elise's spirit had inhabited Jessica's body and Jessica had channeled her music, but this was a closeness of another kind. Looking into Elise's eyes, she recognized deep in her soul the impish light and the loving smile. She saw them every day when she looked in the mirror.

Unable to tear her gaze from the face that was so much like Jenna's—like her own—Jessica wanted to speak, but the words wouldn't come.

Looking directly into her eyes, Elise spoke to her in her mind. *You don't have to be afraid, my beautiful girl. You're safe. Look—*

Jessica followed the spirit's pointing finger to an oar lying in the bottom of the boat. In her fright she had overlooked the means to escape her plight. "But I can't, I—"

You can. Trust yourself.

Elise blew a gentle kiss and sent her one final thought. *I've always loved you; I am always with you.*

Having delivered the message, the spirit form began to fade. "Please wait," Jessica burst out. "Don't go! Stay a little longer."

The dazzling blue-white orb shimmered around her for one more prolonged moment like an embrace. Then, in a flash, it was gone.

She looked, hoping she had been mistaken and Elise was out there somewhere. But Jessica was alone in the rain on the lake. Across the black expanse of water, she faced the stand of tall trees that hemmed the west side of Herron Pond. That meant the house was behind her.

Moving as if in a waking dream, she reached down for the oar Elise had showed her, and as if she had performed the act hundreds of times, dipped it into the water. As she moved the oar in a narrow arc the canoe began to gradually rotate in the direction of the house.

Jessica paddled toward the bank, seeing in a flash of lightning Sage on the shore, stripping out of his clothes, preparing to swim out to her. He knew she was afraid of water, had never mocked her for it. She heard the desperation in his shout, even though he had to know that to enter the lake would be a risky and dangerous act.

Faster and faster, she paddled, yelling as loud as she could manage; telling to him to stay where he was. The rain had slowed to a drizzle, a half-moon peering out from behind a bank of clouds, bright enough for her to meet his gaze. She saw him freeze and knew he had heard her warning.

As surely as she knew anything, she knew that Elise would not let any further harm come to her on that night. Keeping her eyes fixed on Sage, she rapidly closed the gap between them. When she was close enough for him to reach out and grab hold of the bow, he dragged the craft onto the sandbank. Before he had a chance to speak, Jessica jumped out of the canoe and threw her arms around him. Her eyes were shining with tears of joy.

"Are you okay?" he asked with the stunned bewilderment of someone who had expected a very different reaction.

"I couldn't be better." She wanted to shout it to the world. "I just met my mother."

thirty-three

"Vadim Evanov was our grandfather." Jessica tested the words and found they tasted strange on her tongue, with the sourness of a lemon drop. "I was starting to suspect something, but I didn't *really* imagine it could be true."

Spooned together in bed, dry and warm again, Sage's arms were wrapped around her in a grip that hardly let her catch a breath, and she didn't mind at all.

"When I woke up and you were gone; finding you in the middle of the lake. That was one of the biggest scares of my life." His lips pressed to her skin, whispering into the crook of her neck. "I'm afraid to let you go; you might disappear again."

She held onto his hands, which were pressed to her heart, and issued a long sigh. "The house doesn't feel so welcoming now that Rostya can come into the new wing and control me like a puppet while I'm asleep."

"I'd like to know how that works. Do you think she's been here and you didn't feel her presence?"

"That's possible, I guess. What I think is, Elise was able to come on this side because it's where she died—where the fire burned—and that maybe when she came to visit the little twins, she inadvertently opened a door and Rostya came through it." New facets of what she had discovered kept popping into her mind. "Emily and Sophie are Elise's grandchildren. Isn't that incredible? A week ago, it was just Jenna and me. Now I've not only found out who our birth parents and grandparents were, I've lost them, too." A deep sense of grief swept over her and she wanted to weep at the thought of one more loss. "It feels like I'm experiencing Elise's death as if it just happened."

"It's a lot to handle," Sage murmured. He stroked her cheek with a light touch, comforting her. "It's gotta make you feel off-balance and a bit mixed up. You can't expect to assimilate it all at once."

"Yeah. But I wouldn't give it up for anything in the world. For the first time in my life, I know that I had a mother whose love for me transcends death. Finding Elise and having to let her go is devastating. But there's something that's cleansing about it, too."

He kissed her neck softly, making the fine hairs quiver. "In that sense, you are one very lucky angel."

"Don't forget Rostya. We can't stay awake all night, worrying about her coming for me."

"Maybe I should handcuff you to me," Sage said, only half-joking.

"Except we thought she was handy with keys if she's the one who moved them from the cellar door and back."

"Except we don't know whether it was Rostya or Andrews that locked us in. It's got to be one or the other, doesn't it?"

Jessica wriggled around to look up into the languid warmth of his gaze. She wanted to make love to him, but her thoughts had spun into darker territory and her mind was too busy jumping from one place to another. "Do you think we should confront Amy about it? If Andrews and Dianne *are* scheming something—and I'm positive that it was her I heard on the phone—Amy needs to know."

"Amy needs to know what? We don't have any proof that they're using her the way we *theorize* they might be. *If* she intends to share her commission with them as we speculated, she has to be in on the plan, whatever it is."

"I don't know, Sage, I have a feeling there's more to it than that." Was what she felt a psychic hint, or simply her wanting it to be true? She looked up at the ceiling as if the answers were there. She had wanted to know the truth about the inheritance of Herron Pond. Discovering that Elise was her mother had introduced a disturbing element. She couldn't forget how much Elise had hated it here.

"We do need to know more," she said.

"We'll get it." There was such confidence in the way he grinned at her that she knew he was reading her again. "Otherwise, my clever angel will find a way to trap poor, defenseless Amy into an admission."

"Oh, yeah, I'm a regular Jessica Fletcher," Jessica snickered, referring to the elderly sleuth on the old *Murder, She Wrote* TV show. She gave him a gentle poke in the belly. "We can go back to the courthouse. It turns out, I *do* have a right to the marriage and death certificates. Take *that,* State of California."

"Malevolent spirits and the State of California beware; Jessica Mack is on the warpath."

"Don't you dare give me one of those, 'you're so cute when you're all riled up,' looks."

"Wouldn't dream of it," he said sanctimoniously.

"I keep thinking about Elise's diary. How scared she was to be pregnant. She felt so alone. We don't know how Ilya reacted when she told him."

"If he loved her the way we think he did, he would have stood by her."

Jessica thought about the dark moods of despair that had taken over her life for days and weeks at a time as a sulky teen. She had often taken refuge in her bedroom closet, hiding even from her twin to wallow in her yearning for what she couldn't have that everyone else seemed to—a family where the parents adored their kids. She was fully adult before she could admit to herself the truth, that families who actually lived in that kind of sitcom household were rare.

Elise couldn't give her that, even now, but as she had voiced to Sage, there was something ultimately satisfying in knowing that the mother who had given birth to her and Jenna had loved them after all. He had met his own birth mother only a year ago. But his story was a very different one than the twins.'

"I can't believe she gave us up willingly," she murmured to herself.

Sage propped himself on one elbow and behind his eyes, she could see that he wasn't buying it.

"Right now, you have no way to know whether she gave you up willingly. And judging by the scenario we've read in her diary, chances are, she didn't. We need to find out what happened to Ilya. If he's alive and we can locate him, he's the only one left who can give us the true story."

"We're assuming that Jen and I are 'the baby' from the pregnancy Elise wrote about in her diary." Doubt welled up, rekindling old, dreary feelings. "It's possible that after Ilya married Rostya, Elise might have hooked up with someone else and got pregnant again." Even as she said it, the words rang false in her ears. Sage confirmed it.

"So, you think she either lost or gave up her first baby and then gave up twins she had with someone else, and then ended up married to Ilya with no children? Does that sound like the Elise in the diary and that you've channeled? Or the Elise you met on the lake?"

Hearing him lay it out that way was mortifying. "Okay, it's pretty stupid when you put it like that. And I have to admit, according to Claudia's analysis, 'Grandpa Vadim' doesn't sound like the type to have made us his heirs if Ilya wasn't our father. Even though he did cut him out of his will."

The thrill of wonder that ran through her made her realize she had lived too long in a melancholy world of pain of disconnection. Until Sage appeared in her life last year, she had despaired of meeting someone who could accept her uniqueness and take her as she was. The precious moments she had spent with the spirit of Elise had let her experience the kind of unconditional love she had always longed for from a mother. She didn't have to stop and think about how to answer Sage's question.

"No, it doesn't sound like her at all."

They lay for a while in comfortable silence, unable to sleep. Jessica had no desire to relive waking up on the lake and feel that terror again. She wanted to fill every waking thought with the visit from her mother. The word brought a warm glow. Instinctively, she understood that after the tragedy of Elise's death, she had chosen to stay close to the physical world and watch over her twin daughters. Jessica knew that if she had been killed in their car accident and not Justin, she would have refused to leave the earth plane, too.

"It's only eight years ago that Elise was here at Herron Pond," Sage said. "I wish you could have known her."

"It's a gut punch. Jen and I could have had a relationship with her." Jessica nestled next to him, silent for a minute or two, thinking of how it might have been. She sat up suddenly. "Sage!"

"Hmmm?" He was beginning to sound sleepy.

"That article we read about the fire said she was survived by her parents and two brothers." She looked into his drowsy face, imagining that her eyes must be filled with excitement. "If they're alive, we have more grandparents—not just Vadim—and uncles, maybe cousins—Elise's people. The Marcotts were both only children, which is why they adopted us. We've never had grandparents or family."

"You have a lot of catching up to do." Sage roused himself back to wakefulness. "Now we have the family name, Sharpe, it should make it easy to find them. Elise was taking piano lessons here at Herron Pond when she was young, so unless the family moved away, they would have been within driving distance." He paused. "Maybe you'll want to contact the Sharpes and ask them."

She gave her head a firm shake. "I'm not ready for that. This is all too new. I need a little time to process it, and I want to be armed with information before we go knocking on their door and announcing ourselves as the long-lost granddaughters they may not have known they had. We don't know how close Elise was to her parents. In her diary she says she didn't want to tell them about the pregnancy and disappoint them. They may not have been aware that she was pregnant when she went to Europe. Or if they were, whether they approved of Jen and me being given away at birth. I have to find a way to tell Jen about it, first."

"We keep talking about looking through Vadim's papers," Sage said. "Let's stop talking and get it done, first thing in the morning, see if there's anything official that is connected to your birth. It's time for Vadim's secrets to be revealed."

"I also want to know what happened after the fire. Where did Ilya go? His father was hospitalized and Elise was dead. Would he have stuck around Big Sur or gone home—wherever home was that he and Elise lived?"

A shadow clouded Sage's face and Jessica got a sudden psychic flash. He had told her what happened to him and his siblings—the horror and the loss he had suffered—but never had she felt it as strongly as she did now.

"How could he go home, knowing that Elise wouldn't be going with him?" His voice was thick with emotion. He cleared his throat. "Knowing she would never be with him again, never lie next to him like you are with me right now. After losing her, I'm sure he couldn't stay here, even if the house had been habitable, which it wasn't with half of it burned to a crisp. Smoke damage, water damage. And can you imagine his guilt?"

"You mean because he didn't leave when she begged him to."

"She warned him about Rostya. If he had only listened to her." Sage shot her a worried frown. "Rostya's not done, Jess. After what she did tonight, taking you onto the lake like that—" Abruptly, he sat up, his face strained. "Maybe Elise showed you the vision this morning to tell us that *we* should leave; that it's too dangerous to stay here."

thirty-four

FOR A SECOND, JESSICA just looked back at him, at a loss for words. They had dipped into the whiskey after her adventures on the lake and it had done its trick. If Rostya came for her now, she would have a hard time getting her to move.

"We can't leave right now," she said. "We're both exhausted and a little drunk. Elise will protect us tonight. We'll be safe."

Sage didn't look convinced, but he was much too tired to argue. "Your call, my love. I hope you're right."

"Why don't we say a prayer of protection."

"I'm listening."

Jessica began to speak, letting the words flow naturally.

Thank you, angels and guides, for being our protectors. We know that we can count on your love and mercy to surround us at all times and keep evil away. We have no fear. We know you will protect us as we sleep and when we wake.

The prayer ended on Sage's wide yawn. Jessica burrowed under the covers beside him. The sun was beginning to rise when the dark fringe of lashes closed over the eyes that had magnetized her from the first moment they met.

***

They slept late and went directly to the Victorian side after coffee, eager to see what Evanov's papers might hold. The study was quiet and still, no glimmer of an apparition lying on the sofa this time. Jessica sat at the antique desk and tried the cabinet. Both locked.

With her anger at her grandfather taking root, she was in favor of opening them with the crowbar they had used to break the cellar window. It was Sage's calm suggestion that they first check his bedroom for the key.

They found it hidden in a small drawer in a valet box on the dresser. The key was concealed under business cards, an empty money clip, spare change, a pair of dice, and two pairs of Aviator sunglasses.

Jessica jingled the coins in her hand. "Not US money."

Sage peered over her shoulder, reading them. "Rubles, I think. And kopeks."

"I read somewhere that a hundred rubles is worth a little more than a dollar." She dropped the coins back into the box and closed the lid.

For the second time, she sat at the ornately carved desk. What if they didn't find anything useful? Feeling a little unsteady, she inserted the key in the cabinet on the left side of the kneehole and turned it with a satisfying click. Opening the cabinet door, she studied the small stack of papers, folders, manila envelopes, and a red Russian Federation passport. For a long moment, she just sat and looked at the cache.

Sage was waiting patiently to see what she would do. "Anything interesting?" he prompted after a several seconds passed and she hadn't moved.

She hadn't thought this far ahead. What else might she find in her grandfather's papers, now that she knew that was who Evanov was? Would there be anything she would be better off knowing?

"I don't know yet," she said, reaching into the cabinet. She took it all out and placed it on the desktop. Starting with the envelopes, she began to sort through the pile.

Birth Certificates jumped out at her from a manila envelope. The two words were written in the same bold, dark strokes as Vadim Evanov's journal on the top of the desk. Her mouth had gone dry. She snatched it up, heart racing. Withdrawing several papers, she saw that the contents were written in Russian Cyrillic.

Sage worked his Google magic and got help from Wikienglish.ru, to translate what Jessica needed to know. She learned that Russians do not choose a middle name, but that it is taken from the father's name, adding the ending -ovich for boys and -ovna for girls. The certificate on top was the patriarch's own, Vadim Ivanovich Evanov. Next, was his son, Ilya Vadimovich Evanov.

The third one differed. Ilya's son had a US certificate of live birth and was named in the American convention, Ilya Evgeny Evanov. "Our half-brother," Jessica said sadly. "And what about us?"

"Don't give up so soon," Sage said.

She gave him a watery smile. "I was hoping for a little instant gratification."

Underneath the birth certificate envelope, a separate, smaller one was unmarked and sealed with adhesive tape. She ripped it open without ceremony and studied the contents with rising excitement. Two more Russian birth certificates.

Together, they figured out the dates. They were the same on both certificates and matched the dates on Jenna's and Jessica's driver's licenses—January 1, 1990.

She sat back in the chair and pulled her hair back, twisting it into a knot.
She knew it was a way of giving herself a moment to process what she had
just found. For the first twenty-five years of her life, she had been Jessica
Marcott; Jessica Mack since her marriage to Greg—she had not changed
her name after the divorce. But now she was learning that long in advance
of all that, she and Jenna had been born in Moscow, and their names on
the birth certificates were Baby Sharpe 1 and Baby Sharpe 2.

Until this moment she had never known who she really was. The shiver
of truth that ran over her was oddly similar to how she'd felt when she'd
recovered her lost memories. How had she and Jenna, born in Russia to
an American teenager, ended up in the hands of Lorraine and Donald
Marcott?

She glanced up, seeking Sage's reaction. He looked as troubled as she felt.

"I thought adoption of Russian kids by US citizens was illegal," he said.

"I'm beginning to get the idea that my grandfather was a law unto
himself," Jessica heard the bitterness in her tone. She would never forgive
Vadim Evanov for what he had done to her family—his family. "If he forced
Ilya to marry Rostya, as it appears he did, and he lived in the US, it probably
wouldn't have been too difficult to grease the wheels with a bribe or two.
Especially when the adoptees had an American birth mother. I'd love to
know whether he chose the Marcotts or they were random people trolling
for babies. They always claimed they didn't know where we came from."

"There was probably a middleman to handle those details," Sage said.
"Marrying his son into an oligarch's family must have given him a lot of
power and access to money. With his musical career going so well early on,
it had to have opened a lot of doors for him."

"I suppose that's how he bought this land and the house. It makes sense now, his changing his will to leave it to Jen and me. Unless he was keeping tabs on us—and I don't think he was—I probably guessed right, that he must have seen us in the news after we were kidnapped and escaped. It's the time frame for when Dianne said he changed the will—about six years ago. He cut Ilya out and made us his heirs." Jessica chewed on her bottom lip in contemplation. "Why didn't he reach out to us? Didn't he want to meet his granddaughters?"

"That's something you may never know."

"Maybe he was ashamed of what he'd done, separating our parents." Jessica huffed a cynical laugh. "No, probably not that."

"How are you going to tell Jen?" Sage asked, reaching into her thoughts as he so often did.

"It's not gonna be easy. You've seen how scared she is of the 'ghost stuff.' She tries, but it's not easy for her to accept the spirit world, especially now that she has the girls. I mean, how freaked out was she the other night?"

He gave her a dubious look, then laughed. "Well, yeah, but having your kids wake up to a spirit sitting on your bed, even a nice spirit—"

There was a rueful twist to Jessica's lips. "I'll ask Elise not to do that while they're so young."

Sage had raised a good question, though. How *was* she going to tell her sister? Jenna had always been the one who strove to be good and, above all, to do the right thing. For her, that often started with pointing out Jessica's flaws. But to be fair, Jessica had to admit, her twin would point out her own faults too. It was all part of her driving need for self-improvement, to be perfect. Jenna was the serious twin; the one who followed rules and got things done. Stepping outside of those rules made her anxious and distressed. No two ways about it. What Jessica had to tell her was far outside the set of rules her sister had constructed and lived by.

How was Jenna going to react to learning who their birth mother was? If she even accepted Elise, which was iffy, she would never achieve the kind of closeness that Jessica experienced as a medium. Elise had helped her more than once over her stay at Herron Pond. That was a secret Jessica would keep just for herself.

Bottom line, Jenna being Jenna, it would take some convincing. She would probably demand a DNA test to prove they were Evanov's natural descendants. Not that he was available to spit in a test tube.

A text pinged in Jessica's phone. She checked the screen and showed it to Sage. "Jenna."

Jenna: I had the weirdest dream last night. You were in a boat—yeah, I know, crazy, a boat—you! But it was terrifying. RU OK?

Jessica: I'm good. I had the same dream. Tell you later.

Sage was looking at her expectantly. "The twin thing?"

Jessica nodded. "I knew I felt her when I was on the lake. It's too much to text or talk about on the phone. When we go home—"

"Makes sense to me. Now, are we done with this side of the cabinet?"

Jessica sifted through the rest of the items on the desk, not finding anything of interest. The folders seemed mainly to hold forms. Applications for passports and other such official documents.

"Yes, we're done. Let's see what's behind door number two."

Ready to move on to easier tasks than figuring out what to do about Jenna, she unlocked the second cabinet and opened the door. A stack of thin blue envelopes bound by a large rubber band met her sight. She knew right away what they were, even before she saw that the airmail letters were addressed to Ilya Evanov in the hand of Elise Sharpe. The return address was in St. Petersburg, Russia. Blood rushed to her cheeks in a hot wave of indignation as she flipped through one sealed envelope after another.

"He intercepted her letters and never gave them to Ilya," she blurted angrily. "How could he be so reprehensible?"

Sage was silent. Nothing he could say would change the betrayal of the son by his father.

Holding the letters in her lap, Jessica quietly asked Elise what she should do. The spirit failed to respond, and who could blame her if she didn't want to be in Evanov's study, where his energy lingered.

"I'm not going to open them," Jessica said at length. "It's one thing, reading the diary she led me to—"

"It's something else, reading what she wrote to her lover," Sage finished for her. "The maestro was quite the control freak."

"I'm beginning to hate him the way Elise did." She read the dates on the postmarks. "The first one is in July, 1989. That's when Elise was slated to go to Europe for her tour. The last was January 2, 1990, the day after we were born. Can you imagine how she must have felt, being so young, in a strange country and presumably not knowing the language. Giving birth and losing her children. Since the letters were locked up here, they obviously never made it to Ilya. He wouldn't have known where she was or how to reach her. And she didn't know that he didn't receive them."

"Ilya might not have known she was pregnant," Sage said. "Depends just how far Evanov went to keep them apart."

For a long time, Jessica stared at the letters in her lap. "We keep talking about Ilya as if he was just some third party," she said. "But he was our father. He was deprived of the girl he loved, and he was deprived of his children—all three of them if you count his son—our half-brother, little Ilya—just the same as we were deprived of—" Her voice cracked and broke. She could no longer hold back the sobs that wracked her body. Gently, Sage drew her out of the chair and gathered her into his arms, holding her until the emotions had played out.

She returned to the desk wrung out, questioning whether she wanted to examine the rest of the contents of the cabinet. If it hadn't been only mid-morning, she might have revisited the vodka bottle across the room on the drinks tray. But something was prodding her to pay attention to a final envelope. This one had been opened.

It contained a single tri-fold sheet of high-quality letter stock printed with the letterhead of a Monterey accountancy corporation. Jessica read the letter, dated last October, a few days ahead of Vadim Evanov's death, and felt as if she'd been kicked in the stomach. She rose and handed it to Sage across the desk.

"Just when I thought things couldn't get worse."

thirty-five

SAGE READ IT, HIS look of shock reflecting hers. He handed the letter back. "Darryl Andrews was skimming money off the books?"

"According to this letter. There's a whole lot of cold, hard cash missing and it happened over a long period of time." Jessica refolded the sheet and returned it to the envelope. "This is pretty damning."

"How the hell did he get away with it for so long?"

"Evanov must have trusted him with all the estate accounts. But it makes no sense. From everything I've learned, my grandfather wasn't the forgiving type. So why is this—" She broke off, suddenly aware of the aroma of pipe smoke. It curled into her nostrils, a pleasant cherry vanilla scent. A spirit had entered the study. It had not taken on a material form, but she knew who it was.

The edges of her peripheral vision were beginning to soften, a halo-ish aura forming on each side of her as if she were inside a bubble. The room lost its definition and began to get hazy, a prelude to—

"Trance," she heard her own weak gasp, warning Sage as the feeling of unreality grew. She felt his arms around her, guiding her into the chair.

She is still in Evanov's study, still at his desk, and she *is* Vadim Evanov, wearing evening clothes, dressed to go out.

A knock comes at the door and Evanov calls brusquely for the visitor to enter. Darryl Andrews strides in, tall and confident, his square jaw jutting self-importantly. "You wanted to see me, boss?"

"Yes," *Evanov says, standing. He is not tall like the estate manager, but his regal bearing makes him appear taller.* "You have worked for me for nearly ten years now, Darryl, is that right?"

"That sounds about right," *the estate manager agrees warily.*

"During that time, I believe you have been paid quite well for your services."

"Sure, boss, you've been more than fair with compensation. What's this all about?"

Evanov ignores the question. "Someday when I die, you are to also receive a rather robust bequest. Did you know that, Darryl?"

Andrews shrugs his wide shoulders, but something is guarded in his countenance. "You've never told me that, Mr. Evanov, but if it's true, I'm honored. I never expected—"

"It is true that I have not told you." *Evanov interrupts.* "But it occurred to me, the intimate conversation of pillow talk—"

"Excuse me?"

"I am referring to my attorney, my...friend, Dianne Maggio. I believe she shares your bed, does she not? And, as such, I have no doubt that she has also shared with you the terms of my will."

"What the—do you have someone spying on me?" *Andrews sputters.* "What I do outside of Herron Pond is—"

"None of my business? Is that what you were going to say?"

"That's right. My personal life—who I sleep with—has nothing to do with you."

"Oh, it does if my estate attorney is sharing my private matters with you."

"I didn't say she—I—"

"No, and you did not have to. The guilt is written on your face."

Evanov picks up a sheet of paper from his desk and looks at it dispassionately. "I think you know that my only son, Ilya, scorns me. He refuses to understand that I have always acted with his best interests in mind. Ilya is unfortunately a romantic. He blames me for everything bad that has happened in his life. He takes no responsibility for the consequences of disobeying my wishes. So, I have nothing to give to him. And when you came along, I was impressed with your strengths. I hoped you might be a man I could groom to eventually become my heir."

He goes silent and for a long time regards Andrews, who seems to be stupefied by what he is hearing. "Ah, Darryl," Evanov says when the other man begins to fidget. "You know where I am leading, do you not?" He waves the sheet of paper at him. "In my hand I hold a letter from my accountant. Does this worry you? I see from your face that it does. I cannot begin to tell you how disappointed I was to learn that all this time you have been stealing from me." As Andrews starts to protest, Evanov holds up his hand. "Don't bother to deny it, Darryl. The proof is incontrovertible.

"It seems that as long as our accounting was done by hand, by you, you were able to get away with what you were doing. But now I have been forced into the twenty-first century and the books have been computerized—" Evanov heaves a long sigh.

"You set up payment accounts for false companies and paid yourself a few thousand here, a few thousand there. You have stolen nearly two million dollars from me, Darryl." Evanov's face is a thundercloud. His narrowed eyes reflect his distaste.

"Do you know what would have happened to you if we had been in my country?" he growls, all pretense of cordiality gone. "A year or two in a *corrective labor camp if you were lucky. A lot less pleasant if you were not. Poison, perhaps. A fall from a high place, maybe. But here in America, I am just a piano teacher. We are civilized, yes?" His eyes harden to flat black disks.*

"Mr. Andrews, your services are no longer required at Herron Pond."

"Hey, hold on. You're firing me?" Even after Evanov's calm recitation of the facts, Andrews seems nonplussed, unable to believe what he's heard. "I've worked my ass off for this place for ten years. So what if I took a few kickbacks, kept a few extra bucks for myself? I deserve it. You can't do this. I'm not—"

"You are not what? Leaving? Did I give you the false impression that you have an option?" Evanov's harsh laugh holds no trace of humor. "Tomorrow morning, I intend to instruct my accountant to contact the Monterey Police Department and request they issue a warrant for your arrest on charges of fraud."

"The police? Hey, wait, I'm not a criminal. You can't do that."

"You are. I can. And I will." His jaw taut, Evanov points a long finger at his soon-to-be-former employee. "You are fired. Leave my property immediately. By the time I return from my engagement in Paso Robles tonight, I expect you to have vacated the apartment."

"Oh, yeah?" Andrews retorts. "And who's going to drive you to Paso if I'm not here? You can't drive that road at night—your cataracts. C'mon, Mr. E, you don't have to do this."

Andrews's tone has acquired a whiny quality, but Evanov continues as though his former employee had not spoken. "Any belongings you leave behind will be packed up and sent to your address in Carmel. Before you go to prison, of course. Now, get out of my house."

The scene flickers in Jessica's mind as the location changes to outdoors behind the mansion.

Vadim Evanov, wearing a long black coat, a white opera scarf around his neck, opens one of the garage doors and climbs into the Bentley Bentayga.

Driving away from Herron Pond, he veers onto the dark, narrow section of Cabrillo Highway, arrogantly unaware of the vehicle following at a discreet distance.

Behind the wheel of Evanov's own BMW, Darryl Andrews waits for his chance. They are approaching Pitkins Curve when he mashes his foot on the accelerator and floors it. Coming up fast on the Bentley as it starts to leave the covered bridge, Andrews switches on the high beams. The BMW speeds up and taps the Bentley's rear bumper.

Evanov's eyes fly to the rearview mirror in confusion. The harsh glare of the headlights in the mirror momentarily distracts him, making it hard to see through the darkness ahead. His hands tighten on the steering wheel, trying to keep the Bentley on the narrow road, but the BMW taps it again, harder, and he overcorrects. The Bentley fishtails.

All of a sudden, his chest is burning, squeezing the breath out of him. Evanov knows what this is. He's had a heart attack before. As consciousness fades, he is aware of his hands slipping off the steering wheel, his foot leaving the pedal.

The Bentley plunges through the guard rail over the cliff's edge and flies through the air, rolling over and over down the shale and dirt. Finally, the vehicle splashes on its roof into the water, bumping to a halt on the rocks. Ocean waves crash around it, but Vadim Evanov, his body held in his seat by the seatbelt, is already on his way to the spirit world.

"Andrews killed him," Jessica cried out struggling to free herself from the trance into which the spirit of her grandfather had placed her. "He ran him off the road, right over the edge." She was stuttering, unable to wipe the sight from her mind—the luxury vehicle plunging down the cliff, rolling over, landing upside down on the rocks in the furious waters of the Pacific. Regardless of the bad things Vadim Evanov had done, he didn't deserve to die like that.

Rushing to tell Sage everything she had seen, she spewed it all out, hardly able to believe what she was saying, ending with, "He murdered him to stop him from calling the cops."

She had disliked Andrews from the start; had believed him capable of dirty dealings. But this was as far from what she and Sage had suspected him of as the moon.

On the other side of the desk Sage looked at her with a puzzled frown. "Why wouldn't the accountant go ahead and call the police anyway?"

"Probably because Evanov wasn't around to pursue it and they thought his death was an accident. I doubt the accountant would call the cops on their own. But *we* can put it all back in motion. We can call the cops."

"And tell them what, that you had a vision? I don't think that's gonna fly."

"We've got this letter. As an heir, I can instruct the accountant to do what my grandfather was going to do."

From the doorway, Darryl Andrews's deep, raspy voice said, "that's not gonna happen."

thirty-six

JESSICA LEAPT OUT OF her grandfather's chair. A bolt of adrenaline shot through her, waking every nerve ending dulled by the trance. Darryl Andrews was standing there in a brown leather bomber jacket and jeans. The hard expression on his face and the gun he aimed at them told her that he had heard everything she'd said, or close enough.

Covering her fear with bluster she glared at him. "You should stop sneaking up on us like this, Darryl. Eavesdroppers rarely hear well of themselves."

Without missing a beat, Sage stepped in front of her, shielding her. "What the hell, Andrews?"

"I just dropped by to tell you I took a look at the broken cellar window." The estate manager's face twisted into something frightening. "Who knew I was gonna hear such an interesting story?"

Moving out from behind the desk, Jessica placed herself next to Sage. She loved him for putting himself in danger to protect her, but as freaked out as she was by the gun, she wasn't going to cower behind him.

"C'mon, dude," Sage said, "there's gotta be a better way than threatening us with a gun."

The estate manager huffed a mirthless laugh. "Oh, okay. When you figure it out, you let me know, would you?"

"*Anything* is better than what you're doing."

He shrugged. "Yeah, killing wasn't in my plan. But sometimes you have to improvise, and lucky for me, I carry." He raised the gun a little, as if they needed reminding that it was pointed at them.

Jessica could feel the quiet rage building in Sage, but though his eyes glittered dangerously, his voice was steady. "Do you really expect to get away with killing two people?"

Andrews's vibe held no insight or mercy, just grim determination. "Oh, don't worry, *boss*, I'm not gonna shoot you in Mr. E's study and bloody everything up; leave a bunch of forensic evidence. That was the great thing about doing Evanov on the highway. No fuss, no muss. The ocean took care of everything."

His smirk held the self-satisfaction of a full-blown sociopath. "That was spur-of-the-moment, too. Mr. E used to say he admired how good I am at thinking on my feet. Ready for anything, that's me."

From behind him, a nervous female voice that Jessica recognized said, "This isn't necessary, Darryl." Dianne Maggio stepped from the hallway into the study. From across the room, Jessica could see that she was trembling. Was she an ally or a co-conspirator? She put her hand on his and tried to push it down. "Put the gun away and let's talk about it."

Andrews shrugged her off. "What's there to talk about, Di? Didn't you hear what she said? She's got the whole story down pat. I got no clue how, but she knows everything." His gazed bounced from one wall to the next, eyeing the corners of the ceiling. "Maybe the old man had the room bugged without telling me. Cameras. I didn't think he was that tech-savvy."

"There are no cameras," Jessica said, and with nothing to lose, she told him the truth. "A ghost showed me the story, Darryl. The ghost of Vadim Evanov, the man you murdered in cold blood."

Dianne's face paled and Jessica saw the instant it dropped that she had hit home. It took another second for it to register on Andrews's face and another for him to dismiss it. "Evanov's *ghost* told you?" he scoffed. "You must have been listening to the staff. There's no *real* ghost here."

"How else could I have known what you did? I guess you hadn't heard that I talk to dead people, had you, Darryl?" Jessica's voice, which had started out pitched high with nerves, was growing stronger. The tingle on her scalp told her that she had backup. "Remember the day you surprised me when I was playing the piano in the salon? Well, guess what. I don't play the piano. But you know who does? Elise Sharpe."

"Elise Sharpe is dead," he said with an edge of uncertainty.

"Exactly. She died right here at Herron Pond. And she still plays the piano, Darryl. Usually in that room you kept padlocked. Since I've been here, she's left that room."

"What the holy hell are you talking about, woman?" Angry red blotches bloomed on his face. His eyes narrowed with suspicion.

"She inhabited my body, Darryl. It was her playing the classical music you heard that day."

"You're crazy," Dianne said, but she looked scared. "We kept the door locked because the cleaning staff refused to go in there."

"Right. Because they felt her presence, or they heard her playing, didn't they?" Jessica gave a derisive laugh. "You locked up the wrong ghost. Oh, and by the way, did either of you know that Vadim Evanov was my grandfather?"

Dianne's gasp and Andrews's open mouth gave it away. "You didn't? Well, that's okay, I just found out myself last night. His son Ilya, and Ilya's second wife, Elise, were my parents. Surprise. You met them, didn't you, Darryl?"

The gun, still pointed at them, didn't waver. "Sure, I met them," Andrews said conversationally. "They stayed here for a couple of weeks after the old man had surgery."

"Then Elise died in the fire," Jessica said.

He nodded. "The son got the old man out and tried to go back for his wife, but it was too late. She was trapped in the bedroom. The smoke got her. Carbon monoxide poisoning."

His cold indifference chilled Jessica to the bone. With no one else in the house to worry about, Andrews seemed in no hurry to discontinue the conversation, and she was in no hurry to find out what he had planned for them. When Sage's hand brushed hers, she got a psychic message: he wanted her to stop talking. But the longer they talked, the more time it gave them to figure a way out. There were no windows in the study. The only exit was through the door where Andrews and Maggio stood. No place to go, Jessica realized. Even Elise couldn't help them out of this impasse.

All she could do was try and strike a little fear into him; at least enough to make him wonder. "Did you know that Ilya's first wife started the fire?" she said.

That stopped him for a moment. He frowned. "Whaddya mean, his *first* wife?"

"He was married to a woman named Rostya long before you arrived on the scene. She caused their child's death, and killed herself here in the house. All those years later when Ilya and Elise came back to take care of his father, Rostya was jealous. She hated Elise and used the opportunity to kill with the fire." A lot of it was guesswork, but it made sense. And for the moment, it was distracting the man with the gun.

He took a step forward. "What the—if she was dead, how could she start a fire?"

Jessica shrugged. "This place is full of ghosts—spirits. They're watching you right now, Darryl."

"Shut up," Andrews ordered, but his eyes practically spun in his head. "You're out of your mind. There are no ghosts."

Behind him, the study door slammed shut.

Dianne screamed and bumped up close to him.

Jessica laughed. "A slamming door. How's that for irony? It's not so funny when it's you, is it? Which one of you locked us in the cellar?" Seeing the shift in Dianne's posture, she shook her head in disappointment. "It was you?" She had been so wrong about Dianne, thinking she'd had a relationship with Evanov when all along it had been Darryl Andrews, who was nervously eyeballing the study for evidence of her ghost claims.

"What does it matter who it was?" Andrews said roughly, not giving his accomplice a chance to give her own answer. The gun in his hand wasn't so steady now. "You got out, didn't you? No harm, no foul."

"What was your point?" Jessica asked. "To scare my sister and me into selling? Why? Amy already has a client who made an offer. A big offer."

"Far too big. We needed to get the price down. Spreading a few ghost stories around—*fake* ghost stories, of course—that oughta do it. Nobody wants to buy a haunted house."

"Wait," Sage interjected. Tension was coming off him in waves. "You're saying you and Dianne want to *buy* Herron Pond?"

"Why not? I've worked my ass off, saved—"

"Saved the money you stole from your employer," Jessica said with contempt. "That air of entitlement. You worked here for all those years, so you deserved to own the place, and buy it cheap? Is that your reasoning?" She saw the truth flicker in his eyes.

"Yes, Darryl, dear old granddad showed me what you did. It was just like watching a movie. I saw him fire you for stealing millions from him. I saw you follow him and run him off the road, like the sniveling coward you are."

She was on a roll now, and couldn't seem to make herself stop. The voice of Vadim Evanov himself echoed in her icy tone. "Man up and turn yourself in, Darryl. Let us go. We won't press kidnapping charges. Maybe we can cut a deal."

Something snapped Andrews out of the stupor he seemed to have fallen into while Jessica was speaking. "Pull your head out of your ass, little lady. If you think I'm going to walk away and let you and your sister waltz in and take everything I've worked for all these years, you ain't nearly as psychic as you seem to think you are." He gestured with the gun towards Evanov's desk. "Leave your phones on the desk, both of you, and if you try to tell me you don't have them with you, I'll kick the shit out of the little lady and let big boy watch, so don't bother."

He waited until they had complied. "Now, let's go, *Jessica.* Maybe you can ask grandpa to save you and your boyfriend." Andrews backed up to the study door and reached behind him to wrench it open. "You go first, Di, and keep an eye on her. You're bigger than she is, you can handle her."

"But I don't—"

"Just do it. You're in too deep now."

He was right about the size difference between the two women, and it was not that Dianne was a large woman. She didn't look happy to follow Andrews's directive but she didn't argue with him, just clamped a hand around Jessica's upper arm and dragged her through the study as easily as she might deal with an unruly kid.

"Don't let him make you an accomplice," Jessica hissed at her, resisting every step. Her petite stature had rarely been the kind of liability that it was now. "He's wrong, it's not too late for you. You can be a hero."

"Shut up," Andrews shouted at her. "Do you think this is a game I'm playing?" He stood aside, far enough from Sage, who was silently fuming, to exit in front of him without getting near the gun. Andrews brought up the rear.

"Let's go. Dining room. Move it."

In Evanov's study, as long as she was able to keep him talking, scaring the two of them with her talk of ghosts, Jessica had felt more in control of the situation. It was different now. With Andrews making a show of pressing the gun against Sage's spine, warning both of them that he meant business, panic slammed back, packing a wallop and turning her brain to syrup. She bit down on her lip, terrified that he would pull the trigger just to prove he could. If keeping her mouth shut would save Sage for now, she wouldn't make another peep.

Andrews directed them through the wide hallway at the front of the house, and into the dining room. A weak sun, high in the sky, brightened the windows overlooking the gardens. How was it possible that it was the middle of the day when it felt like the darkest night? Less than twelve hours ago, Jessica had been in the canoe on that lake with Elise. Beyond the gardens, a low mist drifted over the lake like an eerie stage set, waiting for the spirits to appear.

The four of them filed past the marble table to the rear of the dining room. Dianne, with a hard grip on her arm, pushed Jessica out the French doors. As they passed Sage, she sensed the silent rage bristling off him like an aura; a fiery heat that promised violence if he could just make an opportunity to deliver it.

Stepping out into the stiff breeze, she couldn't be still any longer. "What are you doing, Darryl?" Dianne was holding on to her when she planted herself in front of him. "I have a sister and she isn't going to be in the mood to sell if she's grieving her twin. Sage has a brother. You haven't thought it through. There's no way you can get away with it. This will all be for nothing."

His hostile scowl held a threat. "Keep your trap shut and walk."

"Takes a real big man to bully a woman," Sage said in a voice tight with anger.

"Screw you, Boles. You better remember the big man has a Springfield XD pointed at you."

Seeing Andrews shove the gun harder against Sage's back, Jessica wanted to scream at him that he could have the mansion, the land, the money, anything he wanted. But deep down, she knew that it wouldn't make any difference to what he was set on doing—getting his revenge on Vadim Evanov for spoiling his plans—even if he had to do it through his granddaughter.

They followed the pathway past the garage, continuing around the lake. It was when they were passing the hidden graveyard in the neglected copse of trees that Jessica knew with a nauseating certainty where they were going.

thirty-seven

THE CLIFFS WERE CLOSE to a half-mile from the house. Leaving the formal path that terminated at the end of the gardens, they trudged through the muddy grounds, closing the gap between them and the ocean one step at a time. What would it be? A shove over the wood railing in a parody of Vadim Evanov's death, ending up in the rocky water below, without the buffer of a vehicle? Or down that long, steep flight of stairs? Jessica was pretty sure a fall like that would result in a broken neck. Either solution would do the trick for Andrews, though how he would explain it to the authorities, she couldn't imagine. Maybe he didn't have to. There was no one around to tell what had happened. Except for Dianne.

When Dianne, walking next to her, dropped her arm, Jessica said nothing, hoping Andrews wouldn't notice. But as she walked ahead of him and Sage, she slipped on a particularly muddy patch of grass and would have fallen if Sage had not reached out and grabbed the back of her pullover.

"Don't do that again. If she falls, she falls. No shenanigans between you two." Andrews's irritated bark infuriated her. What did he expect, for them to go meekly to their execution and not help each other? She righted herself, clenching and unclenching her fists as he turned on Dianne.

"You're supposed to keep a hold of her, what the hell's wrong with you?"

A look of disgust flashed across Dianne's face. Apparently, she'd had her fill of Andrews's abuse. She poked him in the back with a sharp finger. "Who the hell do you think you're talking to? I'm not your child or your subordinate."

"Oh, for fuck's sake, Di, get over it."

"Or what? Are you going to shoot me, too?"

He shrugged her off and kept walking. They were closing in on the towering seaside cliffs, inching closer to death. And with every numbing step, Jessica felt like she was attached to a succinylcholine drip and her body was shutting down, cell by cell. She had read a book once about something called 'walking corpse syndrome,' a condition brought on by sudden extreme stress. The sufferer believed they were dead or simply didn't exist. That was how she felt, like a walking corpse.

She chanced a look at Sage. His face was set like granite, focused on the cliffs. It stung when he kept staring straight ahead and didn't acknowledge her glance. Everyone reacted to impending doom in their own way, she supposed, and being her romantic partner had put him in danger more than once. He had never complained or threatened to leave her because of it. Early in their relationship they had agreed that they had shared many lifetimes. Was this how their love ended in this one, with Andrews's gun at his back?

Ten feet from the railing Sage came to a sudden halt. Andrews cocked the hammer and shouted at him, "Keep moving."

"No," Sage said calmly. "I'm not getting shot in the back." Slowly raising his hands, he turned around to face Andrews. "And I'm not going any closer to that cliff."

Andrews had not anticipated defiance, Jessica was certain, but he still had the gun. In the 0.2 seconds he had before deciding to shoot, she saw the flash of indecision on his face. Sage must have seen it too, and rushed him with an elbow to the face, knocking his gun hand up.

Andrews, thrown off-balance, fired, but the shot went wide. Dianne screamed and suddenly, everyone was yelling.

Jessica threw herself at Andrews from the side and Sage wheeled on him, landing a hard roundhouse kick. The kick pitched the gun out of his hand and into the tall grass. Andrews dove for it.

Sage, younger and faster, took him down with the savagery of a street fighter. A kick to the ribs, punches to the face. Blood streamed from Andrews's mouth and down his chin. He was bulkier and the bomber jacket slowed down his moves but protected him, too. He landed a vicious punch to Sage's cheek, and while Sage was recovering, he got to his feet, roaring like a wounded bear. Andrews slammed into him.

Jessica threw herself on Andrews's back and got her hands around his neck. She didn't have the strength to throttle him, but she clawed at his Adam's apple with everything she had. The move choked him, but Andrews was strong. He tossed her off him as easily as swatting a bug. It was a momentary distraction that gave Sage the opening he needed to move in with a finger jab to the throat.

Jessica scrambled to her feet, looking for the gun. And then she saw it, dangling from Dianne's hand as if she didn't know what to do with it. Still rasping from the blow to the throat, in one smooth move, Andrews snatched the gun and turned it toward Jessica. In that instant, all she could see was the little round hole—the muzzle where the bullet would rocket out and tear through her body.

She would never forget the way Andrews's movement suddenly arrested. He was staring at something behind her, his eyes widening with fear. Something that had contorted his face into a rictus of utter horror.

The next thing she knew, Sage yanked her out of the line of fire. Suddenly, as if time had slowed down for everyone but her, he froze, too. Jessica spun around.

Hovering three feet above the ground in a long dark coat, a white opera scarf around his neck, was the fully materialized figure of Vadim Evanov.

"What the—you can't be here." The strangled cry burst from Andrews's tortured lips. "You're dead." And just like in the movies, he aimed his weapon at the apparition and emptied the clip.

Dianne took off running, back the way they had come.

With a bitter smile, the spirit floated slowly toward Andrews, who backed up until he was touching the guard rail. Evanov lifted his hand and Andrews rose into the air, just high enough to clear the railing. With a flinging motion from the spirit, the estate manager flew past the barrier, his terrified screams echoing all the way to the rocks below.

Jessica heard the spirit's harsh laugh and his words, which would haunt her dreams for a long time to come.

I'll see you in hell, Darryl.

thirty-eight

ADRENALINE KEPT HER ON her feet, propelled her to the railing. She stared down at the broken body, the limbs twisted in angles they were never intended to go. The tide, on its way in, was already lapping at him.

When she turned back, the spirit was gone.

Her legs gave way. She sank to the wet grass, dizzy with shock.

Sage's face was streaked with blood and mud. Looking confused and a little wobbly, he was staring at the empty space where, just seconds ago, Andrews had stood. He came and gave Jessica his left hand to help her up. "What the hell just happened?"

"What do you mean, 'what happened'?" Jessica repeated slowly, still feeling as though everything was moving in stop-motion. "Vadim Evanov threw Darryl over the cliff."

"Evanov threw him—" he broke off with a question in his voice.

Jessica gaped at him. "You didn't see him, did you?"

He shook his head. "All I saw was Andrews taking a flying leap over the railing. Are you telling me it was—"

Her legs were weak, her hands shaking as the adrenaline rush wore off. Her mediumship skills had deserted her. She was just an ordinary person who was as shocked to see the man she had come to know was her grand-father as Andrews had been. To see what he had done.

"Evanov's spirit was here, Sage, as real as you and me. You really didn't see him?"

"Apparently, only you and Andrews did."

"He was wearing the same clothes as in the vision of how he died. I swear, the moment Andrews saw him, he *knew* what was about to happen. I guess you might call it poetic justice, but..." Jessica pressed her hands to her face, wishing she could erase the sight of Andrews's body on the rocks. As horrifying as it was, maybe he deserved his fate. It was her being forced to participate in it by witnessing it that was unfair. Which seemed typical of Vadim Evanov, who had made far too many tyrannical decisions for his descendants.

"In a sense, my grandfather got his vengeance," she said to Sage, leaning against him. "Though you have to wonder. I heard him say—" She broke off, no longer sure whether she had dreamed it or had perhaps misheard.

"What did he say, angel?"

"He said— *'I'll see you in hell.'*"

There was a wry twist to Sage's split lip, which was starting to swell. He swiped away a streak of blood. "From what we've learned, Evanov wasn't the nicest of people, so if you believe in hell—"

Jessica saw him again in her mind, her grandfather. It had all been too much, too fast. Her feelings toward him held no affection. "I believe we create our own hell based on what we do here on earth and how we deal with it afterwards," she said.

"I guess we'll find out the truth about it someday. Thank God, not today." He put his arm around her to prop her up, and maybe himself, too. "We have to get back to the house and call 911. Andrews might be alive and—"

"He doesn't look alive," Jessica said. And then she got a good look at his face. "Oh, Sage, you're covered in blood."

"Uh, yeah, ole Darryl got in a couple of good punches." He held up his right hand, which was grazed and swollen. "So did I."

She felt like a jerk. "I'm so sorry, I didn't realize. I was too wrapped up in—"

"It hurts like a bastard, but I'm lucky he didn't shoot me. And that it's not my drawing hand"

Of course that would be the first thing an artist would think of, as she would have, too. She pushed aside the residual disorientation of the whole experience. "Let's get back to the house. You're the one who needs medical attention."

"I'm fine, but I'm gonna have one helluva shiner."

They were halfway back to the mansion, when Jessica stopped and listened. "Do you hear that? Sirens."

"Dianne must have called 911."

"She took off in a big hurry when Evanov showed up."

"So, I'm the only one who didn't see him?"

"Don't look so disappointed," Jessica said. "It was a pretty scary sight."

By the time paramedics had managed to retrieve Darryl Andrews's body from the water and patched up Sage, a police detective was waiting in the old parlor to interview them.

Dianne had given her side of the story, and to her credit, had not made herself out to be a victim. But neither did she admit to being an accomplice. Remembering her own bad relationship choices in the past, Jessica was content to let the matter go. And the detective seemed content to accept the easy self-defense version of what had happened. Nothing involving ghosts. Just the almost-truth. Andrews had schemed to get Herron Pond, he planned to kill Jessica and Sage, they got into a fight and Andrews tripped down the steep cliff stairs and plunged to his death.

The next challenge was going to be in telling it all to Jenna. But now that they were safe, that could wait.

***

"Tomorrow, we go home," Sage yawned.

"And with you injured, I get to drive."

He grinned, then winced. His lip was going to take a few days to heal. "Haven't I risked my life enough for one week?"

"If you weren't hurting, I might hit you."

"And if I wasn't so tired, I'd make love to you."

"I like yours better."

They kissed goodnight and Sage was asleep within thirty seconds. Jessica reached up to turn out the light and curled beside him. Fatigue scratched at her like a cat at the door, at war with her mind, which wanted to keep spinning. During the police interview, which had taken place on the Victorian side of the mansion, she had not felt any spirit activity. Nor had she when they picked up their cell phones from Evanov's desk, where Darryl Andrews had ordered them left. Later, when they came to the new wing, it seemed clear of spectral energy, too, and they had eaten a light supper in peace.

There had been no further sign of Rostya's energy during the evening. Was it too much to hope that she had finally been banished to wherever it was that murderous mothers were sent?

Hedging her bets, Jessica had done her protection ritual before climbing into bed. Aside from Sage's light snoring, Herron Pond was silent.

As silent as death.

She couldn't help it. The words insisted on being heard. Yes, there had been far too much death and unhappiness in this house. She no longer wanted any part of the estate. The money meant nothing to her. If they lost the entire inheritance, that would be fine.

Sage's truck was already packed, ready for an early departure. Elise's diary and letters were coming along with them. Those, she would share with Jenna. Her only regret was leaving Elise behind. But her greatest hope was, now that she had seen her daughters, their mother would find peace and fully cross over to the other side of life.

thirty-nine

THE TWINS MET AT Tatiana's Coffee & Tea in Ventura, their favorite place to get together for a chat when Jenna's little girls were in daycare and their mother had an hour to spare. Diego and Tatiana, the owners, fussed over them as usual, and brought tall mugs of their favorite beverage, London Fog—one of the few things the sisters agreed on. At the little café table, Jenna listened in silence while Jessica caught her up and told her everything. She had decided that whether Jenna wanted to believe in the spirit world or not, she could not keep Elise—or Rostya—from her twin, her other half.

When it was all done and Jessica stopped talking, she was astonished that her sister had no caustic comments about her dabbling with 'ghosts and evil spirits' as she often did. In fact, Jenna, excited to hear about their mother, chose to ignore everything about Rostya.

"Elise shouldn't have scared Sophie, waking her up like that," was her only objection. "But I get that she wanted to see her grandchildren." She looked wistful. "I wonder if she will ever appear to me."

"Ask her," Jessica said. "I wouldn't be surprised if she did." She took a deep breath. "But what I wanted to say is, I'm more than willing to sell Herron Pond to Amy's client."

Jenna's eyes opened wide in surprise. "I thought you were in love with the place."

"Well, I was, but then I found out that our mother died there. Horribly, I might add. And after the whole 'Darryl Andrews trying to kill Sage and me' business, I changed my mind. Too many bad memories."

"You mean it didn't have anything to do with our benefactor being our grandfather and finding out he'd torn our lives apart from day one?"

"Oh, that." Jessica grinned, and added, "Think what we could do with eighteen million bucks."

Amy, as they expected, was delighted by the news. Hours later, she called back to say that her client was ready to sign the deal. He had read in the news what had happened to Jessica and Sage at Herron Pond, and wanted to meet her and Jenna in person.

The client understood that they would not want to return to the mansion in Big Sur, and by lucky coincidence, he had business in Los Angeles. So, not long after Darryl Andrews's involuntary nosedive off the cliff, the twins found themselves back where they started, at the office of Tanya Stewart in Beverly Hills.

After taking a call from the front desk, Tanya rang off with a smile. "Our buyer has arrived, right on time. Are you ready?"

"What's his name?" Jenna asked. "All we know is the corporation, Big Sur Enterprises. We don't even know what they do."

"Kind of like how this all started," Jessica added. "We didn't know who our benefactor was. Now we don't know who wants to buy our inheritance."

With a perfunctory smile, Tanya Stewart rose from her desk. "Let's all find out together, okay? I'll go and get him."

No more than two minutes after she had left the office, there was a knock on the door. Both sisters turned simultaneously. A distinguished-looking man in his mid-50s stood framed in the doorway. His beautifully-cut grey suit and charcoal tie left no question of his wealth and stature. Clean-shaven with a generous mouth, his thick, dark hair was fashionably tousled and shot through with plenty of silver. But it was the intelligent blue eyes, deep set under dark brows, that seized Jessica's attention.

He had aged since she last saw this handsome, broody man in the vision with Elise, but she knew right away who he was. The sisters rose from their chairs as he moved toward them, clearly nervous.

"I don't know whether you can ever forgive me." His outstretched hands trembled; his voice was shaky, too. "I am Ilya Evanov. I am your father."

He was a stranger to Jenna, but Jessica felt as though she had always known him. When he gathered them into his arms, he knew little about his two daughters, but the genetic bond that connected them could not be denied—the immediate link that confirmed the truism that blood is thicker than water.

After the hugs and tears, the questions came in a torrent.

"There are things we need to know," Jessica began, once the preliminaries were out of the way. "What happened when Elise—our mother—went to Europe, pregnant?"

"I thought she had left me. I didn't know until much later that my father had convinced her I would be better off without her, that it was a sacrifice she needed to make, for me and for her music. I didn't know she was pregnant, though I knew something was on her mind. My father had guessed and confronted her." Ilya closed his eyes. "She was so innocent, and so afraid of him that she would have done almost anything he told her to do. He promised to take care of her, that her family never needed to know about the baby and be disappointed in her for ruining her career when it was just starting. Her family thought she was going on tour in Europe. Back then, we didn't have email; people wrote letters with ink and paper. There were no cell phones and it was very expensive to call overseas. Father took her to St. Petersburg, to stay with an aunt of his. Elise didn't speak the language, she had little money and no way to directly contact me."

When he learned about the unopened letters from his father's desk, and Jessica promised to give them to him, Ilya broke down and sobbed unashamedly. Finally, he dried his eyes on a monogrammed handkerchief and gathered himself. "Much, much later, when had found each other again, Elise told me she had written to me every week and was devastated that I never wrote back. Obviously, I didn't know because my father intercepted the letters. And had no way to know where she was, what was happening to her. I'd had an inkling that she might be pregnant, but—"

"As she wrote in her diary," Jessica said. She would give him that, too. He should have the chance to read it and Elise's letters in private, keeping his grief to himself if he wanted to.

"I like to think I would have stopped it had I known what my father was doing," he said bitterly. "When she was in labor, my great-aunt took her to the maternity hospital—what they called a 'birth house.' A horrible place, she told me when we found each other again. Like a little jail, though my father could have afforded to pay bribes and get better treatment for her. I believe he was punishing her for having the temerity to continue seeing me in secret after he had forbidden us to meet. She was young, and her whole life had been devoted to the piano." His breath caught on a sob. "All those years later, she died never knowing she had borne twins and that they were alive. My father knew, of course, and never told us."

"According to the birth certificates in your father's desk," Jessica said, "we were both very small at birth; just over five pounds each."

"My aunt told her that her baby had died during the birth, strangled by the umbilical cord."

Jessica gasped at the barbaric inhumanity of what these people had done to her mother. It was more than any human should have to bear.

"My father thought she would 'get over it' and return to the concert stage right away," Ilya said. "He didn't understand what the death of a child might do to its mother."

Jessica understood all too well. Something she would share with her father at some later date—that he had lost his grandson, too.

"By then, Elise had grown to hate him and everything he represented. I'm sure he was shocked when she refused to perform and eventually wanted to return to her family." Ilya paused and a big smile brightened his face. "I can't wait to introduce you to them. They will love you."

"We have a whole bunch of new relatives," Jenna said excitedly, grabbing her sister's hand.

"You do indeed," Ilya said with a big smile. "And that will happen soon. But first, let's finish catching up." He took a deep breath. "It wasn't until after my first wife's death that I was able to find Elise again and we each learned of the terrible deception. We got married immediately and moved to Italy. We lived there happily until a few years ago, when I received word that my father was on his deathbed—which wasn't the case, more's the pity. We flew home and took care of him after his surgery. Elise refused to see him, but because I was there, she was, too."

Jessica wanted to ask him about the fire, but to make him remember that night would heap more cruelty on him than she could bear.

"What about our adoption?" Jenna asked.

"I can only guess that he probably arranged it through a lawyer. As you know, Americans can't adopt Russian babies, but you had American parents. I don't know how the Marcotts were chosen. It appears they took you from the maternity hospital the day after you were born, and returned to the US six weeks later."

Ilya bowed his head. "When I found out that Elise had gone to Europe, I was frantic, didn't know what to do. I wanted to contact her parents, but my father convinced me they wanted nothing to do with me—another lie, I found out later. Then he brought Rostya here and insisted that I marry her. Poor girl, she was in a similar state to Elise, in a foreign country, separated from her family. I didn't speak much Russian. She didn't speak much English. For a while, I tried to make the marriage work, but I couldn't stand to look at her face. She wasn't my Elise. Honestly, it wasn't fair to her."

"But you had a child with her," Jenna said.

His face hardened. "Another sin to lay at my feet. A sweet little boy who I failed, utterly and completely. Even more than I failed you. I *knew* he was my son and that his mother was terribly depressed, yet I left him alone with her. You have to believe that I had no idea what Rostya was doing to him until it was too late and he had died. The police came and investigated, but it was clear to me that my father paid someone off and the truth about what had happened was covered up. He made a deal for Rostya to be locked up for a while in a program for mentally ill people, supposedly to protect herself, but the truth is, it was to keep the Evanov name free from the scandal. When she returned to Herron Pond, she was reminded every day of what she'd done. I don't know whether she felt guilty—she never admitted to hurting our son. But she couldn't deal with it. I was not there for her then, any more than I had ever been. It wasn't her fault that I loved someone else."

"That's no excuse for what she did to little Ilya," Jenna said. And Jessica thought of what Rostya had done to Elise, causing the fire that killed her.

"No, there can never be an excuse," Ilya said. "But I was spending as much time away from home as I could, building my career and trying to forget Elise. I was home when Rostya committed suicide, though. So, your father is responsible for the deaths of three people. Little Ilya, Rostya, and Elise."

He kept talking. After losing Elise, the love of his life, only eight years earlier in such horrible circumstances, and now finding that he had two daughters, it seemed cathartic for him. He wanted to explain as much as he could.

"Growing up in Soviet Russia, my father truly believed that Leonid Rashnikov, Rostya's father, could protect our family. But Rashnikov fell out of favor in the 1960s and my parents decided to make a new life in the US. I was born four years later." His eyes filled with fresh tears. "I will never stop regretting that I allowed him to control my life for so long. All of our lives. If only I had been stronger—"

"You were young," Jenna said with a heart full of forgiveness. "You had grown up obeying a controlling dictator. You had no mother to intervene on your behalf."

"It's kind of you to make excuses for me, my darling, but my punishment is a life sentence."

"For the loss of Elise," Jessica said.

Ilya bowed his head in assent. He looked from her to Jenna in bemusement. "I see her in your faces. My father stole so much from me, and from you, but I could never have been given a greater gift than finding you. I don't know whether I can ever make it up to you, but I hope you'll let me try."

He didn't know that it was Rostya who had stolen Elise from him the second time, and it was too soon for Jessica to let him in on the secret of her mediumship. Maybe someday, when she knew him better, she could tell him about her meetings with Elise. Maybe Elise would play the piano for him through her.

"How did you find out about us?" Jenna wanted to know.

"When my father died last October, Dianne Maggio sent me a copy of the will. I wasn't surprised that he had cut me out and I didn't care. But as you can imagine, when I saw your names, I was curious, wanted to know who you were and why he made you his heirs. I hired someone to look into your backgrounds." Ilya stopped for a moment, choking on emotion.

"As soon as I saw the photos of you, I didn't have to look any further. There was my beautiful Elise, smiling back at me in both of your eyes. I didn't understand what the connection was then—as I said, we thought our baby had died at birth. So, I went to Russia and questioned my aunt." He gave them an ironic grin. "Well, I suppose it would be fair to say I interrogated her. Since my father was already in his grave and she had nothing to fear, except from me if she didn't tell the truth, she told me everything. Please understand that by the time I got this news I had already made the offer to buy Herron Pond. It was only a few days ago that I returned from Russia. It has been completely overwhelming for me, as I'm guessing it must be for you."

"Why did you want to buy Herron Pond?" Jessica asked. "Was it because Elise died there?"

Ilya shook his head. "I hate the place with all of my being. I want to tear it down, obliterate it from the face of the earth. The money Rostya left will pay for the purchase. It seemed to make some kind of karmic sense to me."

"I loved it at first, but it feels as though the misery has soaked into the walls," Jessica said. "I thought I might want to live there, but after what

I've learned and all that happened, I don't think I ever want to set foot in that house again."

Jenna said, "I knew something was wrong there right away."

"Of course you did," Jessica retorted with a fond smile. She turned to look at their father, who had suffered so much, and would for the rest of his life. She sent a silent message to her twin. They did not have to bow to Vadim Evanov's manipulations.

"Since we aren't allowed to change the terms of the will and just give you the place," Jessica said, "If Jenna agrees, we can sell Herron Pond to you for one dollar. After that, you can do whatever you want with it."

Ilya Evanov took out his wallet and laid a crisp one-dollar bill on the table. "What would you think of building a music school?" he asked. "I have connections with people who would jump at the chance to come to Big Sur and teach."

For once, both twins spoke in agreement. "I love it."

epilogue

JESSICA CHANGED HER MIND about not wanting to see Herron Pond again. A need for closure, a need to take back the control she had given Rostya there. She didn't know for sure what would happen to the two spirits who had occupied the mansion, but she had a strong sense that they had each completed their journeys and that each would go where she belonged.

Before the mansion was to be emptied and demolished, Jessica and Sage went to say a final goodbye. Entering the foyer, where the stained-glass window wall seemed to glitter and glow, throwing a riot of jewel colors across the staircase, Sage tipped his head to the side. "Do you hear that?"

From the second floor came the sound of the piano. Exchanging a quick glance, they ran hand-in-hand up the stairs. When they reached the landing, Jessica led the way to the last door, which was ajar. Gently, she pushed it open.

Seated at the piano, her thick blonde hair swept into an updo, was Elise, wearing a shimmering silver gown fit for Carnegie Hall, playing Chopin's *Ballade in G Minor*.

Acknowledgments

Writers often talk about the solitary process of producing a story, but it's not just about the author. There is virtually always a great support team who help in research, editing, beta reading, and more. I have a regular group to thank for their help and support, and there are usually additions to the team, so, here goes: Bob Joseph, Raul Melendez, Gwen Freeman, Sara Taylor, Ellen Larson, Jennifer Windrow, and everyone who has ever read one of my books. A heartfelt Thank You.

A special mention goes to Dianne Maggio and Amy Herron of the Hillside Book Club. They'd both won character names in a drawing at one of my launch parties. There is never a guarantee of whether a winner will end up as a hero or a villian, or just have a walk-on part, so I hope these two ladies like what they did in The Last Door.

One last special mention to Mary Vickery, whose off-hand comment at a party gave me the title for the book.

Dear Reader,

Thank you so very much for spending this time with me and my characters.

If you enjoyed this book, I would appreciate it if you would post a brief review on your favorite review site, whether that is Amazon, Goodreads, BookBub, or some other. It helps an author when you tell others how you feel.

Be well,

Sheila Lowe

Also By Sheila Lowe

About the Author

Sheila Lowe is the author of eleven novels, including the award-winning Forensic Handwriting series and the Beyond the Veil paranormal suspense series. She is also a real-life forensic handwriting expert who testifies in court cases. In addition to writing stories of psychological suspense, she writes nonfiction books about handwriting and personality. She lives in Southern California.

Ways to reach Sheila

www.sheilalowebooks.com

https://www.sheilalowe.com

https://www.facebook.com/SheilaLoweBooks

https://www.instagram.com/sheilalowebooks/

https://www.goodreads.com/SheilaLowe

https://www.bookbub.com/authors/sheila-lowe